SHOCKING,
COMPASSIONATE,
UNFORGETTABLE

Enid Harlow has created a woman so real that each
new page and each new pain will stamp its awesome
power indelibly on your heart. "She focuses her vision
more steadily and with greater intensity than any
writer I know."

—Feenie Zinner,
author of *Within This Wilderness*

"Fascinating, absorbing, and very frightening. It's
extraordinarily well done."

—Diana Trilling

"Marvelously convincing."

—Joyce Carol Oates

"Keen tension sustained throughout the story makes
for a powerful, insightful creation."

—*West Coast Review of Books*

CRASHING

Enid Harlow

BANTAM BOOKS · TORONTO · NEW YORK · LONDON

For Michael Odysseus

CRASHING

A Bantam Book / published by arrangement with
St. Martin's Press

PRINTING HISTORY

St. Martin's edition published May 1980
Serialized in Red Book May 1980
Bantam edition / April 1981

ISBN 0-553-14626-2

Published simultaneously in the United States and Canada

Bantam Books are published by Bantam Books, Inc., Its trademark, consisting of the words "Bantam Books" and the por-
trayal of a bantam, is Registered in U.S. Patent and Trademark
Office and in other countries. Marca Registrada. Bantam
Books, Inc., 666 Fifth Avenue, New York, New York 10103.

PRINTED IN THE UNITED STATES OF AMERICA

0 9 8 7 6 5 4 3 2 1

CRASHING

Flat white walls, steady lights, blinds pulled to even lengths, and a sense of boundaries. Heavy white plastic chairs and long, low wooden tables set at right angles to the walls.

Around the tables, the occupants of the room: men and women both, bound together by certain failed mechanisms and misperceptions, by fantasy and obsession, by love's stillbirth and the disorientation of boundaries crossed and recrossed and crossed again.

They sit rigidly, move with difficulty, speak only with their eyes. Some turn away from the work at hand and fold themselves into closed, inaccessible postures, paying close inward attention or none at all.

Gray clay in the center of tables offers to the daring clumps of amorphous challenge: a self within, extract its shape.

Elsewhere: pots of paint and glue, scraps of paper, strips of balsa wood, easels angled away from lunacy, blunted scissors, crayons worn from many pressings—a range of media at their fingertips to imagine themselves into being.

Minds cast back over the years, minutes, days. Decades brought to the surface in nets of distortion and transformed by pen and ink, pastels, watercolors, even blankness—a line, begun, abandoned, that too bearing the shape of a life.

Half-finished clay figures lie on the tables exposed or partially draped by wet towels through which here and there a cavernous eye, emaciated cheek, rudimentary limb pokes through: ghostly stare, gaunt desire, loosened grasp.

Silence, like shadows, slips down from the screened win-

1

dows, plays with its back against the dead white walls. Papered feet scuffle across linoleum smelling of daily doses of disinfectant. Fingers struggle to release trapped forms, lips move by rote over soundless articulations, a sudden smile, an occasional shriek, a flash of anger, paper tearing like pain, paint spilled, shattered, healed over again by silence.

Carefully, the white-coated woman moves among them, lays her hand on their arms, their shoulders, admires their work, goes from one to the other, comes up close, speaks plainly, raising her voice as if she could not be heard above the silence.

A newcomer stares at the wall while her fingers, unguided by sight, squeeze wet clay between them. Her hands move relentlessly into the water, into the clay, carrying more and more water to the clay, needless amounts, prodigious amounts, squeezing the clay in her hands until, sodden, it runs like mud through her fingers, spills over the edge of the table, drops down onto her lap, and splashes there in dirty pools. Her eyes, open, fixed, remain on the wall opposite as if the institutional whiteness were a screen on which by constant, frozen vigil she might prevent the least image from taking shape.

The white-coated woman approaches, pauses a moment as at the entrance to a strange house and, as she might lift her foot on an unfamiliar stoop a bit too high, raises her voice:

"My name is Frieda, Sara."

Sara . . .

I

Sara Richardson stood outside the partially open door to her husband's den and listened to him on the telephone. Even seated, his great height rose with authority into the room.

"I'm going to pass on this one, Bob." He spoke dispassionately into the phone. "She was referred to me by another patient, but the way I put it together on first examination it's really more up your alley. . . ."

Even on Sunday Harry attended to business. Sara watched him through the crack in the door: fine strong face, serious eyes, dedicated doctor's hands—always clean, purposeful, the nails clipped short. She admired those hands, watched them now, one confidently sorting the papers in front of him, arranging them in some kind of order, the other gripping the receiver.

"No, I don't need to see her again. . . . She'll do fine with you. . . . Of course, Bob. . . . Yes, I'm sure. . . . No, I only saw her once. That was all I needed. You were the first one I thought of. . . . You two'll get on very well together. . . . I'll have her call. . . . You're just the man for the job. . . ."

Disposing of patients, passing them back and forth, pairing physician with disease, symptom with treatment. The calm with which he did it amazed her, the absolute self-confidence as if these were colors he was matching up, or patterns—not people.

She would like to have the merest fraction of his certainty, she thought, her eyes falling on the wastebasket next to his desk. Crumpled papers spilled from the basket next to his desk. Crumpled papers spilled from the top—the notes Harry was

3

constantly taking, constantly discarding, notes on his patients, on articles he had read, on those he was writing, indications for new drugs, diagnoses transferred to permanent files, notes written on the backs of envelopes, on pages torn from medical journals, around the margins of letters—the mountainous jottings of a demanding mind.

A mind ever engaged elsewhere, Sara thought, watching Harry replace the receiver now, look up from his desk across the room, his solemn dark eyes directed toward the door, toward her, but filled with some important matter, some medical matter, not seeing the door, not seeing her. His eyes held there a moment then returned to the desk, seeking paper and pen. His hand moved firmly, decisively—she always felt in awe a little of the way he wrote—bearing down hard on the paper, the pen nearly going through, the quick scrawl, heavy, black, illegible.

She ought to have emptied the wastepaper basket. It was something Harry was fussy about. *Don't forget the basket, Sara, please,* he'd say on his way out the door. *The papers I bring home will bury me yet if I don't have a place to dump them.* Perhaps she should do it now. She took a step into the room and a step back. Perhaps she should leave him alone.

Sara liked to study his face while he worked, attempt to memorize its lines. He was home so seldom that sometimes when she thought of something he'd said to her—yet another reminder about the pills, perhaps, *you've got to cut them out, you're destroying yourself,* or that horrible phrase he used to describe his day at the office, *brutal day, brutal schedule*—and tried to imagine the expression on his face when he said it, she couldn't quite remember what he looked like.

But today was a beautiful, clear bright Sunday and Sara wanted to be cheerful for Harry. She wanted to match him in energy and strength today. And so she'd thought, getting out of bed that morning, one little pill wouldn't hurt. And Harry needn't know. He couldn't always tell for sure. She just wanted to take a drive. Justin and Julia had other plans for the day, so that would leave herself and Harry and the younger children and it was so seldom they did anything at all with them. But she'd certainly need one for the drive. Just fifteen milligrams, she'd thought, going into the bathroom. Practically nothing for her. And she'd quit again next week, she decided. Or, better yet, the first of the month. That was a good time for a new start.

She'd tried this time, she really had. And she'd practically broken her record. Gone nearly three whole days without a hit. But the fatigue, finally, and the depression had gotten to her. She knew what she was like when she was trying to kick—no strength to lift a finger with the kids, irritable, worthless, bursting into tears for no reason, dying for sleep—not the kind of person she wanted to be for Harry on his day of rest, the one full day of the week he spent at home.

She'd do it again soon. She'd keep her promise and quit for good. She knew she could. No matter what Harry said, she could quit any time she wanted to. It was just getting through that second day. The second day was always the hardest. Unless it was the first. Unless it was the third. Sara didn't know about the third. She'd never made it all the way through the third before.

She'd made it through weeks, months even—seven, eight, nine months in a row—with only one capsule a day (one every other day when she was at her best), but never three whole days without anything at all.

Harry didn't understand what the pills meant to her. The strength they gave her. She'd been taking them for so long now they were like insulin to a diabetic—a lifesupport for her and not, as Harry said, a threat to life and health. Often she was able to skip a day here and there and over the months and years these unused pills had piled up. A secret supply for emergencies, for days when the prescribed dosage wasn't enough. Hidden in the linen closet, in the backs of drawers and the pockets of coats, in old handbags and special envelopes—her assurance of getting through that day. What Harry didn't know wouldn't hurt him. The pills he prescribed were on the shelf in the medicine cabinet. No need for him to know about the others stashed around the house.

Some day she'd quit. Harry's predictions frightened her. Logically, she knew he was right. She'd been on speed ever since college. It was only luck (or a strong constitution) that had so far prevented some really disastrous medical consequence. Harry was right. Her luck was bound to run out. Lapses of memory, sudden, uncontrollable anger—these things had happened already, were happening more and more frequently, she had to admit, and they frightened her. Certainly, she'd quit some day. She'd take up pottery again, maybe even pursue her dream of becoming a sculptor.

It helped her to work the clay when she was trying to quit. Gave her a feeling of power she rather enjoyed, squeezing the clay in her hands, molding it into a shape. And something to do with her anger too, slapping it back and forth from one hand to the other. But this last time the fatigue had won, her fingers simply couldn't work the clay and, defeated, she'd picked up the figure she'd begun, a little dove, and smashed it on the kitchen table. Smashed it again and again and finally threw it and every square of clay she had in the house into the garbage.

She'd try again, she thought. But not today. Today she wanted to go for a drive. She wanted to take Harry away from his patients and critical decisions, away from his papers and notes, and have him for herself.

She pushed the door to his study open, walked straight in without a pause. "How about taking the kids for a drive?"

Instantly Harry was immersed in work, shuffling papers, taking notes. "I've got a ton of work to do."

"Oh come on, Harry. It's a lovely day. And I'm dying to drive the Mercedes. Just come along and hold William."

"Can't, Sara, really. It's out of the question."

"Nothing's impossible if you put your mind to it. Isn't that what you're always telling me?"

Harry looked up, eyed her critically. "You're in good spirits today."

"Why shouldn't I be? It's a beautiful spring day."

"That the only reason?"

"What else?"

"You tell me."

Harry's doubt, like his devotion to his career, often seemed to Sara the one absolute constant in their marriage. But then she couldn't really blame him. She'd never kept her promises for very long before.

"I just want to get out of the house and go for a drive. Please, Harry. It'll be fun." She tugged at his hand across the desk. "We haven't been for a drive together in ages."

Someday she'd surprise him. She'd look him straight in the eye and say: *There, I've licked it. I'm off for good.* He'd be proud of her then. But not today. Tomorrow maybe, or next month. But today all she wanted to do was go for a drive.

"Well. . . ." Harry looked at the papers on his desk, looked back at Sara. "I suppose this could wait."

"Oh, sure it could. Thanks, Harry. Thanks. Of course it could." She'd get him out of this room with its piles of notes and papers cluttering the desk and overflowing the wastepaper basket. "We'll have a great time, you'll see."

Sara spun around quickly and left the room, knowing as soon as she turned her back Harry would tap his finger against his upper lip and wonder if she was on or off. Unless he took her pulse or listened to her heart, he was never absolutely sure. But whenever he was in doubt, he reminded her of what she was doing to herself and those dire predictions now followed her up the stairs: *serious heart problems, possible brain cell destruction. We don't know the half of it yet. It might even make you bald.*

Right now she was feeling too good to care. She ran up the stairs to William's room, stuffed him into a light jacket, called out to Sam to get ready for a drive, rounded up some books and toys, found his giraffe, Elsie, under a chair just as Sam began to whine, "Don't wanna go for a dumb ride in a dumb car."

"Yes you do," she answered as he fled into his room and began throwing things around.

"Can't find Elsie," he called.

"Here she is, Sam."

"Can't find her!" he screamed, coming out red in the face, tears blinding his eyes.

"Here's Elsie. Look. Right here."

Sara tossed the animal into Sam's arms, snatched up William and dashed downstairs to the kitchen, threw some apples and cookies, William's bottle, and a bunch of grapes into a bag. It was going to be a long ride.

"You take the kids and back the car out of the garage." She handed the baby to Harry, yelled for Sam to hurry, and headed back up the stairs. "I'll be down in a second."

In the bathroom, she stopped for a moment in front of the medicine cabinet, picked up her brush and passed it through her hair. Strands of it came away on the bristles. *Classic amphetamine consequence*, Harry had pronounced it. But what the hell, thinning hair or not, Harry had put down his notes in favor of a Sunday drive. One more for the road, Sara said to herself, opening the cabinet, grabbing the container, shaking loose a pill, and downing it with a backward toss of her head. She'd been on them so long she knew how to swallow them dry.

Too long, maybe? Hair falling out, face drained. Memory going, nerves jangled. Was she headed for a breakdown? Dimly Sara recognized things were reaching a culmination in her life. On her next birthday she would be forty. Her children were growing up. William, only yesterday a newborn, was about to turn one. Her babies were leaving her. The first birthday. Absurd as she knew it was, it stuck in her mind as a point of departure. Once they started having birthdays, there was no holding them back. No more babies. No more children to fill the gap between herself and Harry.

She swung the medicine cabinet closed and went down the stairs and outside to the car.

"Okay, Harry," she said, opening the door on the driver's side. "Hop in back."

"You sure you want to drive?"

"I'm sure. Here, take William with you." She slid in behind the wheel and handed the baby out to Harry. "He wants to sit with his daddy. Don't you, little one?"

"Me too," Sam yelled, crawling across Sara's lap, reaching for his father.

"No, hold on there, son," Harry said, closing the door and getting in the back with William. "One's all I can manage at a time."

"Try four why don't you?" Sara said and gunned the engine.

Sam started to cry.

"Stop that." Sara straightened him on the seat beside her. "No screaming kids today. That goes for you too," she said, smiling up into the rear-view mirror at William. Her sunny baby was smiling too. He never had been a screaming kid. "Nobody's going to spoil this ride." She gave a fast glance out the window and stepped on the accelerator.

"Wait a minute, Sara," Harry shouted.

Sara braked. Sam slid off the seat and opened his mouth to let out a cry. Sara pulled him up quickly, rocked him back and forth to cut off the threatened sound. "It's all right, Sam," she said to him. "You're not hurt. You're not. . . . What is it, Harry?"

"I just thought . . . don't we have a car seat?"

"Oh never mind that. It's in the garage. Just hold him on your lap, can't you, and let's get going."

The streets of the town were quiet on Sunday afternoons. It was a family community. People had their relatives in for the day or took their children out for a drive. Sara was just like anybody else today, doing what people did.

Her house, a three-story white clapboard structure with green shutters, set on one acre of land with both a front and backyard, was like many other houses in the area: large, comfortable, expensive. At least on the outside it looked like other people's houses and Sara was glad of that. Harry should have a nice house, a good wife. Their children deserved a good home. But so often the house got away from her. The contents of its many rooms, the possessions of six lives accumulating dust, getting mislaid, getting out of hand, piling up, rising to consume her. *For Christ's sake, Sara, get yourself some help*, Harry said, and now and then she did on a day-to-day basis but she didn't like to have anyone in full time. A stranger in her house, touching her things, going through her children's belongings—no, she didn't like that at all. Besides, there were some things she had to do herself. A point of honor almost, and to show Harry that she could.

"Isn't he too hot in this?"

Harry's voice came like a jolt from the back. For a minute, Sara had almost imagined herself alone.

She glanced in the mirror, saw Harry struggling with the zipper on William's jacket. Her precious baby, the last of four. In less than three weeks he will have lived a year. She'd have a party for him, she decided, a huge celebration for the first year of life.

"Open the window, why don't you?" she said.

"Won't he be in a draft? I don't want him getting sick."

"Take his jacket off then. And close the window. My vent's open." She loved the sound of the wind careening off the glass, slamming hard against it, and whizzing past.

"I'm hot," Sam said and rolled his window all the way down.

"Sam, it's awfully breezy back here."

"Shut the window, please," Sara said, forcing her voice down.

"Too hot. Want air."

"Sam," Harry called to him. "That's too much wind in the back."

"Hot up here. Need air."

"There's plenty of air," Sara said. "Roll it up, sweetheart." She would be gentle today, keep herself under control.

Sam glared straight ahead.

"Do as you're told!" Harry shouted.

Sara wished he wouldn't shout. His voice made her nervous. Sam's stubbornness made her nervous. The double dose taking hold quicker than she'd expected because of the two days' abstinence was making her nervous too. *Agitated,* Harry called it, *overstimulated,* but nervous was the word Sara preferred. "Shut the window," she said.

Sam didn't move.

"Shut it!" she ordered, her voice higher and harsher than she'd intended. But she couldn't help that. She was off balance, between gears, not quite where she wanted to be yet. She couldn't stand the smirk on Sam's face, his refusal to obey. "Goddamn it!" she yelled. "I said shut it!" Like a shot, she reached across him and rolled the window up. Sam inched his fingers toward the handle again. Sara anticipated that move and slapped his hand back down.

"Ow!" he cried. "That hurt. I wanna sit with daddy." Sam flipped around in his seat and kicked Sara in the head as he threw one leg up and tried to climb over into the back.

"Damn it!" Sara said, keeping her eyes on the road as she grabbed him by the seat of his pants and pulled him down next to her. "Sit still, will you?"

Sam began to whimper, and held the hand she had slapped as if it were broken.

"I'm sorry, sweetheart," Sara said, repenting. She would be kind today. She would stay calm. "I didn't mean to hurt you. But when I say close the window, I mean close it." She put her arm around him and felt his body go lax against hers. "Stay here next to mommy, okay? And tell me what the kindergarten crowd is up to." God, she thought, it was good to be out of the house.

"You didn't have to hit him, Sara."

Oh, Christ! Men! "Forget it, Harry." Just when she'd got it out of Sam's mind, he had to go and put it back in.

Sam stiffened and pulled away. "Wanna sit with daddy."

Why had she brought them along? With the wind whistling against the vent, the energy rising in her blood, she'd really rather be alone.

Maneuvering the last of the smaller roads and about to pull up the ramp and out onto the parkway, she nearly rammed the car ahead as it made a sharp left without signaling. In a split second Sara's window was down, her head sticking out. "You stupid son-of-a-bitch!" she yelled into the spring air, switched gears, and felt herself just about where she wanted to be as she moved out onto the open parkway.

"Take it easy, Sara."

No, she wouldn't. The flat, nearly empty road stretching for miles sent a rush of excitement through her. Stepping on the gas, she let heart and car accelerate simultaneously. This is going to be *my* drive, she thought, nobody else's.

Sam turned around quickly and threw himself over the front seat.

"Oh go ahead," she said. "Go to daddy." She gave him a nudge propelling him harder than she'd intended over the top and into the back.

"All right, Sara. You don't have to throw him."

"And take this damn thing with you." She tossed Elsie back over her shoulder and heard the cookies crunch as Sam, jumping forward to catch his giraffe, stepped on the bag.

"Broke!" he screamed. "Cookies all broke!"

Sara looked up, saw Harry shifting William into one arm, trying to comfort Sam with the other. "There, there, son. It's all right. Calm down, son."

"Why do you call him that?" she asked, seeing her chance to pass the blue Capri ahead.

"Call him what?"

"Son." She pulled alongside the car, glared in at the driver—just as she'd thought, a haughty, smart-assed kid—and sped out in front.

"Well he is, isn't he? Hey, watch what you're doing."

"It sounds like you've forgotten his name or something. You don't call Julia daughter."

"Sure I do. I . . ."

"Oh I don't mean that." Sara knew what he was going to say. He'd say he referred to Julia as his daughter, introduced her as his daughter—*my daughter, my wife*. She saw his whole lengthy argument spread out interminably before her and dismissed it at once. "It's not the same. You wouldn't say there, there, daughter."

"I might."

"No you wouldn't."

"I might if . . ."

"Bull."

"I could imagine myself saying it if for instance . . ."

"Oh shut up, Harry! You wouldn't say it. Not ever."

Sara was pleased to have the front seat to herself. She imagined moving it away from the rest of the car, lifting it off like the nose cone of a rocket, blasting into outer space.

"Don't you think you'd better slow down?"

If anything, she thought she should go faster. Faster and faster until she was way out there on her own, entered in the Indianapolis 500, riding the bumps in the road, taking the curves, swaying now to one side, now to the other. The brightly glaring center line catching the sun, throwing it back in her eyes. Goggles were what was needed, yellow-tinted aviator's goggles and a dark brown leather cap pulled on tight.

"Watch the road, Sara."

"I'm watching it."

Massive trunks of trees, huge flowering branches, cherry blossoms and magnolias spreading from the sides of the road, dropping down over it, over her, a dazzling, living canopy. Something darted out from the grassy divider. Sara swerved, braked, released the brake, skidded to the side of the road, steered into the skid, thanked God for the Mercedes—what a joy to have a heavy car—straightened her wheels, and drove on. At least she hadn't hit it.

"What the hell are you doing?" Harry shouted, bracing himself against the back of her seat.

"Fucking rabbit," Sara said. "Didn't you see it?"

"It was a squirrel, Sara. You'd kill us all for a goddamned squirrel."

"It was a rabbit, mommy," Sam said, jumping forward. "I saw it."

She loved Sam then more than she could say. "You've got eagle eyes, honey."

"I'm glad you didn't hit it."

Sam was on her side again. He often seemed to pick up what she was feeling—especially when she was on a high as good as this one—to join in her excitement and be carried along on her vibrations.

"Go, mommy, go!" Sam pounded the back of her seat.

During the diversion with the rabbit, the blue Capri had gotten ahead of her again. Sara pressed down on the gas and took off after it. If she was stopped by the highway patrol, she could always say Harry was on his way to an emergency somewhere.

"Catch him, mommy! Catch him!"

"Don't pound, honey," she said, closing the distance between herself and the car ahead while feeling each of Sam's thrusts driving like spikes into her back. Sharp, jagged spikes like the pieces of metal the car would become if it were to fly apart. A piece of her flying free on each piece of the car: an ear on the hubcap, a forearm impaled on the windshield wiper. Her severed hands, severed feet flying through the air on bits of metal wreckage. What freedom they would feel, these various parts of herself, no longer attached, no longer confined, rushing ahead to Harry's emergency. She could almost feel it now. Cool, empty places between her joints. Hips and knees sliding free, coming unhinged.

"Take it easy, Sara!"

She speeded up to pass, gaining momentum on the hill, felt the thrusts of Sam's pounding fists running wild through her back, saw the glare of the sun—or was it ice?—on the road and wavered. Yes, it was ice. No, sun. Something—a car?—coming at her down the center, not of her lane but of the divider itself. It wasn't possible. It couldn't be. She blared her own horn against the steady scream of the Capri's warning and saw the silver car pick itself up and jump back across the other side of the road. She pulled the Mercedes back in line and caught a glimpse of the kid's look of triumph as he took the Capri out like blue lightning from under her.

"Goddamn it!" she said, arching backwards to put a halt to Sam's hateful pounding. "I told you to stop!" She slapped at his hand, missed, slapped Harry's knee instead, felt him

13

jerk away, heard William begin to cry. Her baby. The birthday boy who never cried. The one with the sunny disposition.

"Hey, Sara . . . now see what you've done." Harry patted the baby on his shoulder and leaned forward. "How about changing places?"

"Not on your life." She was just beginning to have a good time. "Give him his bottle. He'll stop."

She could spin them all to pieces. That was her power. Her control to lose control. The Capri was out of sight now. A clear road lay ahead. Cars came at her through blossoming trees. Faces hurtled through windshields, bodies spiraled in air. The possibilities of collision were infinite. Two-car, four-car, eight-car pile ups. Jagged edges, raw flesh everywhere. They might all end in a hospital where Harry would be in control.

"Slow down, Sara."

Not two days ago she'd seen a double car collision on this very parkway. Bodies flung over the road, blood drying in the sun. Not wanting to look, unable to look away. It was an outcome she had in some complicated way willed, wanted it secretly for herself—to have it all over with at once. Sudden, violent annihilation. And when she saw it there on the road, she couldn't look away. So that's what it's like. That's how it ends. Horrifying yet intensely satisfying. The perfection of finality.

William was crying louder now.

"Where's his bottle, Sara?"

"What am I, your nurse? Look for it, Harry. This is a car. How many fucking places could a bottle be?"

"Watch your language in front of the children."

"Oh shit, the children! One's not quite a year, and the other doesn't know what the word means."

"Do too," Sam said.

"Betcha don't."

"Betcha do."

"Sara, really."

"Harry, really."

"Harry, really. Mommy, really. Daddy, really."

Sam was getting into it now. She liked him when he was like this. She could get something special going with him then, some quick, special kind of understanding she didn't have with

14

any of the others. He was plugging into her mood, getting off on her high. She loved him for it. Really loved him. "Say fuck, Sam."

"Fuck!" came the screaming answer.

"For Christ's sake, Sara."

Harry didn't approve. Harry was a prude. A prude who didn't approve. Harry could go stick his head in the lake. "Suck, muck, puck."

"Suck, muck, puck," Sam shot back.

"Luck, tuck, zuck."

"Luck, tuck, zuck."

Sam was quick—much quicker than his father. Harry was an old stick-in-the-mud. What kind of stick was that?

"Take it easy, will you, Sara? Please?"

Billboards, road signs, speed limits dropped down out of the sky. Green trees, soft branches, spiraling clouds whirled past out of the blue. Nothing was attached to anything. Nothing was rooted or held down. It's all right, children, she thought. It's all right, Harry. Never fear, Sara's here. Sara is in control.

Meteors splintering in space. Whole galaxies colliding in air, the sound reaching them billions of years after the fact. She was like that now—free, unaccountable, all at once on the other side. This was what she did it for, this perfect escape, perfect freedom. She was as good as anyone now. As good as Harry. Nothing could get to her now, neither Harry's reproaches nor his constant doubt. She was free and loose and off on her own in a place where no harm could reach her. Could he understand that, she wondered. Could a dedicated, prominent internist like Harry Richardson understand a simple thing like that? "Can you?" she asked.

"Can I what?"

No, Harry couldn't understand. Only Sara knew. Only she understood. She knew you had to join it, go straight to the center, become one with it, become as dangerous as the danger itself, then it was nullified, there was no danger at all. Nothing at all. Only Sara. Only Sara's tremendous, limitless power free in the world. She could do anything then—fly through the air, make Harry tender, make him proud. Anything at all. Make him love her. Even that. There was nothing she couldn't do.

Blue metal flashed into view, took the curve up ahead.

Only two cars between herself and it. She'd catch that Capri if it was the last thing she ever did. Nothing would get away from her again. She was a different woman now. Invincible and free. The old Sara was gone. The new Sara was here to stay, riding high in her seat, cool and loose and powerful and free.

"Sara, the speed limit. You'll have the cops after us."

She was beyond reach of them all now—Harry and the law and any other force that might try to bring her down. She had no physical limits, no boundaries between herself and the car. She could pass through any object, through trees, billboards, houses, gaudy advertisements. That gray sedan in front, the toy dog in back wagging its head, glassy, red staring eyes—she could enter those eyes, go straight through that wagging head into the heart of danger, but she steps on the gas instead, pulls to the left and passes.

"Sara, you almost hit him. What the hell's the matter with you?"

Faster now, faster. Only one more car before the Capri. Its driver sees her coming, glances into his rear-view mirror, catches her eye, looks back at the road, back at Sara, his eyes latch on to hers, seem to hook inside her head, drop back to the road again. Sara gains on him, pulls up alongside, his full face coming up opposite hers now like a moon. She presses her foot to the floor and streaks on out ahead. He's left in a path of spitting pebbles, dust and exhaust, shattered sunbeams, and a trail of distance.

"For Christ's sake, Sara, slow down! I know these roads."

Sara knew them too. Better than Harry. Better than anyone.

"What are you trying to do? Get us all killed?"

She was one with the road now, one with the car and the wind, the pedal and the steering wheel, the engine, the hood. Energy both inside and out were hers alone now. The fury in her speeding wheels, the fury in her blood. She was free now. Free of Harry. Free of the children. Free of the house, the thinning hair, the dire predictions.

"Is that what you want? To get us killed? Are you on those pills? Is that what it is?"

Harry was shouting. Harry was afraid.

"They'll kill you yet. I've told you that. One way or another."

Sara saw the fear in Harry's eyes, heard it in his voice. She saw the sweat on his brow, the glassy, staring eyes. She was beyond fear now, beyond them all. She had no arms nor legs to be severed. No flesh to be blown apart. Sara could never die.

"Sara!"

The blue Capri is within range now. All the world is within Sara's range. The kid at the wheel crouches low. He plays it like a game, but Sara knows it's fear he's racing. She feels his fear and Harry's too. It comes over the front seat, rises by her ears, envelops her face. Her strong, confident, important Harry. It comes in through the window, travels the air waves between the two cars. The kid and Harry will live and die in fear. But not Sara, not her. She's beyond that now. She's into the eye of the unpredictable, into it and gone.

Throwing back her head, she lets out a laugh and, blending body with machine, swoops down on that flashy blue speed king, down and past, and holding up a finger flies by and tears on down the open road loose and free as air itself.

A hundred yards further on she pulled over onto the shoulder of the road and stopped.

"What the hell were you doing?" Harry demanded and the Capri drove past.

Turning and looking at Harry, at his solid, capable face, at his great height looming from the darkness in the back of the car, she thought she could say that she just wanted to show him. But as she shook her head, all reason seemed to fall from it.

"I don't know, Harry," she said. "I just got started and then it was like someone else took over."

"I'll drive," he answered. "Get out and change places with me."

In the back seat, Sara sat clutching her children to her—her Sam, her William. Her precious children. She wouldn't hurt them for the world. No, she thought, not for the world.

17

II

Sara was determined to be careful after that. If she had been alone, that would have been one thing, but to take the children with her. . . . And Harry. No. She didn't want to do that.

That wasn't the sort of person she meant to be: reckless, irresponsible, frightening her children, frightening Harry. It occurred to Sara how rarely she saw Harry frightened. She saw him obsessed with work and basking a little in the central position he played in so many people's lives—*help me, doctor, save me, doctor,* they rang him up at all hours of the day and night—she saw the tyranny of that position and its enormous satisfaction. She saw Harry's enviable confidence, even his vanity, professional not personal. And he was entitled to that, certainly, she believed, watching his eyes twinkling, his lips moving rapidly as he spoke of the rightness of a particular diagnosis, the efficacy of a controversial treatment. She saw the pride he took in the success of a critical article, the alacrity with which he had copies made and upon the least pretext handed out.

But rarely did she see his fear. No more perhaps than three or four times in all the years they'd been married and then it came to him, as so much of his feeling did, by way of his work. The news of a patient's death reaching him by phone at night. His good, strong hands falling loose in front of him, palms up, fingers fluttering. A man normally so intent upon a task, rushing into action, taking command, left suddenly unoccupied, adrift. Sara couldn't bear to look. Was it his fault, perhaps? Did he think he had failed? Failure, she once would

18

have said, was the one thing Harry feared. Now it seemed he feared her as well.

The sight of his face in the car, his eyes wide, frantic, the feel of his fingers digging into her arm as he helped her out—no, she didn't want to be the sort of person who could make Harry afraid. She'd get off the stuff, she swore she would.

Harry was right. Harry was always right. Speed was tearing her apart. Speed was rotting her teeth, destroying her brain. She must have lost count yesterday of how many she'd taken. She thought it was two, but two would never have done what they did to her in the car. She'd been on them too long for thirty milligrams to have much of an effect.

She meant it this time, she had said to Harry in bed last night while he nodded and turned a page of his medical journal. She wasn't addicted. Not truly, hopelessly addicted. She could stop any time she wanted to.

"We don't know the full effects of long-term use yet," Harry had said. "Severe dependency, of course. But the effects on the heart, the brain . . ."

Yes, she had nodded, knowing he was right. The drug was affecting every part of her body. It seemed to start at the top and work its way down. Hair and memory had been first. She repeated the same story over and over. *We've heard it before, mom,* Julia would say, her eyes glazing over. Was that pity in those eyes, or was what she saw there perfect adolescent contempt? Sara likened the drug rampaging through her vital organs to a monstrous termite gnawing its way through choice cuts of lumber. Teeth were going now. What would be next? Lungs? Heart? Liver? The last would be her toenails, bitten off, chewed through, discarded like wood shavings on the floor.

"Short term use, okay," Harry had continued. "For weight control, fatigue, even depression. I used them myself in medical school. Everybody did. But you've been on them for years. They can trigger a psychosis, you know. And you're paranoid enough as it is."

She'd get off them, honestly she would. First thing in the morning. For good. Harry had nodded and turned another page. He didn't believe her. She didn't deserve his trust, she knew she didn't. She lied. She cheated. But if only Harry were behind her . . . if only he believed . . .

"I'd like to believe you, Sara," he'd said. "But how many times have we had this conversation before?"

Endless times, innumerable times. Seventeen years worth of times. The words piling up, the promises, the reproaches, the narrow stretches of success turning on hairpin curves into failure. A marriage worth of vows spoken in good faith, broken nonetheless.

There must be something for it, she had said. There is, Harry had answered. Strength. Willpower. Willpower? No, she had never had much of that. Willpower was what Harry had. Inner direction, inner strength. Sara imposed her will from without. She went along haphazardly until she felt a breaking point was near and then she reared back and put a stop to it. She'd give up the drug someday, she told him, and not because of her willpower but because of the power of her will.

Down the hall her four children slept. Next to her, Harry read his journal, went over courses of treatment in his mind. His patients had real diseases, were, in some cases, near death. What were her problems compared to theirs? Sara stared at the back cover of his magazine. How many nights had she gone to sleep looking at that photograph, carrying that image of a wild-eyed, disheveled woman surrounded by the words "anxiety" and "Valium" with her into sleep?

"You said you were completely out. Is that true?"

Yes, she had nodded. That's true.

"You don't have any stored in the house?"

No, she had lied. She didn't.

She had tried to get to sleep, but the speed still in her system lifted her off to a place suspended between sleep and waking where she hovered over herself just out of reach. She might count sheep, but how much more comforting to visualize the Dexedrine lying loose among the linens in the closet where she'd hidden them and count the capsules piling up between the sheets milligram by milligram like coins in a secret bank account.

But today was a new day. She'd keep her promise today and make Harry proud. It was important to get things done, to feed the children and get the older ones off to school, to take care of William, do the dishes, tidy the kitchen, to keep busy, keep her mind off it, walking by the linen closet a hundred times a day telling herself there was nothing in it, nothing she needed, nothing she couldn't do without. She'd do it this time, she really would. If only she weren't so tired . . . but she mustn't think about that. Thoughts of sleep, of stretching out somewhere . . . that chair, that rug, any one of the beds upstairs . . . of sinking down, drifting off . . . but no, she mustn't give in to such thoughts.

She gave William his bottle and put him down for his morning nap. All the same, the thought of a nap, sleeping while her baby slept . . .

But if she took a nap she'd never get up. She'd sleep straight through the day. And who would take care of William then? Who would be up to greet the children when they came home from school? *Get someone in to help*, Harry insisted again and again and through the years she'd tried it. But always it was a failure. And always Sara let them go. Strangers in her house. Spies touching her things, looking after her children. She didn't trust them. Strange women up to no good. *That's nonsense. That's paranoid*, Harry had said. *It's not*, she'd protested. But what did he know about it? What did he know about anything that went on in that house?

The phone rang suddenly, startling her. Sara stared at it and thought at first perhaps she wouldn't answer it.

Telephones to her meant trouble with Justin at school, intrusions into her private life, disturbances of sleep or routine. Only when *she* made the call—usually high and late at night— did she enjoy the instrument.

"Hello," she said, finally picking it up on the fifth ring.

"Hi. It's Jennifer."

Immediately Sara pulled herself up in her chair, shook her head briskly and widened her eyes. Even over the phone she imagined Jennifer could perceive her state. So if she was on when she talked to her, she forced the words out slowly and distinctly, and if she was off, she filled her voice with a false brightness.

"Hi, Jenny!" she cried. "How are you? Good to hear from you. How's Peter? And Edward?"

"Well I'm fine and Edwards's fine, but Peter's in bed with some kind of virus."

"Oh what a shame. I'm sorry to hear that. Anything I can do?"

"Thanks, Sara. Not a thing. I just called to talk. It's not so bad being stuck in the house actually, I've got loads of work to do. That's another reason I called. Just finished developing the pictures I took of you and the children that day in the zoo. Remember? They turned out quite nicely and I'm dying for you to see them."

"I'd love to. The ones of the children that is. I hate the way I photograph. Dumpy and disagreeable."

"Not in my photographs, you don't. You look great in these, but then I only take good pictures of friends."

"Really?" Sara laughed. "Must've been one of my thin days."

Her weight tended to go up and down, not so much anymore according to whether she was on or off the pills—they had long ago ceased to affect her appetite—but more in response to the degree of emptiness she was feeling within. Some days it was vast and then she would stuff herself with enormous amounts of food—thick slices of bread covered with butter and jam, huge snacks of cold meat and crackers and cheese devoured between meals—and after dinner in the kitchen she would surreptitiously finish off every bit of food the children left on their plates. Other times she didn't eat a thing all day, and even at supper stared at her plate with disinterest.

Sara knew she wasn't a bad looking woman. She liked her dark eyes—they were the same color as Harry's—and her large-boned, sturdy looks. She was just a little on the short side and tended to look dumpy, she thought, when overweight. She envied Jennifer her slimness and her height and her work too. Having something of her own, the way Jennifer had her photography, might make all the difference, Sara thought. How she would like that—to have a work of her own—but where would she get the time? Jennifer Talbot had only one child. And a lover who cooked.

"We'll have to get together as soon as Peter's well. You could come over or . . . Oh, that reminds me . . . William's birthday is two weeks from Friday. I'm giving a party for him . . . out in the yard if the weather's nice. I hope you all can come."

"William's birthday? Is it a year already? It seems like

yesterday that you brought him home. I know people always say that but it's true, it does. Of course we'll be there. Wouldn't miss William's party for the world. . . . The kids all right? Harry doing well?"

Harry? What did she know about Harry? Harry was busy, Harry was never home. At this very moment he was probably saving a life somewhere. But it exhausted Sara to think of it and other than that she couldn't say. Fine, she said. Harry was fine. They were all fine. She'd love to put the phone down, curl up in this chair, go to sleep, but she had to keep talking about the things she was expected to talk about, childcare and housework, sibling rivalry and the dust on the top of the fridge. What about the life of the imagination and the other Sara she could, with a dip of her hand in the linen closet, become? The Sara that's free of these expectations and as good as her doctor husband or her photographer friend. Free and confident and absolutely certain of every move she makes, free of this house and its rooms with their dust piling up, their clothes piling up, free of possessions rising like a flood above her, closing over her head.

"Do you need any help?" Jennifer asked.

"Help? No. What for?"

"For the party, of course. I'd be glad to help."

Jennifer was her friend. Sara could talk to her. Two things she thought she wanted most: to talk to a friend, to sleep forever.

"Maybe you could come over," she said. "We could sit and talk."

"Today, you mean? But I can't, there's Peter . . ."

Of course. She had forgotten Peter.

". . . and I've got a mountain of film to develop. But soon, Sara. We'll do it soon."

Yes, soon.

Sara hung up and made her bed, straightened her room. She wondered why Jennifer couldn't come over. Did Peter really have a virus? Couldn't Edward look after him for an hour or two? Or? . . . Oh, but she hated to be like *paranoid*, Harry called it. Mistrustful of her best friend, her only friend. She wanted to be normal, to be like everyone else. Like Harry. Like Jennifer—calm and rational and successful and thin.

The linen closet was just down the hall. She could take one. No one need know. One was nothing. One was all she needed. But no, she decided, raising the blinds and turning back to dust the dresser, she had promised.

At first she didn't recognize the young woman in the wedding photograph. For seventeen years she had stood there on top of the dresser next to Harry, and Sara had thought she had known who she was. But today a stranger returned her glance from inside the frame, frozen in time. She was not that young, hopeful girl holding eagerly to her new husband's arm, certain everything would turn out all right. She'd make him a good wife, be a credit to him—hadn't she just finished speaking those words when the picture was snapped?

Harry had advanced rapidly in his career. Sara had struggled to keep up. She went to the obligatory parties, gave her share in return. She met the right people, the ones who might do Harry some good. But she never felt she knew what they were talking about, never was sure how to reply. The parties frightened her. Did she really have to go? She didn't know how to dress or what to say, and she really was too tired. *Here's something for energy,* Harry said. *It'll see you through.* Harry was right. Energy was hers. And courage and strength and wit and humor. She was a different person then, the life of the party. She could carry on a conversation with anyone at all. And Harry was proud. Through the crowd she'd catch him beaming at her, *my wife,* he'd say, coming over, handing her around, *I'd like you to meet my wife.* It was just until he got himself established, she told herself. Until he had the right people behind him. Then she would stop. She'd give up the pills and go back to being the girl he had married.

But she'd never get back to her now. The girl in the photograph wasn't waiting somewhere, as Sara had once imagined, for her to return and bring her back to life. Yet she still believed, she had to believe, that anytime she wanted to— today, for instance, this could be the beginning of it—she could be a different person, lead a better life. Any day she decided to, she could renounce the pills and turn herself into the decent, drug-free wife Harry deserved.

She scrubbed out the tub in the bathroom, rested her head a moment, just a moment, on its smooth, cool rim, closed her eyes. . . .

* * *

A small repetitive sound at the back of her head—familiar, unfamiliar . . . urgent yet not urgent, a kind of chirping . . . a bird perhaps . . . no, not a bird . . . human sounds, but not words, not quite words. Oh, my God! Sara bolted awake. It was William beginning to cry. William who hardly ever cried, and here she was asleep on the bathroom floor. How long had her baby been awake, sending his pathetic little calls tentatively down the hall? Not long. It couldn't have been long. A few minutes at most. And her sweet William patiently waiting for lunch. Lunch! Not even lunchtime yet? Not even noon?

She changed his diaper, put a clean playsuit on him and carried him down the stairs. Passing the linen closet, she told herself there was nothing in it. Nothing she needed. Nothing at all. Look away, she said. You're doing fine. Just keep walking. You made a promise, didn't you?

"And we'll keep that promise, won't we, sweetheart?" she said to William, feeding him his lunch. "We'll stay off the hateful stuff."

He smiled up at her between mouthfuls, laughing as the food ran down his chin. Her easy, happy child. The one among them she could trust.

Dishes again, the highchair to wipe, the spots on the floor. Laundry to do, vacuuming. She liked for the house to be neat, for her children to have clean clothes to wear. She wasn't so different from other women, other mothers—but the thought of those stairs, those cluttered rooms. She wanted what other people wanted—to do a good job, to be worthy.

She put William in his playpen, watched him from the door. It was better to stay on her feet, she thought, and if anything could keep her awake it was watching William chase sunbeams across the floor. He'd pounce like a cat on one, give a short, high laugh, then wait as if expecting it to move out from under him. After a moment, he'd spot another, give a joyous shriek and pounce on that one too. Born on a brilliant day in June, he had always loved the sun, sought its company like that of a dear friend. She should take him out into the yard, Sara thought, but that was such an effort. She'd have to go with him, follow him around, keep him safe. Here inside nothing could harm him. Here in his playpen she knew he was safe.

Again she forced herself up the stairs, once more past the linen closet on the landing. My God, what a mess four children could make. How many things they had—toys, books, records, papers, tiny metal pencil sharpeners, tapes, pocket calendars, calculators, rulers, tennis rackets, all kinds of bats and balls and shirts and socks. Nobody could have so many socks!

She made the beds, forced herself to ignore their soft appeal, picked up the clothes, did the best she could in Sam's room. Julia and Justin were supposed to take care of their own, after all.

Downstairs again in the kitchen, she separated whites from darks, put a load in the machine, wondered what she'd make for dinner, and remembered the wastebasket in Harry's den.

There it was overflowing at the side of his desk. She emptied it, straightened his papers. Folders in one place, letters and notes in another, xeroxes of his published articles, outlines of those he was working on. As if his practice weren't enough, Harry was always writing for one journal or another. *Next time I'm going to turn them down*, he swore. *It's not as if I don't have enough to do.* But he never did. Harry couldn't say no to seeing his name in print. He wanted to be everything, Harry did: writer, physician, teacher, psychiatrist—the last was a dream so secret he didn't even know Sara knew. Anything worth doing, Harry did, or could if he wanted to. It was hard keeping up with a man like that.

Time seemed to have stopped. Sara passed a clock, passed another, no movement, no advance on the day. Would it never end? Would it never even begin to come to an end? She had to consciously lift each foot, to force it ahead of the other. Everything she picked up now was heavy. Her body was heavy. The air was heavy. She had to push herself against it.

She should take something out of the freezer for dinner. She should take William for a walk. Happy as he was, it wasn't fair to keep him in the house all day.

Her eyelids were heavy. Her arms hung at her sides. It was warm in the house. Still and dry and warm. William was better off indoors. She went into the living room and saw him there at play. A sweet, happy child. No trouble. No trouble at all. Where had he come from?

She pulled up her favorite chair and smiled at him through the bars of his playpen. He smiled back. A huge, generous, toothless smile. He made soft, gurgling noises at her. Nice noises. She nodded. Pleasant noises. She settled back in her chair. Happy noises. She closed her eyes.

Suddenly there were voices all around her. Loud, high voices. Low, deep ones. Questions, demands, accusations, entreaties. Dozens of voices speaking at once. A confused jumble of sound in her ears. Fingers tugging at her sleeves, her hair. Plucking at her skin as if she were a chicken. A dead chicken. Couldn't they leave her alone and let her die in peace?

She opened one eye, then the other. She shut them both. The children were home from school.

"She's awake. She's awake. I saw her eye!" Her little Sam.

"Leave her alone. Let her sleep." Her eldest boy.

"Hiya, mom. Whatcha doing?" Her only daughter. "Kicking the habit again?"

III

Sara awoke on Wednesday and wondered why she wasn't dead. The morning of the third day without a pill. Surely the fatigue and depression, the immense effort of withdrawal were enough to kill her. To say nothing of the internal emptiness, vast enough to drown in. Perhaps she could simply drift off again and die in her sleep, the sleep of the deprived addict being a kind of death itself—profound, airless, black. But the power of her will, as she had said it would, was prevailing. If she wasn't going to die, she deserved a reward. Some little gift to mark the occasion.

Surviving this day, she might look at Harry and say, *there, I've done it, broken my record, I told you I would.* Wouldn't that be reward enough, she asked herself, to see the smile on his face, the pride in his eyes, to feel worthy of his good opinion? *Do it for them,* exhorts the smooth, censorious voice on television. The happy family grouping, mother and father and several children delivering the National Heart Association's message: *take your medication for them.* That parent with high blood pressure, herself lying here visualizing husband and children before her—both drug-dependants being urged in the one case to continue, in the other to desist. For them. Do it for them, Sara told herself, dragging herself out of bed, for Harry's good opinion, for the good of her children.

Could she make it through? Crashing was such an ordeal. Her limbs ached with fatigue. Her body didn't want to move. She had to use her hands to push herself up off the bed.

"You're doing fine," Harry said, already up, already washed. "You know what they say . . . one day at a time."

28

She pulled on her jeans, a shirt, no shoes, and walked out of the room to wake the children, make breakfast, make lunch, begin the wearing routine of her day.

Justin was out of bed, as she knew he'd be, and down the hall in the bathroom. An early riser, he did what had to be done. With no unnecessary movements, he got himself up and out of the house in the mornings. He was like his father in that. Only in that. He wouldn't be a scholar or a doctor like Harry, but whatever he chose for himself it would be right for him, Sara was certain. If only Harry had more confidence in the boy. If only he wouldn't push him so. But she couldn't lean here against the doorjamb, staring in at Justin's empty room, and think about that now. She had to get moving, to force her legs to move.

Julia and Sam were her two slug-a-beds. She sat down next to Sam's sleeping form and gently rubbed his forehead to wake him. His hair, matted and damp, his cheeks flushed and sweaty, he always seemed slightly feverish to her in the mornings. And his bed looked as if he'd spent the night engaged in battle upon it. The quilt was pulled loose and thrown on the floor, the topsheet and blanket were shoved to the foot of the bed. The pillow was tossed against the wall, its case had come off and was wedged between mattress and headboard. What dreams could a five-year-old have violent enough to leave a bed so torn apart?

"Sweetheart," she said, rubbing her hand through his hair. "Time to get up."

He squeezed his eyes tight and flung himself over onto his stomach. "No. Don't wanna."

Such was Sam's characteristic stance toward the world. Not mommy or daddy, but no was the first word he'd ever uttered.

"Get up now," Sara urged him gently. "Breakfast will be ready soon."

Julia used her pillows as soft living things to clasp against her body or cast aside in sleep. Objects of comfort or disdain, they were alternately held in the strangling embrace of her arms and legs, or flung to the four corners of her room. Some mornings like this one, upon coming in, Sara found her daughter lying so absolutely still with the pillows over her face that

29

it made her stop up short and catch her breath a moment before rushing to her side, as she did now, to snatch the pillows away.

"Don't do that," she said. "You can suffocate that way."

Julia groaned deeply and groped for the sheet to cover her face. In some ways Sara feared more for her than for any of the others. The only girl. The one most like herself. Yet in saving graces, least like. Julia was warm, outgoing, open. She seemed possessed of a sense of self, contented with it. From whatever source that trait had come—and Sara knew it was not herself—she thanked heaven for it. Was it Harry's confidence this child had inherited and, by some genuinely elegant act of her own creativity, infused with a sweetness and humor not to be found in her father? Whatever its origin, Sara honored it. It was what she thought would save her daughter from herself.

"Time to get up, darling," she said. "You don't want to be late."

She tugged lightly at Julia's arm, then began to rub her back. The skin was as smooth as the day she'd been born and Sara could recall the child, even at two or three, reacting with curiosity and confusion to her use of drugs. All that time. So long ago. Was Harry right? Was her luck running out? Julia would cock her little head and narrow her eyes as if to ask what made her mother talk so fast, what made her different from the day before. And back in those days she wasn't taking nearly the amount she took now. Lately, very lately, it seemed to Sara, perhaps just since William's birth, things had begun piling up. She was under constant pressure. The responsibility of caring for a newborn—of even one child, let alone four— the size of the house, its insurmountable tasks, and then there was her age. Perhaps she was too old for a baby, too nervous. Perhaps it had been a mistake. But the others were growing up. They'd be leaving her soon. She'd be alone with Harry. Speed helped her get along. It masked her fears. Soon one was no longer enough. Two now hardly got her off the ground.

And through the years, Julia had watched it all, taking everything in. Children see everything, Sara had always known. And Julia, with her green eyes, clear as the sea, saw with a special acuity, perhaps. *Cool it, mom*, she'd say. *Your addictive personality is showing*. The only one of her children who could joke about it. The one who was most afraid?

"Come on now. You've got to get up." Sara gave her one more tug and moved on into William's room.

Her baby was already up and playing in his crib. He gave his usual morning shout and the sight of him—his face lighting up as he saw her at the door, his arms stretched out, hands reaching for her—was enough to make her forget for a moment the consciousness it required to take another step. No, she thought, picking him up, no mistake here.

Downstairs in the kitchen, she sat William in his highchair and gave him a banana to eat while she undertook the simultaneous preparation of breakfast and lunch. It was an expert act of juggling she'd perfected over the years. Making sandwiches, scrambling eggs, spreading mayonnaise, spreading jam, packing juices, filling glasses—now breakfast, now lunch, folding them in one after the other. Her mind working easily on two levels hours apart—coffee perking, salt and pepper for the eggs, some raisins for Sam, chicken salad on rye. The fruit was on the table, the eggs on low. The first sandwich made before the eggs needed stirring, toast pressed down with one hand, sandwich wrapped with the other, toast buttered and sliced, eggs stirred, another sandwich made, lunch bags opened, napkins folded, apples and oranges packed while at the table her family ate.

"And how is everyone this morning?"

Harry sat up tall—closely shaven, eyes bright, hair slicked back, fingernails scrubbed—uncorrupted and brisk.

"Fine, dad." They kissed him. They asked how he was.

"Great. Just great. Never felt better."

Never sick a day in his life. His appetite robust, his energy vast and possessed of a power to increase proportionately as Sara's declined.

"Elbows off the table, Sam. Your head'll stay up by itself."

Obscurely, she counted on it: her lows playing to Harry's highs, her weakness to his strength.

"How's school, Julia?"

"Terrific. I hardly have any. Rehearsals take up all my time."

Off the drug she was no match for him. Alone with Harry and straight—the idea frightened her.

"And you, Justin?"

31

"Not bad. Vacation's coming up."

"Vacation? Shouldn't you rather have your mind on chemistry? I seem to be paying for you kids to spend more time out of school than in it."

But the prospect of their highs seriously clashing, Harry's natural omnipotence pitted against hers, chemically induced—now *there* might be a battle worth watching.

"More eggs, mom."

"Patience, Sam. William hasn't had his yet."

"He's got a banana."

"I want him to have eggs too."

"He doesn't got to go to school."

"Take it easy, Sam," Harry said. "We'll all live longer if we learn to take it easy."

Sara knew what he was doing. She could feel his eyes on her back.

"Nice and easy," he continued. "Everything in its own good time. William will get his eggs. Sam will get his. We'll all have a nice calm breakfast. Then we'll get on with our day—each of us doing what has to be done—calmly, cheerfully."

A message meant for her not very subtly disguised as a general communique to the group. Sara turned toward the table, William's dish in her hands, and saw that Julia had picked it up too. The girl's green eyes flashed from her father's face to her own.

"Trying it cold turkey again, mom?"

"Julia, help is what's needed," Harry observed. "Not levity. If we'll all just take it easy and help one another, everything will be all right."

"Keep it up," he said to Sara as she saw him out the door. "You're doing fine."

He turned to go, turned back. His fine, dark eyes holding on hers a moment, dropping away, finding hers again.

"Go ahead, Harry," Sara said quietly. "I know you have to ask."

He looked away again, looked back, asked it as routinely as he could. "You don't have any in the house, do you?"

"No. I don't," she said, looking him in the eye. "Go along now and make everybody well."

Justin was next out the door. "See ya, mom. Oh . . . I'll be late tonight. I'm working at the garage after school."

"And I've got rehearsal," Julia said, giving her one of her green-eyed glances. "This must be your lucky day. Two of us off your hands. You can crash early tonight. Seriously, though, try not to get too down. Don't take any either. Downs, that is. Get it?"

Sara nodded wearily. She got it, she said, but she wished Julia didn't. She wished none of them had to know anything about this.

Sam was the last one ready.

"You wait for Sam now," Sara called to Justin who had started on down the street.

"Julia'll take him," Justin yelled back. "I've gotta run. Gonna be late."

"Oh, mom. Why is it always me?"

The entreaty she heard in her daughter's voice, as if she would pull an answer from her, the battle she foresaw with Sam, the protestations, attacks and counterattacks, the deadening movements back and forth, the predictable words—*hurry up now, am hurrying, no you're not, yes I am*—all moving before her as if she had seen it before, heard it before, as if she were listening to two people other than herself and Sam saying these words to each other, making these movements, it was more than Sara thought she could take.

"Maybe you'd better go see what he's after," she said to Julia. But then there he was coming toward her, his face tight in anger and Sara's heart sank. She didn't have the strength for this today.

"Not going!" Sam yelled. "Can't find Elsie. Not going without Elsie."

"Come on, Sam," Julia coaxed. "Leave Elsie home for the day. She'll be all right with mom."

"No she won't, you big dummy."

"Yes she will."

"No she won't."

"All right, Sam," Sara said, seeing the tears in his eyes, feeling them rise in hers. "All right. Think now. Where did you have her last? Julia, you'd better come in. This is going to take some time."

"I don't *have* time, mom."

"Make it then," Sara snapped. She couldn't deal with them both. She turned to Sam. "Where were you when you had her last? In the living room? The dining room? Did you have her at dinner? Did you take her up with you to bed?" Sara remembered she hadn't put him to bed. She'd been so tired last night Harry had had to do it. "Did you leave her in the den? The bathroom?" The possibilities were limitless, exhausting just to list. They could search the house for days. Sam would refuse to go to school. She'd have him as well as William at home and on her hands forever. "Sam," she said. "Think!"

"Don't know," he cried, the tears spilling over.

"Don't cry," Julia yelled. "I've got to get out of here."

"Don't yell at him, Julia. Help."

"Help? What can I do?"

"Look for her. Find her."

Julia headed toward the dining room and Sara sent what strength she had in the form of prayers behind her. Find her, please find her, find the giraffe and save my life. She bent down to Sam, wiped away his tears, smoothed back his hair. Forgive me, she almost said. For not finding Elsie, for being too tired to put you to bed. Maybe she could make it up to him, sing him a song tonight, make him a giraffe out of clay. If only she could get her fingers to move, force them to mold a shape, but she remembered how hard it was the last time she'd tried. She'd given up in defeat and thrown out all the clay she had in the house.

"Got it!" Julia screamed from the hall, running back in, swinging Elsie over her head. "Now let's get going."

One disaster averted, one crisis resolved. An auspicious beginning to the day, Sara thought. No reason the rest shouldn't follow accordingly, if only she could stay awake.

"Bless you, Julia," Sara said. "Now the two of you go on and be good."

The memory came back to her, with its attending comfort, later in the day of how she once had dreamed of becoming a sculptor. Huge pieces cast in bronze. No modest goals for her. Henry Moore was her exemplar. She never got farther than

34

throwing pots but even that was an accomplishment to Sara's mind, and a source of great joy.

Harry had been impressed with her pots when they first met. Sara smiled now to think of it. He had been different then—softer, with an area still accessible to her, not entirely closed up as it very nearly was now beneath his expertise. *Nice. Very nice,* he said picking up a piece she'd done, turning it slowly in his hand. *Wish I could do that.* He said it sincerely. Not the way he'd say it now, implying he could if he wanted to or if he had the time or if it interested him, but acknowledging a skill beyond his reach. Sara could do something Harry couldn't do. He looked at the pot in his hand and was impressed.

She ought to have kept it up. She was getting quite good at the wheel and firing the glaze. But after they were married and moved out here where there was no kiln . . . and then when the babies started coming. . . .

Sara looked up from her favorite chair at the ceiling overhead. William was asleep in the room directly above. He'd been fed, been changed. She'd even taken him out into the backyard to get some air for a few minutes after lunch. She wasn't doing badly. Not badly at all. The whole morning got through. . . . The whole afternoon yet ahead.

She'd like to do something nice for Harry. Make him a pot, perhaps. Sew a button on his coat. She didn't have any clay. His buttons weren't loose. There was so little one could do for Harry.

Self-sufficient, was how he described himself. He was proud of that. His ideal. An ideal man. Closed up now. Complete. She wondered where that little area had gone, that narrow space in his soul that once had room for her.

She really ought to get up now, clean the house, make the beds. . . . He'd let her in once. . . . She didn't want the children coming home seeing nothing done. . . . Maybe he would again. . . . Not nothing. They couldn't call it nothing. She'd played with William, fed him. . . . Maybe another space would open up some day. . . . She'd got through the morning, kept him alive. . . . Maybe Harry would need her again. . . . They could hardly call that nothing. She'd kept them all alive. Justin was sixteen, Julia two years younger—fourteen years, sixteen years—so many years to keep them alive. That wasn't nothing. They couldn't call it that. . . .

The chair beneath her was soft and giving. It molded itself to her shape. To sit there, just as she was. . . . As she molded the clay in her hands. . . . It received her. Accepted her as she was. . . . But she had to get up. There was something she meant to do. Something for Harry. Fix Harry's. . . . Get Harry's. . . . If she didn't get up she'd fall asleep. Well, why not? Just for a minute while William slept . . . the house was so quiet, so empty. . . . But what was it she had meant to do? . . . Something for Harry . . . She tensed her legs as if to rise. They stayed where they were beneath her. Her intentions were honorable, Harry would be proud. It was her legs that failed to respond. She'd try again . . . she tried so hard . . . she'd do what she had to do . . . the innumerable rooms upstairs . . . she'd make him proud . . . the unmade beds . . . the mounds of socks . . . Look! One right here. Loose in the living room. A sock on the floor in front of her. She stretched out her leg, angled her bare foot, strained her toes in its direction. She could get it, she could. Sliding down a little in her chair . . . stretching her leg, toes splayed and straining . . . almost . . . a little more . . . look, there! She's touched it . . . concentrating hard, she's made it move . . . half an inch, an inch . . . she did that for him. . . . Closer now, concentrating, her whole mind on the task. . . . For him . . . when all she wanted to do was sleep . . . a little more . . . just a little . . . she's got it now . . . seized it in her toes. . . . Look, Harry, look! One sock less at large in the world . . . the minor triumphs of man, of woman . . . she was trying so hard . . . didn't he see? . . . wasn't he proud? . . .

Sara snapped awake, shook off images of floating pieces of cloth, rising free like sails filled with wind, falling suddenly, losing the wind, dropping down on her face, on her eyes, her nose, covering her mouth. She couldn't breathe—she gasped for breath, stood up, shook her head, she wouldn't let this happen to her. Not today. Today was the day she'd break her record. What was needed was a change, a walk downtown with William, an act of determination to propel this endless day to an end.

Maybe she'd buy herself some more clay, get started again. She could begin with simple figures, bowls or little animals for the children—"You'd like that, wouldn't you?" she asked William, changing his clothes, carrying him down the hall—work her way up to something more complex. This time she wouldn't give up.

It really should be a possibility, Sara admonished herself, to raise her children, take care of the house, have something of her own like pottery, and also lead a reasonable life without resorting to drugs. *Millions of women do it every day,* Harry reminded her. *Why do you need the stuff?* To feel alive, she might have said, she thought, pausing a moment on the landing, shifting William to one hip, staring at the door of the linen closet. Therein lay her hidden treasure, she imagined a capsule in her hand—brown on one end, clear on the other, the tiny letters SKF—the magic properties within to feed her blood, transform her soul.

To feel worthwhile. But Harry wouldn't have understood that. *Millions,* he repeated for emphasis and Sara wondered just how right he was. Soap operas and tranquilizers, vodka in the orange juice, steady sipping all day long. There were more out there like her than Harry imagined. Closet drinkers and chain smokers, pill poppers of all kinds. Julia had brought the literature home from school, left it where Sara could see: women take fifty percent more tranquilizers than men, they make up half of America's twelve million alcoholics. Millions, Harry? Yes. It all depends on which group you're counting.

William issued a shriek of delight as they stepped outside into the sun. He loved the brightness of day, sat up straight in his carriage, waved his hands in greeting to every tree and house and person they passed. If Sara slowed down or had to stop for a light, he squealed in displeasure and shook the side of the carriage to make it start moving again.

Passing the book shop which Edward once owned, Sara thought she might go in and say hello, but she'd never had much to say to Edward. To tell the truth, she couldn't quite see what Jennifer saw in him—a man that young, so much younger than Jennifer herself. But, then, maybe that was why—to keep herself young, to avoid the crisis of her first marriage: middle-aged man seeking a younger woman. How typical that was. Common enough to be a cliché. Harry was probably doing it, Sara wouldn't be surprised, with his hospital visits and late night calls. Not that she actually blamed him, she hadn't been much of a wife to him in that respect. It was something she could very well do without, and did, more and more, lately. All the same, she'd kill him if she ever found out.

Passing "Aileen's," she stared at the negligee in the window—long, pale gray silk. Ordinarily Sara wasn't attracted to silky things, but this flowed like a river gently down the sides of the mannequin. She wondered if Harry. . . . Pulling William over to the side and letting him fuss, she gazed at it. Soft, flowing, elegant lines. Simple but elegant. Something about it touched on Sara's desire to be another kind of woman. . . . Claudette Colbert floating down the stairs. Harry would say it was extravagant, for it was bound to be that, she could tell just by looking. All those layers of silk. No, it was out of the question. She moved the carriage forward to William's satisfaction, reconsidered, and pulled it back to his renewed annoyance. But, why not? A treat for her day of record, a little surprise for Harry.

"Take it easy, little one," she said, braking the carriage to William's cries of outrage. "I'll be back in a flash."

The saleswoman looked at her jeans, her sandals. What did she expect, Sara wondered. Designer clothes to push a carriage through the streets?

"May I help you?"

Sara didn't like people looking at her like that. This was when she needed a pill—to make her as good as anyone else, to protect her from the hostile looks of strangers. A salesgirl, no less. Didn't she know who she was—a doctor's wife. She could have anything in the store. Certainly a little flimsy thing like that. She asked the price.

"Seventy-five dollars. Isn't it beautiful?"

Yes, it was beautiful and Harry would be right to chide her. Sara turned around and left the store. Outside, she released the carriage brake again. Seventy-five dollars indeed. It was unthinkable. She pushed William on down the street. Absolutely out of the question when all she'd really come for was a lump of clay.

When she stepped inside the art supply store, ancient, buried feelings were revived with force. There she was, twenty years younger, childless, unattached, filled with noble aspirations for the creative life. She wandered slowly up and down the aisles, touching jars of paint, examining pens and drawing boards, pulling out reams of papers, checking for quality, testing charcoal pencils, running the soft heads of brushes against the pads of her fingers. She would have liked to be a painter, to capture likenesses, reproduce expressions, but she couldn't draw to save her life. Some kind of artist then, a molder of forms, and yearnings welled within her for a different kind of life.

She bought two squares of plastalena. One green, one maroon. *Permanent modeling clay, non-hardening, pliable, will not crumble or break.* That was what she needed—something permanent of her own, something that would not crumble or break. Just having the clay in her possession, knowing that soon she would be squeezing it through her hands, filled her with a pleasure she hadn't felt in months. She dropped it in the case on the handle of William's carriage and headed home.

Passing "Aileen's" again, she pulled up abruptly in front of the store. What the hell? It would give her a lift. A non-chemical boost. A sculptor in a gray silk gown.

"Charge it, please," she said. "To Dr. Harold Richardson."

She'd make something nice for Harry, something to make him laugh. She kneaded the clay in her hands. Some little figure—a frog with bulging eyes, perhaps, or a horse or cat—something to cheer him up after the "brutal" day he undoubtedly would have had.

Rolling the clay into a ball, throwing it from one hand to the other, she enjoyed the slapping sound it made as it hit against the flat of her palm. She liked the feel of it, throwing it into her hand, taking it out, throwing it in again—just as she had so often seen Justin throw a baseball into his glove. It was a good gesture, Sara thought, a good sound. Not quite the same as throwing the wet clay onto a wheel, but nearly as good and maybe she could work her way back up to that again in time.

In the meantime, she was doing all right, she told herself. The day was passing. It was nearly suppertime. Harry wouldn't be home, but the children had to be fed. The third straight day and she still had her eyes open, her mind on something.

Every once in a while William looked up from his playpen and laughed at the sound of the green ball landing in his mother's hand. He was such a good baby. Such a joy. Sara wanted his party to be especially nice, the yard looking lovely and the weather perfect. What would she do if it rained? It angered her to have something as crucial as the weather beyond her control.

Maybe a little lamb instead of a frog for Harry. Or an elephant . . . she wasn't the only one showing disinterest . . . his trunk straight up in the air, of course. For luck, she'd heard. And if Harry should be inspired that would be luck indeed. Sara couldn't remember the last time they'd made love. It had never been totally satisfactory—Harry always seemed preoccupied, wanting to hurry and finish and get back to whatever more important thing he was doing. But it had never been altogether absent as it had been now for . . . oh, she couldn't remember how long. She'd read somewhere the first year without sex was the hardest. After that, a marriage was home free. Would it come to that between herself and Harry? Was he seeing someone else?

But Sara didn't want to think about Harry and another woman—someone younger, prettier, no doubt. She thought instead of the gray silk negligee upstairs in her drawer. Would that revive his interest? She wasn't foolish enough to insist on love. She was thirty-nine, after all—they'd been married for seventeen years. But some warmth, a little affection. Her body craved it so. Yet, she wondered, looking down at the clay in her hands, wouldn't she be as out of practice in that field as she was in this one? Already her fingers were weakening. Her arms ached right up to the elbows. It took more strength than she'd remembered to mold even the smallest piece. She was glad she hadn't opened the other pack.

"What is it, mommy?" Sam ran into the room and peered at the thing in her hands. "A unicorn?"

"No, honey. It's an elephant."

"Looks more like a horse to me," Justin said, slouching in after him.

"A horse with a unicorn's horn," Julia amended, home from rehearsal.

"Don't make fun," Sara told them. "And Justin, please. Stand up straight. Put your shoulders back."

"I know!" Julia shouted, inspecting the figure more closely. "It's an abstract."

"What's an abstract?" Sam demanded.

"That!" Julia pointed to the clay and laughed.

"When will dinner be ready?" Justin asked. "I've got to go out again."

"Back to the garage?"

"Yup. I didn't finish the job this afternoon."

"You're spending so much time there," Sara said, beginning to think Harry was right about that place.

"It's my job, mom."

"And what about your schoolwork?"

"It'll get done. Don't worry."

But she did worry. That was one thing she had in common with Harry. She worried about her children doing well in school. She worried about the images they had of themselves. Justin, a mechanic? Wasn't he selling himself short? Wasn't Harry right?

"Are you keeping your grades up?"

Sure, he said, and she let it go. She was far too tired to fight with anyone tonight. Her fingers were too weak to work the clay anymore. She put it down, thought of the negligee upstairs, thought of the other woman she might be.

"Julia," she said. "Come here, sweetheart."

Julia came obediently. "What, mom?"

"Nothing." Sara pulled her down into her lap. "I just want to hold you a minute."

Justin was too big to hold and Sam too impatient. But Julia filled Sara's lap nicely. Her only girl. She loved her so. Wrapping her arms around her, Sara leaned forward and rested her head a moment on her daughter's shoulder. Holding on, she thought, she was doing that, holding on until the day was done. Holding up too, holding herself up against her little girl. Or holding back, was that it? Holding Julia back from her own proper pursuits, entrapping her in a matter which even to Sara seemed so often beyond her power to control. She prayed it wasn't that. She would do anything to spare her this, to be a fit mother for this lovely child.

"Rough day, mom? The third's always hard, I know."

Julia knew. Julia had been counting, been going through it in her own way with her. Harry never knew for sure. With all his medical knowledge, he had to ask. *Stay off today? Didn't take any, did you?* But Julia knew just by looking. Sara held her tighter and tried to keep her body still as the tears poured from her eyes. Silently she cried against her daughter's back. Then Julia's arms were around her, her face pressed up against hers.

"I'm sorry, darling," Sara said. "I'm sorry. It's just that I get so tired."

"I know, mom. It's okay. Why don't you go on up and I'll make dinner?"

Her splendid, loving daughter, holding her now, everything was all right.

"Better yet," Sara said. "Why don't we make dinner together?"

Sara looked at the lopsided piece of clay on the table. The kids were right. It didn't look like an elephant. It didn't look like anything. She squashed the green, pathetic thing, gave it to Sam to play with and went into the kitchen with Julia.

After the children were fed, Sara went upstairs and took a bath. She looked down at her body in the tub. Not a very exciting body, she thought. The breasts were flatter than they should be, the hips fuller. Jennifer would be making love to Edward right now, Sara assumed. She tried to picture the two of them together—Jennifer's taut, slim body, Edward's short stubby one. No, she couldn't understand what Jennifer saw in him at all. The attraction of some people for others was positively incomprehensible.

Take herself and Harry—now that had made sense all those many years ago. She knew what she saw in him: his certainty and strength, the way he went straight to the heart of a matter, taking control, knowing what had to be done. And he for his part had wanted a mother for his children, someone to take care of his house. An equitable arrangement, it had seemed to Sara. And wasn't that what most marriages were about?

Cupping the ring, applying the jelly, she inserted her

diaphragm. It was something, like a touch of rouge on her cheeks, she sometimes wore that Harry never knew was there.

In a sense, she thought, pulling the gray silk negligee out of the drawer, shaking it loose, slipping it on, Harry himself wasn't there. It wasn't just that he was rarely home. In some profound way he eluded her. He closed himself off and became inaccessible. She had to fight for admittance.

Hours later, when she heard him in the room, Sara was nearly asleep.

"Sorry I'm late," he said. "Brutal day. You all right?"

'All right,' in the tone he asked it meant, she knew, drug-free. "Yes," she said, trying hard to focus on him. She was too tired to fight tonight. Harry's height, his firm chin, strong cheeks, high, intelligent forehead seemed a defense against her. A tower of strength. He lived in the tower. Apart from her. He lived within his strength. Protected from her. Harry depended only on himself. Anyone inhabiting such natural strength was to be forgiven for finding her dependency contemptible. Did he truly despise her, she wondered. Did he find her contemptible?

Sara watched him empty his pockets. Coins, keys, paper clips emerged. Pens, pencils, address books, articles torn from various journals. Notes written on scraps of paper and the usual collection of things he brought home with him from the office: stethoscope, thermometer, prescription pads, phone messages, drug samples, laboratory results. Night after night Sara watched these medical paraphernalia streaming from Harry's pockets and thought she wouldn't be at all surprised to see sections of patients' organs, vials of their blood and urine coming out of those pockets and taking their places on the dresser as well.

These things were the facts of life to Harry, and watching him undress, Sara thought the most pertinent information she had about her husband came to her in the form of these facts. Harry *was* the things he pulled from his pockets—his notes, his articles, his overwhelming concern for his patients' well being. Harry was his office, his practice, and his den at home, that den she could not enter without fear of disturbing some delicate arrangement. Harry was the reflected fame of his celebrated patients. He was his writings, his success, his fine reputation. But what was he in himself?

Sara liked the touch of the silk next to her skin. It was almost enough, she thought—its sensuous embrace of her body. Feeling it, she understood why some women surround themselves with silks and satins. Even with no one else to touch her, the softness of the silk, its gentle clinging, that in itself seemed nearly sufficient.

"Don't read tonight," she said to Harry as he got into bed with a medical journal.

"Got to," he said. "There's something I want to check."

Professional journals, medical facts completed him. They exhausted her.

"Had to pass on a patient the other day," he explained. "Don't like to do that. There's an article in here that pertains to the case." Harry flipped through his journal, then tossed it on the bed. "Stuffy in this room, isn't it? I better open the window," he said and jumped out of bed.

Even now, at this hour, he was full of life, conscious of temperatures, able to correct mistakes.

He looked so tall to her, standing by the window in his striped pajamas. Her father had been tall, too, Sara recalled, and equally preoccupied with business. She remembered how as a small child looking up at her father as he left for work, she'd felt as she felt now looking up at Harry, watching him walk back across the room . . . tall and distant . . . so distant a walk . . . what height, what power in those bones and muscles . . . forever unattainable . . . forever desirable.

She held out her arms to him as he got back into bed. Harry held her a moment, kindly but without passion.

"Look," she said, pulling back the sheet to show him the negligee. "I got it this afternoon." It seemed so far away now. . . . "Like it?" Almost lost to her completely . . . the time of purchase, the intention she'd had.

"Very nice," Harry said. "Very pretty."

The silence of the night spread out between them.

"Did you really stay off today?" he asked after a while.

"Oh God, Harry."

"I only meant if you did, I know how tired you must be."

Yes, she was tired. She took his hand and put it on her breast. It lay there, impartial, professional. Immensely tired. Too tired to talk. Too tired to think. There was something she'd meant to do tonight . . . something to do with Harry . . . so tired . . . so very tired . . . whatever it was it would keep. . . .

Sara awoke at 4:33. Frequently, she woke at precisely this time. Harry lay with his back to her, sleeping soundly at the edge of the bed. Carefully, she got out on her side and tiptoed out of the room and down the hall to the linen closet. It had been a victory all right, short-lived and unheralded. She'd never be a sculptor. Harry was seeing another woman. Her children made jokes about her. Harry despised her. Three days off the drug. She was empty, worthless. A record broken. What use was such a record? She slid her hand in between the sheets in the closet and pulled out a pill.

IV

On Thursday Sara was strong again. A sculptor, an artist.
Powerful and free. She didn't want to save lives or make a lot
of money. Harry did that. But she wanted to be more than she
was, better than she was. On speed she could do that. Speed
formed her the way she tried to form the clay, creating an image out of chaos, a shape from nothing. To feel what she felt
when she was high, to feel it all the time, to make it last—
that would be a life, Sara thought.

Sam came hurtling through the door and flung himself
against her knees. "Lucy broke my airplane," he wailed, "and
I said she had to pay for it and she said she didn't and I said
she did and Andy spilled chocolate milk in my sandwich and
I took his and he bit me."

"Bit you? Oh, darling."

"And I bit him back."

"I see."

"And teacher said I started it and I didn't and she made
me sit against the wall the whole play time."

"Poor Sam. Come here to me."

Harry was coming home for dinner. Late, he'd said, but
not too late to eat if she didn't mind putting dinner off a while.
No, she didn't mind. She'd fix something nice—it wasn't
every night Harry was home—get the little kids off to bed.

Sam pressed himself against her, then broke for the door
as Justin came in.

"Up, up!" Sam screamed and Justin hoisted him to his
shoulders, then plunged him down again and wrestled with
him across his knees.

"Hiya, mom," Justin said, looking up. "How ya doing?"

Fine, Sara said. And all things considered, she thought she was. The effects of her early morning dose had long since worn off, so strictly speaking she was straight again. If only she could get through dinner, hold out until it was time to go to bed.

Leaving Sam to Justin, she went upstairs to attend to William.

"What do you think, little one?" she asked, tickling his stomach the way he liked as she put him into his pajamas. "Is mummie going to make it?" William reached up with his hands to pull at her hair and laughed in reply. "Does that mean you're taking bets on it? I don't know if I'd do that if I were you."

Downstairs, Sam began to shriek.

"What is it, Sam? What's the matter?" Sara listened to what he was trying to say, but couldn't quite make out the words. Had he fallen? Was he hurt? "What, Sam? What happened?"

"Nothing," Justin shouted up the stairs.

Sam continued to wail.

"It must be something," Sara called down. "Why is he crying like that?" She snapped William's pajamas in place, watched his face go red and his body begin to strain.

Justin was trying to tell her something, but Sam's screams drowned him out.

"Shut up, Sam!" Justin yelled.

"Don't you tell him to shut up."

"Mommy! Mommy!"

"Shut up, Sam. What'd you say, mom?"

"I said don't you tell him to shut up."

"What?"

"Goddamn it, Justin! Come up here and tell me what's going on. Don't scream at me from the other end of the house." Sara laid William back down, removed the pajamas which were now soaked through, the rubber pants, and soiled diaper. She washed and dried him, rubbed some lotion into his soft, sweet skin, found a clean pair of pajamas and put him into them. Her precious baby—the only one who didn't fight, didn't even talk back yet.

Justin ran up the stairs. Sam was right behind, punching

at the backs of his legs. "Quit it!" Justin said, slapping him away. "Cut it out, I said."

Sam shoved ahead into William's room. "He hit me! Justin hit me!"

"Yeah, well look what he did to my shirt." Justin pointed to a large red stain spreading across his pocket. "It's indelible too. The little pest."

"God, Justin. You're eleven years older than he is." Sara picked up William, took a step and nearly stumbled as Sam threw himself at her knees. "All right, sweetheart. Let go now. I can't walk with you there."

"I hate Justin!" Sam screamed. "I hate him."

"I'm not too fond of you either, twerp. This was one of my best shirts."

"Just drop it, will you?" Sara's strength was giving out now. She handed William to Justin. "Here. Do something useful." She picked up Sam, was overwhelmed by his weight, put him back down on the floor, squatted next to him and hugged him. "There, there, Sam. I'll bet you're hungry, aren't you? Let's go down and see where what we can do about dinner."

At the top of the stairs Sara hung back a moment. She went to the closet, reached her hand in between the sheets, found what she wanted, dropped it into her pocket. It didn't mean she'd take it. It just felt so good to have it there where she could feel it.

It was quiet in the kitchen. Sara hoped there wouldn't be any more fights. No more noise, no problems. She didn't have the strength for any more problems today. What she'd like, she thought, was an evening of silence, a peaceful dinner, peace running like a river throughout her house. Her barefoot children wading silently through the peace, their lips sealed, hands clasped. Peace running down the halls, trickling into each of the rooms. Herself floating in long, cool robes, organizing her children's days, maintaining perfect order with a nod of her head, a gesture of her hand. Life in a nunnery, she imagined it, where she could impose a rule of silence. Silence built like a great stone wall to preserve the peace.

William refused to eat. Sam fussed throughout his meal. He mimicked William's noises, spilled his milk on the floor. She knew she was slipping. She felt the stones crumbling, felt her fingers' precarious grip dislodged, her nails sliding down the wall of silence.

Sam gave William a savage pinch under the table and succeeded in making him cry. As the baby opened his mouth to scream, he spilled out of it the one bite Sara had managed to get in. She took a swat at Sam. Jerking away, he knocked his plate to the floor. William wanted to be held, his pajamas needed changing again, the floor had to be mopped, Harry was coming home for dinner and she hadn't even started it yet or changed her clothes or washed her face or brushed her hair. Oh, God, her hair! More was falling out every day. She looked awful, she knew she did. What was the use? She might as well admit she couldn't do it. She couldn't keep up, couldn't cope. And there in her pocket lay the means of her transformation. With a toss of her head, she swallowed the pill.

"Daddy's home!" Julia shouted, but Sara was ready for him now. She had a chicken in the oven, stuffed, candles on the table, a bottle of white wine in the refrigerator. Her hair was washed, face made up and she was wearing a dress with a long skirt she only wore when they entertained. She could feel her eyes sparkling as energy, like new life, coursed through her veins. Why, if she could feel like this, would she ever want to give it up?

"Hello, Harry," she called, bursting through the swinging doors into the living room. "Have a nice day? Would you like a drink? How're your patients doing? None in the hospital, I hope. None dead. What a pleasure," she said, kissing him, "to have you home for a change."

"No. Nobody's dead," Harry said, studying her closely. "I did have to put one in the hospital though. . . ."

Looking for signs, was he? Her bright cheeks, brilliant eyes?

". . . but he's not dead . . . not yet. I'll have to call in later . . . respiratory problem . . . pneumonia probably, but he'll pull through. . . ."

Critical eyes, medical eyes. Searching, scrutinizing.

"Might even have to go in later. . . . Sara. . . ."

Looking for flaws. For telltale signs. Give Harry a symptom and what a case he could concoct. Offer him dizziness, diarrhea, dislocation of the joints and see his face light up. Out of a pink eye, jaundiced skin, or broken bone he structures a whole body of work. Harry, too, was an artist, it occurred to Sara now, that word conjuring in her mind the image of his strong, skillful fingers expertly sorting through symptoms, picking them apart. Fever, pain, rash. Setting each aside. Bleeding, cramping, vomiting. Each piece a jewel in his eyes. Edema, hypertension, arrythmia. His great height bending to the task. Impotence, headache, hormonal imbalance. Jeweler's eyepiece magnifying the tiniest abnormality. From these precious stones of assorted symptoms, brilliantly isolated, brilliantly categorized, Harry creates a mosaic of disease.

"More wine?" Sara asked at dinner. "More chicken? More stuffing?" She wanted them to have a nice, friendly dinner. Just the four of them. That's what she'd like. "Wouldn't you?" she asked them. "Wouldn't you, Julia? Wouldn't you, Justin? Of course you would. We all would. Wouldn't we, Harry?" He stared at her. Was she talking too fast? Was she not making sense?

"Are you all right?" he asked.

Of course she was. Why shouldn't she be all right? Human beings can adapt to anything. "That's what you always say, isn't it, Harry? That's the marvel of human beings." Sara was feeling good now. She was a strong, marvelous, adaptable human being.

"How's school, Justin?" Harry turned to his son. "Chemistry still giving you trouble?"

"Not much."

"How much?"

Sara wished they wouldn't fight. She wanted Harry and Justin to be friends, to speak gently to one another. "More rice?" She offered Harry the dish. "Wild rice is lovely with chicken, don't you think?"

"Yes it is, but no thanks. Now listen here, Justin . . ."

"Salad then?" Sara pushed the bowl toward him. "Have a little more salad."

"Well, yes, all right. That dressing's awfully good. Something new?"

"Just a few special ingredients," Sara smiled. "I'm glad you like it."

"Mm . . . sensational." Harry plunged his fork into his

salad, into his mouth. "Really terrific. Wish you'd make it more often."

"If you'd come home."

"I do try, Sara." Harry looked at her and took another bite. "But it's always something at the office. Margot was out today and Helen and I had to run the whole show. Can you imagine what that's like, with no secretary and only one R.N.?"

Yes, she could imagine. Sara sipped her wine and imagined it. Harry racing in and out of examining rooms, peering down on prostrate forms, bending now over one, now over another. She filled her glass again and nodded. How well she could imagine. She was an old hand at this . . . forming images of Harry's life through her wine, through her pills. Drugs in her blood, drugs in her glass. Revving up, slowing down. Imagining the doctor's life while using alcohol to balance the speed in her own.

"Seriously, Justin," Harry started again. "I wish you'd take more interest in your work."

"I'm doing all right."

"Straight C's? You call that all right? What about pride of achievement, sense of accomplishment? We used to have things like that when I was a boy."

"Let him alone, Harry."

"Let him alone? He'll be going to college soon. One hopes. He has his future to think about. This is important, Sara. What he does now can determine the years ahead."

"Tell me about your patients, daddy," Julia interrupted. "What famous people did you treat today?"

Leave it to Julia to change a subject. And conclusively, too. Sara looked at her with admiration. If there was one thing Harry enjoyed more than fighting with Justin, it was talking about himself to his daughter.

"As a matter of fact," he said, looking at her and grinning, "I did see someone you'd be interested in today."

"Well . . . who?"

"Some rock star."

"A rock star! Who? Who?"

"Let me see if I can remember his name. I've seen his album in your room."

"Album! My room! Who, daddy? Who?"

51

Harry was a master at this, Sara observed. Playing on his patients' fame to increase his own prestige.

"Fritz something," he teased. "Starts with a B. Fritz Brin . . ."

"Brinner!" Julia shouted. "Fritz Brinner? Of Outside Orange? You know him? He's your patient?"

"One of them."

"You've actually met him? You've touched him?"

"All in the line of duty." Harry smiled.

"What's he like? What's he say? What's he look like without his makeup?"

"His clothes, you mean," Justin said.

"Shut up, creep. Tell me about him, daddy."

"With his face washed, he's just an ordinary looking kid."

"Ordinary?" Julia shrieked. "Fritz Brinner? No way."

"Come off it, Julia. He's a faggot."

"He is not! He . . ."

"That's enough, you two," Sara interceded. "I said I wanted a quiet dinner."

"He's *really* your patient?"

Julia's eyes sparkled as she gazed at her father. And Harry's, Sara noted, blazed with the double triumph of reflecting the glory of his patient's fame first off himself and then off his daughter. It was a game of power he played, going out into the world, attracting the celebrated to his door, turning that power on his family at home, fueling himself with it. Using power to attract power. Harry was a very clever person. Sara was impressed. Harry couldn't lose. But neither could she. Not tonight. Tonight she had her own power source running rampantly through her blood.

"Tell you what," Harry said, gazing adoringly at Julia. "I'll get you his autograph, if you like."

"You could? You would?"

"If I don't forget."

"I'll write you notes. I'll tie strings on all your fingers."

With strings on her fingers and bells on her toes . . . or was it rings? Sara felt like dancing. Harry never danced. She felt like singing. Harry didn't sing. She poured them both more wine. Harry was looking at her oddly. Justin was feeling hurt. Harry expected too much of him, pushed him too much. Sara told Justin how sorry she was about his shirt. She said maybe they could have it specially cleaned. Harry's glances were making her nervous. *Anxious*, he called it. *You've got more chemicals in your blood than platelets*. Nervous was the word she preferred. Did he suspect? Did he know? Was she talking too fast? Too loud? Was she drinking too much? What was the matter?

"What is it, Harry?" she snapped.

"What is what?"

"Why are you looking at me that way?"

"What way?"

"Damn it!" she cried. "I hate it when you do that."

"Do what?" he said, and Sara threw down her napkin and left the table.

"How are you doing?" Harry said later, coming into the living room, sitting down.

"I'm doing fine. Don't I look like I'm doing fine?"

"You look very nice."

"You like this dress?"

"Very much."

"You liked the chicken? The salad?"

"It was a lovely dinner, Sara."

"Then I'd say I'm doing fine, wouldn't you?"

"And you didn't take any today?"

"No, I didn't."

"Not even one?"

"I said no, didn't I?"

Harry looked away.

"You don't believe me, do you?"

"I'd like to, Sara. But how many times have we been through this before?"

"So you think I'll never do it then. Is that what you think?"

"I don't know what to think." Harry looked out the window.

"Don't turn away," Sara said. She needed to look at his face, his confident, strong face. "I started on them to please you . . ."

"For weight control," Harry shot back. "I never told you to continue."

"But they did so much more than that, didn't they, Harry? They made me talkative, energetic, bright. They made me into a woman you liked. I wanted you to like me."

"Oh, Christ, Sara . . . like you?" His voice was low, almost gentle. "All I want is for you to tell me the truth."

All right, she would tell him. He was a good man, an intelligent man. He would understand. "You know what happens when I go off? How terrible it is to crash?"

Harry nodded.

"You know how depressed I get? How all I want to do is sleep?"

"I know."

It was all right. Harry's eyes were kind. His voice was gentle. She could confide in him. "I can't do anything then. It's like being dead. Worthless. Can you understand that?" It was all right. Harry's hands were on her shoulders. "No you can't." She was wrong. He couldn't understand. "You don't know what that's like. You've never felt worthless in your life. And then the children started fighting. I can't take their fighting on top of that." Harry was squeezing her shoulders. "Everything was coming at me at once . . . Sam and Justin arguing . . . William wet . . . and you on your way home for dinner . . . I wanted it to be nice . . . and my hair looks so awful . . . oh, God, I hate my hair. . . ." Harry was squeezing her harder. "I don't want to go bald, I don't . . . I wanted to please you . . . I wanted everything to be nice." He was hurting her now. "I know how you like for me to look nice, to cope . . ."

"Aw, Sara. Did you have to?"

"I did it for you."

Harry took his hands away.

"Only one. I only took one."

He was walking away.

"One, Harry. What's one?"

He was walking away from her.

"One's nothing. You know that. For an old addict like me."

He was walking across the room.

"I did it for you. To feel worthwhile. To feel alive. For God's sake, Harry, don't you want me to feel alive?"

He was walking out of the room.

"Just one. Not to feel worthless. Can't you understand

that, Harry? Really? Can't you? Worthless. Can't you imagine how that feels?"

Justin was coming into the room.

"I'll quit tomorrow. I promise I will. I promise. Tomorrow. You'll see, Harry. I'll do it tomorrow."

Justin was walking into the room. Harry was walking out. They collided at the door.

"Just where do you think you're going?" Harry yelled.

"Out, dad. I've got a date."

"The damn garage, you mean?"

"No, not tonight."

"Don't you have any homework? They used to give homework when I went to school."

"It's Friday night, remember?"

"Don't fight," Sara said. "I can't stand it when you fight."

"Damn it, Justin! Is that what you want out of life? To spend it in a garage?"

"I said I wasn't going to the garage. I said I've got a date."

"Don't you raise your voice to me."

"Stop it!" Sara yelled. She wouldn't have this tonight. She'd do what she had to to make them stop.

"If you've got a date, who's it with?"

"Don't bully him!" she yelled. "Let him go."

"No one special, dad. Just some of the kids."

"Who exactly?"

"Larry and Linda, Mitch maybe and . . ."

"And just where are you going?"

"Stop it, Harry. You sound like a cop."

"No place special. Just hang out. Go to a movie maybe."

"What do you mean, hang out?"

"You know. Hang out."

"No, I don't know. That particular phrase means nothing at all to me. You're just going to have to explain it."

"Let him go, Harry," Sara repeated. She was strong tonight, powerful. She could do anything she had to to protect her son.

"Hang out, you know . . . walk around. Go for pizza or something."

"I thought you said a movie."

"I said maybe a movie."

"And maybe not?"

"That's right. Maybe not."

"Who are these kids you're hanging out with?"

"I told you, dad. Larry . . . Mitch . . . Linda . . . you know them all. They've been to the house."

"And where exactly are you going?"

"For God's sake, Harry. Stop it. It's tyrannical. It's obscene."

"For pizza maybe. Or bowling. Or a movie."

"That's all? Nothing else?"

"What else?"

"No drinking? No grass?"

"Dad, I said . . ."

"Is that what you mean by hanging out . . . smoking and drinking?"

"No. It's not."

"Harry, enough!" Sara grabbed at his sleeve. She'd rip it off, break his arm, she'd do anything she had to to keep them apart.

"What do you do, Justin? Pass out joints under a streetlight like a bunch of hoodlums?"

"If we were going to do it, we wouldn't do it under a streetlight." Justin turned on his heel and walked away.

Harry ran after him, grabbed his arm.

"Where do you do it, then? In the back of that garage?"

Justin shrugged himself free and walked out into the hall.

"Don't walk away from me!" Harry shouted and started after him. He stopped as Justin stopped too and swung around to face him.

"Don't worry, dad. I won't get into trouble. I know how you'd hate the publicity."

"Just what do you mean by that?"

"Your sacred practice. Your reputation. Nothing means more to you than that."

"All I want to know is what you're doing with your time. Who your friends are."

"I don't ask you who you're out with or why you're never home!"

"Damned right you don't. I'm your father and don't ever forget it!"

"Stop it! Both of you!" Sara screamed. She'd smash their heads together, pull out their tongues to make them stop.

"What goes on in that garage of yours? You're not just fixing cars in there."

"What are you afraid of, dad? Dope? Drugs? Why look at me? Mom's right here."

Like white light striking her eyes, Harry's hand came up, shot out—a blaze of light landing across Justin's face.

V

Hit him, will he? Hit her son? Sara was in the kitchen drinking wine and going over it in her mind. Harry's hand shooting out, the sound of the slap reverberating in the room. Harry had gone now. Gone to the hospital to play God. First Harry was there. Justin was there. Then Justin was gone. Then Harry was gone. Gone to give orders to nurses and patients. Doctor's orders. God's orders. It was late now. Very late. Speed was pounding through her blood. She'd taken more, been drinking a lot. Her mind was racing. She came in here to think it out. Orders at the hospital, orders at home. Drinking wine and thinking about his lies, his evasions. She wasn't the only one in the family who lied. Oh no, not by a long shot. The good doctor lied too. Clever, sophisticated lies. Going to the hospital, late night calls. Humanitarian lies. Speed pounding behind her eyes, pounding in her wrists. The wine would bring her down.

A tyrant. A bully. Giving orders. Hitting children. Slapping Justin, never satisfied. Pushing him to be something else. Somebody else. As if what he was wasn't good enough. Wanting him like himself. In his image. Make him over. God's image. Creating people. Giving and taking away their lives.

The half gallon was nearly empty. Misjudging the distance to the glass, red wine splashed on the tabletop. Did he think she was stupid? Or that she didn't know? Arrogant. Egocentric. Of couse she knew. Where else was he spending his time? She wanted to hear it from him. To hear it straight. Harry straight. That was a laugh. But all the same it would show some respect. As if her perceptions mattered. *Yes, Sara, there's someone else,* if he could say that. As if she mattered.

But no one mattered except Harry. The doctor's wife, the doctor's children. They had no identity apart from him. And didn't Harry love that? The great doctor giving orders, ordering destiny. You will be my wife, take one every four hours, you will be good in chemistry, be a boy like me, a man like me. Only Harry existed. Only him.

After a point, Sara didn't want to stop drinking or stop speeding. She liked the place she reached where she was someone else. Harry's equal. Harry's match. A worthwhile, secret self of hers hiding in the closets, hiding in the drawers, emerging now when she needed her. Dependable, reliable. Not like Harry. Couldn't count on Harry. Never home. Never there. Escaping her. Eluding her. She did everything alone. Raised the children, kept the house. Without him. No help from him. *Help me, doctor. Save me, doctor.* Always the patients. They came first. And now it wasn't good enough. She wasn't good enough. The children weren't quite right. Not good in chemistry. A little bit off. Get another woman. Get other children. Create them the way he liked.

Now Harry was back. Standing there flooded in the kitchen light. Out of nowhere. A burning bush. She raised the bottle, poured what was left of it into her glass.

"Ah, the living God returns. Should I fall to my knees? Offer a sacrifice? Or have you already had that wherever you've been?"

"Don't you think you'd better come to bed?"

"No, I do not."

She couldn't imagine ever sleeping again, ever lying down again. Her energy was vertical. Luminous and sharp as a razor blade. It penetrated the room, pierced the air. It could slash through the soft tissues of Harry's brain to his most secret thoughts.

"Who is she?" she demanded. "Tell me who."

"Sara, you're in no condition . . ."

"My condition is fine. How's your condition, Harry? How's your state of affairs? Let's talk about that, shall we? The condition of your dirty little affairs."

"Please, Sara."

"Top notch condition? Is that what you'd say? Or only

fair? A fair affair? Second-rate, I'd call them. Shabby little hand-me-downs. Down at the heels, fraying around the edges, seconds, odd lots, used merchandise, no doubt. Bargain basement goods."

"Come on upstairs. Try to sleep."

"That goes for your famous brain, too. That marvelously astute, exquisitely scientific brain. Why don't you take it out and get it photographed? Publish the pictures along with your articles. Let your public see just where that kind of thinking comes from. Wouldn't that knock them dead? A close-up of the great doctor's gray matter. Then you could perform some miracle. Ressurect your dead fans."

"Sara, come on. You're not making sense."

"Take your hands off me. Are you going to hit me too, you goddamned tyrant? Do you think we're all just a bunch of patients? Helpless and weak and everlastingly grateful?"

Her voice was all over the room now. Darting from corner cabinets, charging through the electrical current into the overhanging lamp. Shattering forth in blinding white light. Shooting up the stairs. Waking the children. She didn't want to wake the children. "We're killing the children, don't you see that?" The children were not involved in this. "We're killing them." This was between the two of them—herself and this man in front of her.

Close now. Very close. Her face close to his. "Who is she?" she screamed. Her voice entering the great God's eyes. She could tear them out, slice them up. "Tell me who!" Her voice shattering the bones in his face. She could gnaw on those bones with her teeth. "I know there's someone. I know it!" Body of His body, blood of His blood.

"There's no one. Come on now." Harry was holding out his hands. "I'll give you something to calm you down."

She'd hack those hands off. Chew them up into little pieces. She'd claw at the lining of his organs, scratch through to the place where he kept the truth. She could do it now. She could do anything she wanted to.

Harry was trying to hold her. "Come upstairs. We'll talk about it in the morning."

Nothing could hold her now. She broke free. Free of Harry. Free of his lies.

She picked up the knife. Suddenly it was there. Materialized out of her will, her power, the power of her will. No knife in sight, suddenly a knife in her hand. A short, sharp blade jumping into life to do her bidding.

"Sara, for Christ's sake!"

It was so easy. Nothing at all.

"Put it down."

Easy to raise a knife, to stick a blade into living flesh. No effort at all. No weight in her arm, no obstruction meeting the blade.

"You're crazy, you know. Crazy."

So easy she couldn't be doing it. Not Sara. Not Sara actually doing this. Sara was watching, standing off across the room, watching a film, a scene of murder.

"I should have you committed."

Watching the woman raise the knife. How easy it was. Watching her plunge the knife. How simple. The blade slipping through flesh. Sliding through blood.

"For Christ's sake, Sara!"

Watching the slit open in the sleeve, the blood seep through. This wasn't real. A horror film. She almost laughed. She didn't feel horror. She did laugh.

"You must be crazy. How can you laugh!"

Watching the man clutch his arm, his sleeve, the blood seeping through. He was a very bad actor. The expression on his face wasn't real at all. His sudden, deep intake of breath . . . ludicrous. His exaggerated clutchings of his arm, his reeling back against the sink . . . fake, all fake. A ridiculous dumb show.

He was stumbling toward the door now, saying something about stitches, going to the hospital for stitches. Oh, Harry, what a lame excuse. He was carrying this a little too far. None of it was real.

"Come off it," she said. "You're not hurt. That's not real blood."

Another voice in the room. A scream. A clear, pure, pellucid scream like rushing water. Ripples of light and water. A high, pure mountain stream with the force of nature behind it.

"Stop her! Do something!"

Vibrating circles of light and water. Reverberations of sound.

"Stop her! Stop her!"

The man with the fake blood running down his arm was coming at her now. Stop him, that's what she had to do. Clutching his arm with one hand, holding out the other. "Give it to me, Sara." She still had the knife in her hand. "Give it to me." His hand was open in front of her. Palm up. Pink flesh crossed by rivulets of blood. The nails in the hands, the blood running free. He was asking for it. He wanted it. It was so easy. In His image. A simple downward thrust.

The pure scream again. A girl's scream. A girl screaming as if her heart were cracked in two. Sara dropped the knife, wheeled around. Julia stood in the door. "Daddy!" she screamed. "Daddy!" Julia was watching. Her own Julia. Her little girl.

VI

Sara didn't think it was all that bad. "A minor flesh wound," she said to Jennifer a couple of days later on the phone. "Barely nicked the skin. But you should have heard him carry on. And for only four stitches. What's four stitches? Sam had six last summer when he fell off his tricycle and split his lip. Remember that?"

"I remember."

Jennifer's voice sounded strained, unnatural, at the other end of the line. Was she horrified? Did she think it monstrous?

"I didn't mean it, Jenny. I still can't believe I actually did it. Having Julia see was the worse thing. I don't know how long she'd been standing there. But when I heard that scream . . . looked up and saw her face. . . . I never wanted her to see a thing like that."

"No, of course not."

"Do you think she'll ever forgive me? Oh, that's a stupid question, I know. How could you possibly answer a thing like that? But I don't want to hurt her. I love her so. And she'll be leaving soon. Justin too. Both of them gone in a couple of years. And me alone with Harry. I think about that a lot, you know. Harry in his office. Me here alone. I'll hate that. I need my children with me. My own flesh and blood. Even William's growing up. My own world. I need that. A world I created."

"Sara, do you want me to come over? Do you feel like talking? Edward's out with Peter. I could be there in no time."

"Not today, I'm in no shape. But soon. Come for lunch, all right? We'll have a long talk. I want to hear all about your new work and how you're doing."

"Okay, Sara. Soon."

"No. If we don't make it definite we'll never do it. How's the end of the week for you? Friday okay?"

"Friday's fine. But are you sure? . . ."

"I'm sure. Friday, then. For lunch. You can help me plan William's party. Can't wait to see you, Jenny. And thanks for everything."

Harry had told her the wound would leave a scar—a thin silver thread in the flesh of his arm as proof. Evidence of her crime. It was a crime. Assault with a deadly weapon. A two-inch vegetable knife. Deadly nonetheless. She might have been arrested, gone to jail. Sara couldn't imagine it. She who was so good at imagining things couldn't even now visualize the consequences of this thing Harry called a crime: a gash in his arm, going to jail. Only the bandage convinced her something had happened. And Julia's scream. But what had she herself actually had to do with it?

Julia was avoiding her. Sara had heard her asking Harry if she was crazy. *No, no. Certainly not. Not crazy. Upset,* he'd said. *Intoxicated. Had too much to drink. But, no. Certainly not crazy.*

And speeding? Julia had asked. *Speeding too?*

Well maybe that was part of it, Harry had conceded. But Julia mustn't be afraid, he'd said. It wouldn't happen again.

Why don't you do something? Julia had asked him. *Get her some help? You're a doctor, aren't you?*

Harry got mad then. Told her to watch the way she spoke to him. He was her father, after all. He said he knew what he was doing, knew just how far her mother would go. He had the situation under control, he said. He was doing everything that needed to be done.

Situation under control. It made Sara's blood boil. As if she were something he was studying in a test tube. Some culture he was growing. She knew what was the matter with Harry. Harry was afraid. Afraid of the publicity, the repercussions. Afraid of losing patients, being talked about. Harry liked for things to be contained. His wastebasket, for instance. This wasn't all that different. Refuse neatly disposed of. *I'll handle it in my own way,* he said to Julia. Sara knew what that meant. Keep it under lock and key. Keep it neatly tied up.

If she got any worse, he'd lock her up. But not in a hospital, Sara knew. That would be too public, too obvious. One couldn't keep a thing like that quiet. Word would get out. His patients would hear. Harry couldn't take a chance on a thing like that. He'd lock her up here in the house, Sara thought, hire a keeper, a jailer, convince himself he was handling it well. *Trust me,* he told Julia. *I know what I'm doing.*

And what, after all, had she done? There'd been no intention on her part, no premeditation. If it weren't for Julia's face at the door . . . the look of horror . . . the sound of her scream . . . she'd almost swear it never happened.

Sara was being careful now. It was nearing the end of the month and her supply was running low. If she didn't watch it, Harry might refuse to write her another prescription. No, he wouldn't. He wouldn't dare. He knew she could always get them some place else—the street, scrip doctors. But Harry couldn't take that chance. She might get busted. Word would get out. People would know. Harry was afraid. He'd rather supply her himself than have people know. Harry's fear came to Sara's aid. Threaten as he did to cut her off, he saw the dreadful possibilities before him—Sara's name in the papers, his practice jeopardized. Shaking his head, shielding his eyes, he would reach for his pen and write her out another prescription.

"Where in hell do you keep them?" Harry demanded and Sara swore there wasn't one in the house.

"Did you stay off today?" he asked and Sara held out her arm and rolled up her sleeve. "Care to do a blood test?"

Two of Harry's patients were in the hospital now and it was that he said that kept him in town late several nights a week. If he thought about that evening in the kitchen with the knife, he didn't speak of it. His reputation was on the line. Occasionally, as he looked at her, Sara read it in his eyes: *My practice. My patients.* A thing like that could ruin him. Harry's fear kept him quiet. And Sara was being good. No trouble now. Everything was under control. Harry watched her closely for a while, then seemed content to let it drop.

Tonight he was sitting in the living room reading his paper. Sara took the army patch she'd been promising Sam for weeks to sew on his jacket and sat in her old comfortable chair across from him.

Harry was so certain. So sure. His face, his body, seemed to Sara like a rock. Solid, unchangeable. Harry had the facts and let them out at his own discretion. He told dying patients the truth or let them believe they had years yet to live. He could produce a drug for every ailment, monitored the course of disease with wisdom and tenacity. Only when it came to her did he turn away. At the very roots of her being he came upon an entanglement he could neither fathom nor unravel. *I don't understand it, Sara. I just don't understand it*, he said and it might have been her father speaking then—that other tall, confident man who also had all the facts, and whose business also left him no time for her, no time to stop a moment there on the steps of the porch, bend down to where she sat and try to make sense of what she was saying. Profoundly perplexed, Harry turned away, as her father had done, and went about his business. She was his one true failure, Sara believed, and failure was something Harry could not tolerate. *In my business when I'm wrong people die.*

It was hard to think of him now, sitting there reading the paper, as a man who had ever known failure. Success was Harry's metier. The careful control and ordering of facts that led to success. Harry could take any number of pieces of unrelated information and establish a relationship between them. From the most incohesive set of circumstances, he created order. Sara found it quite remarkable. She who was so often overwhelmed by world events, feeling them fly about her head in a jumble of disparate, conflicting elements, knew that to Harry, sitting there confidently behind his paper, Iran, Madrid, the Middle East were but more facts to be contained. Health insurance, the energy crisis, he broke them down into component parts. Inflation, unemployment, austerity programs—Harry determined statistical relevance, seized upon causatory facts. Only when it came to her did he falter and, faltering, turned away afraid.

Sara studied him over her needle and thread and thought his face, creased in the light, seemed tired and a little sad. Two deep lines at either side of his mouth drew the whole lower portion of his face down toward his chin. Harry was aging. He seemed tired and sad. All the same, Harry was what he had set out to be, a totally successful man. He had a busy practice, a fine reputation. Success gave him power. Power increased his success. It was a process Sara envied. Harry was continually enhanced. Things flew away from Sara, but Harry captured them in his hands. Where she was scattered, he was centered. It was a kind of psychic wholeness that had attracted her to him the very first time they'd met.

It was at her friend Marianne's party, Sara remembered, and as was usual for her at parties, she was having a miserable time. Then Harry entered and Sara felt drawn to him at once. His height, his strength, his look of confidence, and something familiar about him, too, as if she'd known him before, had made her ask to be introduced.

Sara poked her needle into Sam's sleeve and caught a corner of the patch. Pushing it through, she asked Harry if he remembered the first thing he'd ever said to her.

"Stick out your tongue?"

"No," Sara replied. "You said, 'Someday I'll be treating ninety percent of the people in this room.'"

"Did I? Where was that? Hey, look here." Harry pointed to a photograph in the paper. "He's a patient of mine." He scanned the article beneath the picture. "How do you like that? He just won the architectural bid for that new middle-income housing complex in the Bronx."

"At Marianne's party. Don't you remember?"

"Good for him. What? Whose party? Won't do his ulcer any good, though." Harry turned the page.

"Marianne Tilson's. Where we met. Don't you remember saying that? It turned out to be true."

"What did?"

"What you said . . . that you'd treat ninety percent of the people in that room." She had known it was true the minute he said it.

Harry was lost in his paper. He read it closely, critically, ferreting out facts, leaping on errors, scoffing at misinformation. It was a great pleasure to him to find items in the news about his patients. A smile brushed his lips when he came upon one, and an almost imperceptible movement turned his head. He was as proud of them, and in nearly as proprietary a way, Sara thought, as she was of her children.

"Jim Woodly's play opened last night," Harry said to her now. "The play itself didn't get much of a review, but Jim got a rave. He said he'll get me tickets if you want to go."

Harry's patients in the news. Celebrities who came to him with their private ills, private lives. He had confidential information about some of the most important people in the country. Whatever was written about them, wherever they went in the world—building houses, starring in plays—that knowledge came back to Harry to set him apart. It raised him above the common man reading an item in the paper. Chosen physician to the rich and powerful, he watched his success spin off theirs.

Sara was proud of the way Harry garnered facts, always keeping one step ahead of his patients. She'd hate as much as he would to see him exposed, to have a fact slip by him, his expertise opened to question. She was proud of Harry's certainty and felt something of an obligation to uphold it. She had to be in some way constantly looking out for him. Not merely seeing that he got his meals and had clean clothes to wear, but in some deeper, more subtle way to see that he was upheld. She couldn't bear it if, for instance, the children didn't answer his questions or laugh at his jokes, if they didn't look him in the eye when he spoke to them. To see him slighted like that gave her a turn in the pit of her stomach. *Justin!* she'd yell, for usually it was Justin. *Look at your father when he's talking to you.*

Suddenly Harry sat up straight and shook the paper out in front of him. "Listen to this," he said and began to read: " 'Five percent, or 16,000, of the country's doctors are considered unfit. The figure is based on known rates of drug addiction, alcoholism, and mental illness among professional groups and on the proportion of incompetence uncovered through reviews of hospital case records.' Five percent!" Harry was incensed. "I don't believe it. Three maybe, but not five. Nowhere near five."

Harry had been working too hard. Sara worried about him. She worried about his blood pressure and his lack of sleep. She worried about what he ate when he didn't eat at home. It did no good to suggest he take better care of himself. Doctors were the worst patients in the world.

"For Christ's sake!" he shouted now. "Listen to the way they put this: 'Every year perhaps 30,000 Americans accept the drugs their doctors prescribe and die as a direct result.' *Direct* result." Harry repeated the word. "*Direct.* You'd think doctors were out to poison their patients." He read ahead silently a moment. "Oh, great! And here's their example: 'Not long ago, a fifty-year-old woman went to her doctor complaining of a sore throat. He gave her an injection of penicillin and within minutes she lay dead on his office floor.' And that's supposed to prove the guy's unfit."

"But people do die from penicillin, don't they?" Sara said, turning the sleeve to sew the last bit of patch.

"Yes, if they're allergic to it. But don't you see? They're trying to crucify the poor bastard for not testing her first."

"Well, shouldn't he have?"

"Do you have any idea how long it would take to test every patient for sensitivity before giving a shot? There aren't enough hours in the day. He should have told her to go home and take two aspirins and go to bed." Harry flipped the page. "People who don't know beans about the field should stay the hell out of medicine. And that includes the federal government." He read ahead in silence for a while. "I hear they're even watching Drumson now."

"Ben Drumson?" Sara had heard Harry speak of him. "Your friend?"

"Not friend, exactly. Colleague."

"What are they after him for?"

"Don't know for sure. Could be they suspect him of injecting amphetamines without a prior medical exam."

"Does he do that?"

"Hope not. It's fraud if he does. Stupid, too. I can't believe that of Ben. Anybody who gets a shot of any kind in my place gets an exam first. I'm sure he works the same way."

Sara couldn't imagine taking the drug directly into her veins. The idea of injecting it terrified her. Of being higher than she'd been behind the wheel that day, for instance, or with the knife in her hand. . . . And Julia standing in the door. Sara heard her now laughing in the kitchen with Justin. But that night she'd been standing in the door. Sara heard that scream again . . . saw that look of horror on her daughter's face. Had she done that? . . . put that look on her daughter's face?

Sara heard Julia's laugh just then interrupted by a cough. She wanted to be a good mother. Justin and Julia doing dishes in the kitchen. She wanted to keep them safe. Sam and William asleep upstairs. Sara surrounded by her children. All safe. All protected from harm.

"Is that Julia coughing?" Harry asked, putting down his paper.

Sara, too, had heard the laughter turn just then into an explosive cough, but she knew it wasn't serious. Julia had never been really sick in her life. Sara couldn't explain it. There were so many things about Julia she couldn't explain. That child was like no one in the family. Light hair, green eyes, physically resembling none of them, Julia was a puzzle. Her easy sense of humor was beginning to return. Sara had thought at first she'd never see her smile again.

"It's just a little cold," she said.

"It doesn't sound like a little cold to me," Harry answered. "It sounds more like incipient bronchitis."

"It's not bronchitis."

"How do you know?"

"I just know."

"So you're the doctor in the family now?" Harry put down his paper and pulled out a medical journal.

Julia coughed again and Harry leaned forward listening. "You'd better get her to a doctor."

"She doesn't need a doctor."

"All right, Sara. Have it your way. But there's an excellent bronchial man in the area when you're ready."

Harry always knew who to contact. The names of specialists where at his fingertips. Confronted with ailments of the eye, nose, throat, heart, lungs, kidneys, gastrointestinal or urogenital tract, Harry knew what to do. *I've got just the man for that*, he'd say, rattling off phone numbers, addresses. *A good spleen man. A good proctologist.* He could find a proper destination for every organ in the body. But emptiness befuddled him. Vacuity confounded him. Where could he send someone in search of a center?

The kitchen door swung open and Julia and Justin came in.

Even now, seeing her, Sara's first impulse was to turn away. Avoid the look on her face, the terror in her eyes. But it couldn't have been. It wasn't possible. How had things got so out of hand that something she did made her daughter scream, her eyes go wide in terror?

"How long have you had that cough?" Harry asked.

"What cough?" Julia said, sitting down on the sofa, curling her legs under her.

Light-hearted, resilient, almost back to normal.

"I don't like the sound of it. I could hear it all the way out here."

"Must've been Justin," Julia said and smiled.

Smiling again, cracking jokes, but wary of her, wary still.

"Looks good, mom," Justin said, picking up Sam's jacket, inspecting the army patch. "Sam'll like it."

"Think so, dear?"

"Sure he will. It looks tough. That's what he likes." Handing it back, he kissed the top of her head. Her first-born. At least Justin hadn't seen. At least he could still give her a kiss.

"Well, goodnight, mom," Justin said, walking toward the door. "I've got some homework to do."

"Right this minute? Couldn't you sit with us for a while?"

The four of them together in the living room, a normal family passing a normal evening. Oh, what she wouldn't give for that!

"Oh, Julia, I almost forgot." Fumbling through his pockets, Harry brought out a crumpled piece of paper. "I've been carrying it around for days." He held it out to her and Sara thought for a moment it might still be possible. "It's that autograph you wanted." Promises made and kept. Wishes come true. A normal, happy family.

Julia stared at him a moment uncomprehending, then her face lit up and she threw herself across the room. "Oh, daddy! You remembered! You got it! You did it, you did! Is it really . . . ? Can it really be . . . ?" Slowly unfolding the paper, she read with great solemnity. " 'For Julia, from Fritz Brinner.' Oh, wow. Did he write that, daddy, really? With his own hand?"

"Saw him with my own eyes."

"Let's see," Justin said, going over to look.

Julia held it out to him for one quick glimpse, snatched it back as soon as he tried to take it. "No. Don't touch it," she gasped. "It's sacred." She pressed the paper to her breast. "I don't want your awful germs on it."

"Women!" Justin cried and threw up his hands. "They're hopeless."

"Oh, thanks, daddy, thanks so much. I'll treasure it always." Julia seemed to be in another world as she floated over to kiss Harry, then back, as if the other night were already forgotten, to kiss Sara and across the room to settle herself into the sofa where she gazed at the autograph in her hand as if it were the Holy Grail itself.

Her eldest son. Her only daughter. Her husband reading his journals. Herself, calm, rational, for the moment like any other mother in the neighborhood. Not someone Justin could point to and call dope fiend, drug addict. Not a madwoman Julia might see poking knives into people's arms. Not a woman her children despised, made jokes about. Julia had once quite casually told her that in the hierarchy of addiction those hooked on amphetamines occupied the lowest rung on the ladder. *Even heroin addicts look down on them*, she'd said. Another time, after an argument, Sara had heard her remarking to Justin: *You know what the trouble with mom is, don't you? Speed freaks have no sense of humor*. Did her children think of her like that? An addict? A freak?

Sara went to the window and looked out and thought of the times before Sam and William were born, when Julia and Justin were small, when Harry wasn't always so busy. She remembered the night they'd decided on that old swing set— it sat out there in the backyard, moonlight glinting off its metal bars—ordered it from a catalogue . . . Justin sitting next to Harry on the sofa, playing the man for his father. *Not that one, dad*, he said. *It doesn't have a slide*. Julia on his other side liking every set she saw. *Get that one, daddy. Oh, no, that one. It's prettier*. Harry, in the end, as Sara knew he would, ordered the most expensive set of all. *We want the works*, he said. Slide, swings, teeter-totter, ladder, rings— they got them all. Sara could just make them out in the darkness now. When it arrived, the four of them went out together in the yard to dig the holes—she and Julia working together on two of them while Harry and Justin did one apiece—they poured the cement, planted the stakes, sank the rods, adjusted the chains and *S* hooks. When it was set and dried, Sara went out and sat on one swing while Justin stood behind holding the bar above her head. Harry sat on the other with Julia in his lap. She could see them now, pushing off the ground, laughing. She could hear their voices as the swings rose into the air.

Sara leaned her head against the glass. The smooth, bare rods, the dangling swings and chains formed a strange metallic skeleton standing there beneath the moon. Julia hardly ever used it now. Justin never. Sam was beginning to enjoy it, but William was still too young. Sara stared out into the darkness, seeing shadows of their former selves pounding stakes into the ground, hearing ghostly younger voices—*Our side's in. We win. Look, mommy. Look, daddy*—rising from the soil where they'd been interred so many years ago, released now, she thought, by her overwhelming need to hear them.

It was a question of need, Sara believed. A need to think that, even in all the desperate confusion of her nature, Harry would not abandon her. A need to believe that somehow they might approach one another again, that some day somehow everything would be all right.

Sara turned from the window. Husband and children sitting quietly. It was all right. It might still be all right. The light darkened, a shadow fell, the light resumed again as she crossed in front of the lamp.

"Well, the books are beckoning," Justin said. He took a step, waved good night. "Chemistry calls." He nodded at Harry and left the room.

"Me too," Julia said. "I'm going straight to sleep and dream of Fritz." She floated out of the room and rose, trancelike, up the stairs.

Things were breaking apart. An enormous number of valuable things were at that moment being taken from her, Sara believed. Dropping almost physically like beads of water from her person. Her beginnings with Harry as man and wife. Words she had waited to hear him say and had not heard. A turn she had thought her life would take that it had not taken. A hope for something . . . was it love? Some success at life? Would she never be worthy of love? Was this what her life was to be? Were there no other chances?

"I'm being careful now, you know," she said to Harry as soon as they were alone. "I'm watching it."

"I know." Harry looked up. "But if you want to get off

for good, I've said I'll help. I'll do anything I can. Only you've got to stop cheating. I know they're hidden all over the house."

"No, they're not."

"Sara, I can't help you if you won't cooperate."

She didn't like his tone then. She was trying. She really was. But to get rid of them all . . . not to have a single one in the house. . . .

"You'd be over your symptoms in a week. One week. Think of it. The anxiety, the jumpiness, the tension—all gone in a week. If you could just stick it out . . . sleep as much as you want, the whole week if you like, I'll get someone in. I've told you. . . ."

"No, Harry." She wanted his help but not that way. "I know what I'm doing. I can handle it." He looked hurt and turned away. She hadn't meant to hurt him. Never. Not with the knife or now. She hadn't ever meant that. He was so tired, he worked so hard. It was true what he told Justin again and again. He only wanted the best for him. For all the children. And for her as well. She knew he did. He only wanted the best.

"There really isn't anyone else, is there?"

"Oh, Sara."

"I mean really. Really there isn't?"

"Sara, please."

"There isn't, is there?"

"No, there isn't."

"I'd hate it if there was."

"Don't worry, Sara."

"I mean that. I don't think I could stand it if there was."

"Don't worry."

But she did worry. She needed him so, depended on him so. On his strength, his certainty. Not for sex. She could do without that. If that was what was driving him to other women she couldn't help it. She'd never really felt much of anything when it came to that.

"I've never understood your needs," she confessed. "To me it's just not that important."

"Sara, please. Let it go."

Was that, too, lost to her now? Would she die unawakened? For seventeen years she had been somebody's wife, somebody's mother. Always longing for more. Longing to feel what other women claimed to feel in every magazine she read. She didn't feel it with Harry, didn't feel anything like it. She would go to her grave without having known it. Her children would mourn her, if they mourned at all, thinking they mourned a real woman, when in reality it was more than a function that lay in its box, no deader now than it had been in life—only the outward, visible signs of life had vanished preventing the function from being discharged. Perhaps it was time to give it up, accept its loss. She didn't want it anyway if there was another woman to share it with.

Sara felt a pain in her heart and put her hand to it. How odd that it should hurt. She hadn't expected it to hurt.

"Is she young?" she asked. "Is she pretty?"

"Sara, please. You're just upset. How much speed have you had today?"

"Not nearly enough." How surprising, she thought, to feel this hurt. "There isn't enough on the market to do any good."

"Sara, you've simply got to get yourself under control. You're running the risk of really serious heart trouble otherwise. If you don't care enough about yourself, think of the children. Think of me."

"You?"

"Yes, me. I'm a well-known physician. I've worked hard for that. I have a good practice, a reputation to maintain . . . there are appearances to keep up. A thing like this . . ."

"Appearances! So Justin was right. All you care about is how it reflects on you."

"That's not true."

"Yes it is true. It's all for you. You and your patients. You and your practice. That's where you do it, isn't it? Down at the office in one of your examining rooms. . . . It wouldn't be a patient, though. You'd never risk that. One of your nurses, then? Helen, probably. No, it's Margot, I'll bet. Or is it both? Do you do them both together or back to back?"

"That's enough, Sara."

"Who is it, Harry? Tell me who."

"I've told you. There's no one. All I want to do is help you."

"Help me? How? By screwing around and lying about it? No thanks. I don't need help like that." She backed away

75

from him. "Thanks all the same, but I've got a different kind of help." She walked out of the room and into the front hall. "A kind that doesn't lie and never lets me down."

The air itself seemed to carry her up the stairs. The door to the linen closet opened without her touch. The capsules sprang like Mexican jumping beans into her outstretched hands.

She walked past the rooms of her sleeping children. There lay Sam—his faded giraffe in his arms, his covers on the floor. There was William, slanted in his crib in his own peculiar posture: knees drawn up, bottom raised in the air. And Julia and her pillows crushed against her chest. Was she dreaming of her rock star? There sat Justin at his desk grappling with his chemistry texts. Through their doors in a gentle blessing like a puff of air, Sara sent them each a special wish: be anything they wanted in life, anything at all, but not like her.

She went into her own room and, standing over her bed, slowly opened her fists. The pills rained down, some bounced back at her off the quilt, others rolled across the bed, finally became still. Watching her body as she removed her clothes, she saw the sagging flesh, the puffiness around the knees, the puckered thighs. She lay down on the bed. The pills pressed like pebbles into her back and buttocks, but she felt no discomfort. They knocked against her fingertips as she plucked at the spread. The window was slightly raised. A cool wind billowed the curtains at the sill. Sara didn't feel the cold. The night air crossed the room, crossed her body, and she lay still.

VII

On Monday afternoon, her fingers impatiently clasping and unclasping the strap of her bag, Sara waited for Sam at the school gate. She'd thought she'd start the week off right by doing something nice for Sam. But the light hurt her eyes and she'd forgotten her dark glasses. She'd also misjudged the time and arriving too early encountered this damnable wait. What could she have been thinking of? To please him? Surprise him by taking him with her to the grocery store? Sam wouldn't be pleased at all. He hated to shop as much as Sara hated to wait.

Other mothers were gathering now. Sara watched them grouping themselves in clusters to chat. She was like any one of them, she thought, a typical mother calling for her child at school. But none of them waved to her or called her by name. She didn't saunter over easily to any of their groups, offer her own impromptu plans for afternoon cookies and milk. She stood alone in sneakers and jeans, the sun hurting her eyes, remembering William's sitter's specific request to be allowed to leave early that day, while these mothers stood about in spring pants suits or freshly laundered skirts and blouses looking as if they had all the time in the world.

Why didn't she fit in? Why didn't she ever do anything right, Sara wondered, vexed with herself for misjudging the time, with Sam for the look she knew she'd see on his face the minute she mentioned the store. This was a mistake. She never should have come. She should have let Sam go home with Julia as usual. But there was no way around it now. She couldn't get hold of Julia. She'd simply have to stand out here and wait.

But how did they do it, Sara wondered, watching the mothers arrive. Some pushed carriages or dragged shopping carts behind them, others struggled to rein large dogs in on leashes. How did they manage to organize themselves, to smile so easily as they greeted one another across the yard? Valium? Alcohol? A thimbleful of bourbon before stepping out the door? That Sara could understand. Otherwise she felt no connection with them at all.

But finally the children were coming out. Pouring from the doors, running noisily into the yard that was suddenly sparkling with color, alive with movement. Everywhere children were falling down, getting up, shrieking and racing for the gate. Sam was there among them somewhere.

"Here, Sam!" Sara called, spotting him now. "Here I am!" He was shoving the boy in front of him, being shoved by the one behind. He dropped something on the ground, stopped, bent over to look. God, would he never come? She had a million things to do.

"Come on, Sam. Over here!" Sara shouted, already feeling angry with him when what she'd meant to do was please him. "Hurry up, will you!"

Sam looked up at last and saw her and started to run and Sara thought, good, she'd make it now, he was coming, they'd be on their way in a minute. But then a boy ran up behind and punched Sam in the back and Sam wheeled and gave the boy a whack in return. Christ, she'd never get out of here now, Sara thought, standing on her toes, straining to see above the crowd. They must have fallen to the ground. She couldn't see either one of the boys now.

"Goddamn it, Sam. Come here!" she cried, plunging into the crowd, swinging her hands before her, parting children right and left. She found the ones she was looking for grappling in the mud. "Get up," she yelled, pulling Sam off the wet ground and setting him on his feet.

"He started it!" Sam said the instant he was upright.

"Well I'm ending it," Sara replied, grasping his wrist and jerking him along. "I've got shopping to do."

"Shopping? Toy store?" Sam asked eagerly.

"Toys? No. Food today. Sorry to disappoint you, little one. But Christmas is over."

Sara led him down the narrow sidewalk, across the lightly trafficked street. Skillfully maneuvering him around people in their path, swinging him by one arm up over rain puddles at the curbs, she was pleased by the strength in her body today. She felt strong again, in command once more. No one would talk her out of her pills again.

Harry wanted her to quit. But his way, of course. Even in that he had to have control. Take the pills, stop taking the pills. All as the doctor directs. Well Sara wouldn't do it, that was all. She would control her own body and her own drug habit. Harry didn't understand the relationship she had with those pills, the running questions in her mind. How many would she need today? Would she win? Would the drug win? It was a delicate balancing job she struggled with each day. How many milligrams had she struggled with each day. How many more could she risk? Harry mustn't be allowed to interfere in that. How much had she slept the night before? How much would she eat that day? Everything needed to be weighed, calculated, figured in. She put a great deal of time and effort into her addiction. Constantly planning, constantly thinking ahead. What did she need to do that day? How much energy was required? Could she double up, cut back? It was always on her mind. Could she get by, go without? Could she fool Harry? And the single overriding consideration—Would she run out? Would there be one left when she absolutely had to have it?

It was like a job. Not as important a job as Harry's, perhaps. But a job nonetheless. A complicated and tricky task. Difficult and time-consuming and hers. Sara wouldn't let Harry rob her of that.

"Come on, Sam," she said, hurrying him across the supermarket parking lot and finally in through the double seeing-eye doors.

She grabbed a yellow-handled shopping cart, hauled Sam up from the floor, plopped him in the seat in front and steeled herself for battle.

The harsh, neon lights glaring down from the ceiling, bouncing off the walls, hurting her eyes, but Sara was an old hand at this. Head lowered, jaw set, she took to the aisles, veering left and right, grabbing what she wanted more by instinct than sight. Bottles of soda and juice, boxes of Kleenex and rice, quarts of milk, containers of eggs. Packages of frozen foods flew off the shelves and into her wagon. Party plates and favors, paper cups and napkins, rolls of crepe paper, plastic forks and spoons, frosting and cake mix filled in the space behind Sam.

"Party, mom?" he asked. "Party for me?"

"No, sweetheart, I told you. It's William's party this time."

At the produce section, Sara ripped plastic bags from their rollers, filled them with fruits and vegetables, tossed them on the scale to be weighed, watched the price computed and threw them into the wagon as well.

"Move that, lady! You can't leave it here," Sara called to a woman who had left her cart blocking the aisle while she stretched for a jar of pickles on the shelf. "Damn, I can't quite seem to reach...." the woman began and the sound of exploding glass momentarily hushed the store. Heads turned to look as pickles and glass in green juice floated across the floor.

Leaping up at the crash like a fighter at the bell, Sam jumped out, tilting the cart. "Me want cookies," he cried and before Sara could stop him, he disappeared into the crowd. Sara put one foot out to steady the cart. The bag of tomatoes rolled toward her and caught on the clasp of her handbag. As she pulled it free, the plastic tore apart and two pounds of tomatoes went rolling across the floor. Some were squashed at once, some kicked away, others were caught in the rungs beneath the carts ahead and, mangled, dragged on down the aisle. As Sara bent to retrieve the few left whole, someone shoved her from behind. Straightening up, she banged her head against the yellow plastic handle of her cart. "Shit!" she cried aloud and not a single head turned her way.

"Sam!" she called. "Sam!" She rolled her wagon past the pet food and cleansers, turned the corner at the 7Up and saw him sitting on the floor, mouth crammed full of Oreos, cookies clutched in either hand and four or five open bags around him. "Sam!" she called. "Come here this minute!" Compelled by her voice, he got to his knees, and struggling to gather the bags in his arms, spilled loose cookies out onto the floor.

"Now! This instant!" Sara yelled and Sam ran to her, dropping cookies along the way.

Sara stood in the check-out line imagining the frozen foods and toilet paper, the soap flakes and pickled herring, the soda pop, tomato paste and bottles of apple juice coming to life, leaping down off the shelves, crashing down on the heads of the shoppers, down on the clerks and the packers, down on Sam with his mouth full of cookies, down on herself too. She visualized the market in ruins, burst containers, broken glass, her small son buried beneath an avalanche of packaged goods. She longed to lie down, to have the noise stop, the people vanish, to have silence and stillness and a long dark green space like a path spreading out forever over empty hills without trees or grass or flowers—where she could walk into eternity without ever touching a thing.

It was no good, Sara realized, coming home, swallowing another pill to boost her confidence. These forays of hers out in the world never turned out as she had hoped. A simple thing like going to the supermarket, millions of women did it without event every day. Millions of women, as Harry would be the first to say, and there he was in her mind's eye again toting up lists, computing normalcies, running his finger down the names, not finding hers among them. *Why, Sara? Why can't you be like everyone else?* Why indeed? How she longed for that. Shattered nerves and thinning hair, thirsting nonetheless to be like other women, other mothers, to look like them, dress like them and have friends, to have the same concerns and be accepted—liked, if that was possible, but in any case, tolerated—not to protrude, embarrass herself or Harry, humiliate her children. But somehow it always went wrong. She should stay at home where she belonged. At home with the children and furniture where she couldn't do any harm.

It shouldn't be so hard just to get along, she thought. To do the normal thing, not to be crazy. But personality for Sara was a splintered and incoherent mass. It came and went before her in great swirls of rushing air. Arms outstretched, she spun through the maelstrom striving just to keep her balance.

But tonight she looked to the wine in her glass and to Harry's steadying influence, perhaps, to keep her still. She thought she'd take a Seconal before going to bed. She hadn't slept well the night before, hadn't slept well in years it seemed. Maybe it would help to tote things up the way Harry did, establish priorities, make lists. How did her day add up on the balance sheet? The first dose of speed the minute she got up. A second at lunch time. William was fretting and wouldn't settle down for his nap. She remembered thinking that wasn't like him. Perhaps he was getting sick. Not now. Not with the party coming up. Another when he woke after his nap and another—or was that the same one?—in the afternoon to handle the supermarket and Sam. The last just now before dinner. How many was that? Three? Four? Five? How many milligrams? Forty-five? Sixty? That was nothing for her. Or for lots of other people either. Lots of them, she could tell Harry, she knew it for a fact, took seventy-five or a hundred regularly. Kids were boiling up paper soaked in the stuff, getting as much as two hundred fifty milligrams a day. Three or four hits were nothing at all. She could handle that. She knew what she was doing.

No respite in the maelstrom, a desperate spinning time-lessness. She swirled the wine in her glass. It wasn't even beginning to take her down.

"I'm sorry, Harry. I'm sorry," she said and started to cry. Dry-eyed, dry cheeks, tears the farthest thing from her mind, then suddenly there, surprising her, surprising him, springing to her eyes, streaming down her face.

"It's all right, Sara. It's all right."

"No it's not. I hate myself like this."

His hand on her shoulder firmly, as if to stop the tears, to keep her still.

"I try so hard and it's never right. Nothing I do is ever right."

The world spinning before her, simple choices, obvious actions, spinning out of focus.

"It's all right. We'll work it out."

"Sometimes I think I wasn't meant to be like this at all. Something went wrong in the very beginning. Maybe not even a woman. Maybe a man. Or not even a man. An animal maybe. Or a tree or stone. Something solid that doesn't move—that can just be still and watch and learn. Be still and watch for centuries. Then maybe try it in human form. I think I was meant to have all that time. Something went wrong. I'm not ready. I want to get back to the way I should have been in the beginning. Have all that time I missed. Then maybe I could do it right."

Harry's arm was around her. He was helping her up. "Come to bed, Sara." He was wiping her tears with his hand.

The tears had stopped. Harry had stopped the tears, wiped them away. It was like old times again in the comfort of his arms. She knew what she was doing, would do. Maybe she would make another baby to keep herself safe. Walls of flesh and blood. A house of her own creation. Not clay, but human forms in her own image. Blood ties, protective tissue, no perfidy expected there. No treachery from one's own kind.

It was all right now. Harry was holding her. He, too, remembered. Old times. Good times. She wouldn't let them slip by again. She moved her hands on him to remind herself of how it had been—the structure of his head, the shape of his shoulders, the width of his hips. The model she would copy. Her prototype and guide.

Harry was holding her. She was the woman he loved. The only woman. Children would follow to bless their union, children to keep them safe. Harry was kissing her, calling her his sweet Sara the way he used to when she was young. She was young now, it was safe to let him in. Nothing could go wrong again. Their heads on the pillow, their bodies touching. She was his sweet Sara, his young, sweet, only Sara. She tried to raise herself up to make of her body a pouch to contain him. Harry was sucking at her skin. She tried to make the part he was sucking rise up to fill his mouth. Her body shuddered with pleasure. Harry's tongue was circling her breast, his mouth was closing over her nipple. She tried to make her whole body shrink to the size of her nipple, the whole surface of her skin concentrated like that and drawn into his mouth.

Harry could give her everything she needed. Give her children, give her pills, give her something to take away the pain. Harry had it within his reach, it lay in his power to give her whatever she needed—in his body, in his desk, with a wave of his hand across his prescription pad. Harry was the source of all sensation—uppers, downers, tranquilizers, sex—

the transcendental center of being. *A's*, bennies, chalk, green-ies. Harry could transform her. Hearts, jellybeans, speed, splash. Harry could turn her on to anything. Dexedrine, Ben-zedrine. Harry could hook her straight up to God. She let out a sound. "My pusher. My pimp." Her heart was pounding, her pulse was racing. The room was spinning out of control. She thought she might explode, burst apart right there on the bed. "Help me, Harry," she cried. "Make it stop."

"Just a minute," he said, getting out of bed. "I'll get you something."

All the places on her body where his hands had been felt cold when he left. She watched him walk away, watched his white, wrinkled, sagging buttocks move away from her across the room. It seemed an immeasurable distance. His white skin moving interminably through the darkness toward the bath-room door.

She thought of a beluga whale she'd seen in an aquarium once. A yellow rash across its vast white back. A nervous disorder, the attendant said. What would Harry prescribe for a nervous whale? But Harry was gone. Harry was in the bath-room getting her something to help her sleep.

"Just a light tranquilizer," he said, coming back, handing her the pill, the water. "It won't put you out, but it should calm you down. I can't give you anything stronger because I don't know what else you've had today."

Twisted faces on the bedroom wall scoffed at her. Harry had been gone for years. Harry had returned from a distant shore to place something in her mouth. Whatever he put into her body, she would take. Harry had the power. Everything lay within his reach.

"What would you give a nervous whale?"

"Go to sleep, Sara."

"What could be big enough to make a whale nervous?"

The faces on the wall took their time devouring her. Their mouths opened hugely, opened slowly. Harry's mouth con-suming her. Opening wide enough to consume the world. Everything Harry wanted—pieces of the earth, of her, power, other women—everything fell to him through that hole.

Harry was asleep. Sara couldn't sleep. Lights from the street strained in through the curtains and shadows flickered on the bedroom walls. Perhaps she should get up and close the windows. Perhaps she should turn off the bathroom light. But Sara didn't move. Whatever Harry had given her was paralyzing her limbs. Harry was sleeping, the children were sleeping. Sara wanted to sleep too.

She turned the radio on low—a soothing classical piece—maybe that would help her sleep. If she concentrated on the music, thought only of that, filled her body, her mind with that . . . if she could picture the music, visualize it floating in her mind, floating in patterns through her head, carrying her body away . . . if she could see only that . . . full notes and grace notes . . . she was in need of grace . . . only that . . . in need of grace. . . .

Sara's eyes snapped open. Again, it was 4:33. The digital alarm clock met her stare. Three luminous numbers waiting in the dark to attack, ticking themselves off one by one, waiting through the night to leap out at her when she awoke. She hated those numbers, despised that clock. The three flipped over now into a four. 4:34. It did it for spite. To remind her she couldn't sleep. To torment her with the fact that always her nights were foreshortened, either at one end or the other.

She wondered if there was a pill for early morning insomnia. Harry would know. A three-hour sleeping pill. She'd keep it handy by the bed, gulp it down at 4:35, sleep like a baby until the alarm went off. That was something she might invent: short-acting pills for different hours of the day. Every pill-head in the world would sing her praises then, and she'd know something of Harry's fame. Establish a housewives' treasure-trove of psychopharmacology. A light one-hour tranquilizer to get them through the morning and see the kids off to school. Followed by ten milligrams of speed to get the cleaning started. Ten should be enough. She didn't want them soaring too high too early in the day. That would take them through to about noon, and then, let's see, what little treat could she concoct? The noon blues? Something to get baby fed and down for his nap? Elavil, she thought—an antidepressant—precisely what was needed. But she'd want it mixed with a tranquilizer for a more soothing effect. There was such a thing on the market, she'd heard Harry say—Harry in his doctor's coat, his nurse by his side, avenging angels dressed in white, bringing health, bringing hope. Triavil! That's its name. An upper and downer in one. And later, for the empty hours of baby's nap, when there was not a single other waking consciousness to intrude on their own, they would want. . . . Well that would depend. She'd have to do a little experimenting, Sara thought, seeing herself testing chemicals, grinding powders, weighing potencies, mixing colors: Seconal reds, rainbows, goofballs, bright blue devils, throwing in a dash of Preludin orange, and for old time's sake, basic Dexedrine brown. She'd give them a couple of those, fifteen apiece, her old standbys, while baby slept if they wanted to fly, but if their houses were too silent, the emptiness too threatening as it sometimes was in hers, then maybe Thorazine was more in order, wouldn't you agree, doctor? nurse? Fifty milligrams, let's say, for psychotic agitation, wouldn't that be about right? Or would you suggest Stelazine to minimize their anger and anxiety? Followed by Cogentin, of course, to eliminate the side effects of the other two. You had to be prepared for side effects, Sara knew. Nothing came free in this life. You couldn't have your exhilaration without your paranoia too. Give her a white coat and she'd be on her way. Maybe she could take a course in alchemy. Add a little Dexamyl, a little Librium . . . a dash of Lithium . . . sprinkle in some herbs. . . . She had an urge to wake Harry up so he could watch her at work. But Harry slept so soundly. His side of the bed was heavy with fact. Hers lifted off in speculation.

These early morning hours were Sara's alone. Almost a gift, once she got past the desperation. They were another sort of trip, a gentle hallucinogen pulling her in towards a calmer part of herself, almost a deadly calm, pulling her inward in one long continuous moving stream that lasted as long as the hours themselves lasted, unbroken. But if she allowed herself to go along, she'd suffer for it the rest of the day. She had to get up now and take a hit. It would plug in just in time to wake the children. How she wished she could do that with grace. Float through the house, an angel in white, offering, like a gift to each of her children, the joy of another day. Maybe Harry would know of a drug to bring out different parts of the personality—a pill for poise or wit or understanding, a capsule for humor or grace. That was what was needed. To ask Harry about grace. But she didn't dare to wake him. Harry needed his sleep. The children needed their sleep. They all needed hours and hours of uninterrupted sleep. Sara would die at night so as not to disturb their sleep.

VIII

When he got up, Harry said of course he couldn't go. "You handle it, Sara. See what it's all about." Elongated in his pin-stripe suit, casting slant-eyed glances. "You'll go in straight, won't you?"

"Oh, Christ."

"I'm only asking."

Emptying the drawers of the bedside table, turning the pockets of her robe inside out, blindly sweeping things off the shelves of the medicine cabinet, picking the linen closet clean—her hidden treasure, placed there tenderly between the sheets like other women place sachets—Sara threw it all into a paper bag and handed it to Harry.

"What's this, the makings of a pharmacy?" he asked and tossed the bag up on the dresser.

"No," she said, pressing it on him. "Take it with you. I want them out of the house."

"I thought you were out already. You said . . ."

"I know what I said but this time I mean it. Take them, please." She opened his medical bag and stuffed the paper sack inside.

"It's hard this way, Sara," Harry said. "Slow withdrawal is best. Maybe I'd better leave you some tranquilizers."

"No. Nothing. No more pills." It meant so much to her to show him she could do it right. Harry deserved a decent wife. She could be one for him, she'd show him she could.

"Good luck at the school," Harry said. "I'd go with you if I could, but I've got a brutal schedule today. Helen's even got my lunch hour filled."

Harry had refused the mission and here she was, unfortified, sent out like a knight without his armor to do battle with the principal of Justin's school. It was hardly the right day to enounce her support, but there never was a right day to begin.

Whatever happened, Sara swore she wouldn't go to Harry and beg. She'd done that once. Actually got down on her hands and knees and begged to have them back. She remembered the look on Harry's face then—disgust and horror and pity. She didn't ever want to see that look again. She might try someone else, she thought, find herself a local scrip doctor, never even have to go to Harry. But that was risky, and doctors were being so careful these days, tightening up, some refusing even to prescribe them for weight control.

She'd been out that time, completely out, like now. Not a single capsule in the house. It was like drowning, like being buried alive. No way out. No hope of rescue. And so she'd gone to Harry and got right down on his office floor—she had no pride then, no sense of herself as a person at all—and wept and said she'd do anything he wanted to have them back. Horror, disgust flashed on Harry's face. Pity, too. That was the worst. And he'd turned away so as not to have to look at her and held out the prescription behind his back.

That wouldn't happen again, she swore to herself, getting dressed. Harry was right. All she needed was willpower, a little strength. Certainly she had that. She was strong. The dark eyes blazing back at her from the mirror, the high cheekbones testified to that. They'd see at that school just how strong she was.

But where was the sitter now? Sara didn't want to be late. Perfectly respectable, she thought, twisting to inspect herself in the mirror downstairs. Like any wife. Any decent wife. All except her hair. She really needed to have it done. Perhaps in time for William's party. Not that there was much that could be done with it, but something perhaps. A little styling, a little body. And in the meantime, just for today, perhaps a hat. Oh, but she hated hats. She looked in the mirror and gave it a little pat. But on the other hand, it did hide her hair and hats lent a certain authority to any head. She could use some authority today, she thought, in dealing with Mr. Walsh. The hat, black and drooping, definitely seemed to suit her purposes. It hung far enough down to conceal her face when she lowered her chin: demure, sympathetic mother throwing herself on the mercy of the school. Raising her head, the brim flipped up a woman to be reckoned with rushing to the defense of her son. But could she do it? Would she have the stamina to pull it off straight?

From the way they'd talked to her on the phone, she knew it would take every ounce of strength she had, as it usually did where Justin was concerned. And here she was, without a pill. What a day to give them up. Oh, but she really could kill that boy for getting her into this. With a quick, angry gesture she smoothed her skirt down over her hips. How she hated skirts, and this one didn't fit. She yanked at the waistband and pulled her blouse out over it to hide her stomach. She wasn't fat, only a bit too hippy for this skirt. She pulled on the jacket and swirled to inspect her hem. Not bad from the rear. Matching skirt and jacket, a nice suit. Businesslike, nicely suited to her needs. But God, from the front could they tell? A woman drowning, a woman going down for the count. Why hadn't they called his father instead, summoned the famous New York internist? But Harry was too busy. Harry had his practice. And here was Sara having given all her pills away. Oh what a fool she was.

Hearing the doorbell at last, she pinched her cheeks to raise the color. Rouge was what was needed but that too had been swept, as if by a tide, off the shelf. Rouge, sleeping pills, aspirin, amphetamines. A great wave had covered the house, washing away cosmetics and drugs. Sara stepped back from the mirror. That was the best she could do. Not bad, she thought, for a drowning woman of thirty-nine.

"I'll be back in an hour," she told the sitter and went out the front door squinting her eyes against the sun.

It had rained again last night and the still wet streets looked clean and bright, like a promise of sorts, with the smell of spring in the air. The wind was surprisingly strong, though, and Sara raised her hand to hold her hat in place.

Didn't she have enough before her without having to battle the wind as well? Justin had better appreciate this, she said to herself, walking down the block, but she knew he probably wouldn't. That child had no idea of the efforts she made on his behalf.

Whatever they might say, he was a gifted boy. All her

children were gifted, each in his own way, of course, but Justin perhaps especially, with his quick intuition, his sensivity. It was only natural that such a boy would react to authority as he had. For that was the problem, she surmised, some trouble with one of his teachers. Freedom was at the root of it. Justin was beginning to demand his freedom now, Sara knew, turning right on Acorn Lane. And at sixteen, well he might. She could see that, could even condone it up to a point. But limits must be set. Wasn't Harry always saying so? *Limits, Sara, must be set.* She would see to that, and with her hat on straight, too. Raising her hand again to hold it against the wind, she felt a wave of hatred pass through her—for Justin for calling her out like this into the wind, making her face the people at school, for Harry for refusing to go, for making pronouncements from the safety of his office about limits needing to be set. Everything in Sara yearned now to be sitting safely in her house, in her comfortable old chair with William in her arms.

The first day was definitely the hardest, Sara decided, turning the corner at Jackson, heading down toward Main. But she would show Justin she was on his side. What did those teachers know anyway? The fine flash in his eyes, the defiant stance—all they saw was disrespect.

She would do it for Harry too. Harry was a good man, a dedicated man. He deserved a decent wife. This thing of his with Helen wasn't serious, couldn't possibly be serious. A fling with a younger woman, that was all there was to it. It was his age, his time of life. Sara understood that. It was common among men of Harry's age. He would get over it and she would be there, decent and drug-free, strong, upstanding, a veritable pillar of the community, when he did.

The very imagery made her weak. She felt her body sag and looked around for a place to sit down. A woman passing turned to look. People were always turning, looking. Sara didn't like that about people. She didn't like going out into the streets to be looked at. She longed to be at home, sitting in her own special chair with her knees flung over its arm, her baby in her lap. She could feel herself sinking into the cushions of the chair, feel William's warm, safe body in her hands. God, she was tired. How she longed to go home.

She trudged on, though, resolutely intent on her task,

thinking this was an altogether different woman on her wa
to school to save her son. This wasn't Sara, not the real Sar
The real Sara soared high above the threats of principals an
outdistanced the pull of fatigue. The real Sara was in contr
of her fate, not subject to fears and needs. Debilitating need
she thought them now, feeling a need to have Harry with he
Harry journeying stalwartly by her side. The two of the
united in purpose, marching off to do battle for their son. The
son. Not his or hers, but theirs. Harry would hold her togethe
He would stretch out his hand and keep her on course. On
he never had. Whenever she looked around she found herse
alone. But one day, perhaps, he'd be there when she looke

If it was need that bound her to Harry, Sara understoo
it was love she felt for her children. And a desire to keep the
safe. Protecting them, she protected herself—body on bod
flesh on flesh, intertwining limbs and lives. Perhaps it was f
that she had had them: to be enveloped by a world of her ow
flesh and blood. An environment of her own making—that w
the only truly trustworthy one, Sara believed. And as ye
followed year, so her children had succeeded themselves-
Justin, Julia, and when they seemed ready to break away, Sa
and William—a chronology of her distrust. And of her jo
too. For truly she loved them. And now William was growin
up, moving on. The first birthday. Age measured for the fir
time in years.

Sara would surround herself forever with her children
she could. She would give them whatever she had to. mal
them successful, make them better than herself. And she ha
accomplished that, it came to her in moments powerful enoug
to make the skin on the back of her neck rise in goosefles
to make her breath come in short, sharp peaks and her eye
fill with tears whenever she saw any one of them being real
good at something. That they could do that. Her children! Sa
sliding into second. Julia in the school play. Justin fixing
motor. That they knew how to do such things despite bein
hers. Yes, it was enough to make her cry.

And William was growing up. Age one. Age overtakin
him. How fast the other years had gone. Justin's sixteen
Julia's fourteen. How fast her baby's childhood would go. A
blink of her eyes, her back turned for a moment and William
too, would be leaving her.

The traffic cop was motioning for her to cross. All right, she was crossing Main Street, moving ahead like the other pedestrians. Why did he single her out? She was just like anyone else. Any other mother on her way to school. Only she knew she wasn't. She looked absurd, she knew she did. This skirt . . . this hat. . . . Nobody wore hats like this any more. Couldn't she even do that right? Dress right? Find a hat in fashion? Maybe she could stuff it into the trash, but someone would see . . . and then her hair . . . they were bound to laugh. It was hopeless, she knew it was. She wanted to cry. Who did Justin think he was, dragging her out in the street like this to be laughed at? And in a skirt too. *Please, mom, not to school,* he'd begged and she had promised him she wouldn't wear jeans. That was one promise she could keep.

Only two more blocks to go, but she didn't think she'd make it. Her legs were giving out. She couldn't possibly face Mr. Walsh like this. She needed a pill to bolster her up, just one to give her a boost. She dug her hands into the pockets of her jacket. There must be one there somewhere. One that had fallen loose, dropped out of the bottle, worked its way into the weave of the coat. Just one. Damn! She dug her fingers into the lining. Nothing. But back at home in her jeans. . . . Maybe she had time to run home. . . . She turned, caught sight of the clock in the church tower. No, she was nearly late now. She couldn't go back, couldn't go ahead. *Please, Harry. Give them back.*

Her legs were aching terribly. She had to sit down. She saw an empty bench up ahead in the library park. *Please, Harry.* She pressed the heels of her hands into her eyes. She would make him materialize before her, one hand stretched out to keep her whole, the other clasping the means of her transformation. *Please, Harry.* She wouldn't mind about Helen, she'd do anything he asked. Oh, but she did mind. Why did it have to be Helen? Why did it have to be anyone? Why couldn't she be the one he wanted?

Perhaps she still could. If she kept her promise. If she showed her strength—strength, willpower, that was all Harry said it took. She thought she might fall asleep right there on the bench, sink down into the blackness behind her eyes, let herself be lifted up, blown off the bench and carried out through

space forever. Harry had taken her pills away. Harry had take
himself away. If she weren't so tired she'd despise him for i

Rounding over beneath her hat, Sara sagged against th
bench, seeping through its wooden slats, spilling from i
boards, drifting in and out of herself, she became that othe
self again. The real Sara. Unafraid, unaccountable, airborn
once more, she grazed the heads of her astonished childrer
Her flesh was organdy, her bones spun sugar. Weightless an
free, soaring high on blue lights and yellow skies, the exu
tation of her flight teased her mouth into a grateful smile. Hal
sleep, half smile, half drug diluted in water and filtered throug
cotton, she drew into her veins a far-off flash of remembere
euphoria and with a start, awoke, refreshed.

Mr. Walsh stood up as she entered his office. She hadn'
remembered him as being quite so bald.

"I've asked Justin to join us," he said. "He should b
here any minute."

He leaned forward across his desk to offer her a mint
No, thanks, she said and wondered why he had asked. Wa
her breath bad? Was that it? She'd been meaning for week
to buy mouth wash. It seemed every time she went to the stor
she forgot.

"Justin is not an ordinary child," Sara began and stopped
She'd meant to say adolescent, not child. He could mak
something of that, her thinking of a sixteen-year-old boy a
a child. "He has an unusual mind," she continued. Mr. Wals
was mocking her, smiling thinly, mocking. Ah, yes, Sar
could read his mind. I've heard that before, he was thinking
every mother says that about her son. "It's true," she insisted
addressing herself to his silent contradiction. "He does. H
has a highly independent spirit." Sara pulled herself up in he
chair, placing her arms on the rests. She thought she shoul
make that clear at once.

"Ah, yes," said Mr. Walsh. "Independence. Well, her
he is now."

Sara turned to face her son. In he sulked like some long
thin creature more accustomed to traversing the ground on i
belly than making its way on foot. Why, she wondered, coul
he never stand up straight, pull his shoulders back? When ha

he lost so much weight? And that hair. It grew longer and stringier by the hour. She saw dirt spots on his jeans, grease beneath his fingernails. A dose of anger more potent than amphetamines shot through her then and Sara knew she'd make it all right. What she'd give her life for was to strip him where he stood and throw him in the nearest tub.

"I very much regret," Mr. Walsh began, motioning Justin to a chair, "that we are forced to have this meeting. I only call in a parent as a last resort."

How Sara wished she hadn't worn this skirt. She didn't know how to sit in a skirt, what to do with her legs. She pulled her jacket tight around her and leaned toward the desk. She had to be firm with this man. "From what I was told on the phone," she said, "I thought you might be mistaking independence for insubordination."

"Oh, no, Mrs. Richardson. I don't think we're in the least confused in that regard."

"What exactly has he done?" Sara hated to be put in the position of asking questions. It was a tactical error giving Mr. Walsh the upper hand. But at least she'd voiced it strongly and with a flounce of her hat.

"Well, to begin with . . ." The principal referred to a file on the desk before him. "Out of forty-two days of the spring semester, Justin has had twelve absences. Seven of them unexcused."

That damn garage. Harry was right. Sixteen and his only ambition to be a mechanic. Sara wheeled to confront her son. Justin's arms were looped around the back of his chair, his feet coiled on the rungs. He looked soiled and skinny to her and markedly reptilian. The very sight of him sent another rush of energy into her blood. "Well, Justin?" she demanded.

"Well what?"

"Is it true?"

"Is what true?"

"Have you missed all those days?"

"I wasn't counting."

She could kill him for humiliating her like this in front of a stranger. Making her admit she didn't know what her own son was doing with his time. And Mr. Walsh, the pompous, bald-headed ass, was enjoying it. As Harry might. Sara looked up now and saw his face—the two adult male images merged into one, a superimposed witness to her humiliation. Having refused the mission himself, Harry sent her instead, his emissary of failure out into the world. He sat there himself, complacently now, shielded as by glass behind the principal's face, enjoying the spectacle of her defeat. Sara would like to wring their necks—individually and collectively too, Justin's as well—but all at once she didn't have the strength. Like air from a punctured balloon it was gone from her. Let the men handle the boy. It was too much. You do it, she silently begged. You're knowledgeable, experienced, strong. Your sure hands can mold a skinny boy.

"But that's not all," Mr. Walsh said. "There's more, I'm afraid."

Oh, no. Not more. Sara dropped her head to let the brim of her hat shield her from whatever else was coming. Mr. Walsh's voice droned on. ". . . no respect for his teachers. . . ." Not for her, nor for his father, that was true enough. ". . . answers back . . . talks out of turn. . . ." Right again. She knew he did that. Were men always right? ". . . and only yesterday. . . ." But Sara didn't want to know about yesterday, she couldn't handle any more. Why couldn't he be a good, kind man and stop? ". . . Mr. O'Connor had to ask him to leave the class." Asked to leave? Threw him out? Pulled then by some sense of ancient obligation, Sara's head turned in her son's direction. Arms and legs squirming about one another, reptiles restlessly coiling. "It seems Justin threw an eraser at him." That too. She might have expected it. Sara's head nodded wearily. But now the soiled snakeboy stiffened and sprang.

"Not *at* him."

"You threw it."

"Not *at* him."

Sara really didn't have the strength for this. If they were going to fight she'd simply have to leave.

"You threw an object at a teacher."

Hadn't she heard all this before? She saw the dark brown bottle on the shelf in front of her, the white plastic cap.

"I didn't throw it at him."

It had such a familiar ring.

"You'd been talking all period."

"I had not."

Yes you did. No I didn't.

96

"O'Connor said you had."

Didn't she spend her life settling such disputes?

"He's got it in for me. He hates me."

The brown bottle nearly full, a month's supply within her grasp.

"He does not."

"He does too."

Harry had it now. Harry had what she needed.

"Tell me in your own words exactly what happened."

Please, Harry. Be good. Be kind.

Her son's quick, nervous angry voice beginning a tale by her side. Something about a boy named Frank . . . who was Frank? did she know him? A girl named Linda . . . a phone out of order . . . he tried to call. . . .

". . . Linda said she didn't believe him and Frank swore it was true and O'Connor turned around and saw them talking and threw the eraser. It landed by my seat so I picked it up and threw it back."

This was different. This was something else. "I find it shocking," Sara said, aroused by what she'd heard, "that you have teachers in this school so little in control of themselves they are reduced to throwing objects at children." It was an immense effort and Sara felt drained of the last of her strength as she finished. But she had done it. She'd come to the defense of her son.

That was all she could take now. Truly, she had to leave. But Mr. Walsh was returning to the subject of Justin's absences. She had no way of explaining them, Sara said, and even if she could, she wouldn't.

"What?" Mr. Walsh was leaning toward her. "I couldn't hear."

Sara wanted to lie down. She felt Justin's breath behind her, saw the neat, baldheaded man in front of her and thought they were both probably right. Let them figure it out without her.

"Do you and your husband entertain hopes of sending Justin to college?"

Her husband. Did she have a husband? Ah, yes. The famous internist. The highly celebrated and always absent doctor. No, she said, they didn't entertain much of anything any more. But they still might. She still had hope. If only she could go to sleep, just lie down between the boy's breathing and the man's questioning, never wake up again unless someone handed her a pill. Why didn't someone? Why didn't Harry? She would count it a positive act of love on his part if he walked in right now and returned her pills.

"Because if you do, he's certainly going to have to shape up."

Sara turned to look. Would this long, sinewy boy shape up, fill out, grow into the man behind the desk, the man behind the man behind the desk? Would he wash his face, shave his head? She looked at Mr. Walsh. Had he, too, reptilian origins? He was leaning toward her. Justin was leaning toward her. Why did they surround her so?

"He needs to apply himself . . . show more seriousness about his work. . . ."

Yes, that was right. Sara had heard that phrase before. *Apply himself.* Strength. Willpower. The brim of her hat blocked out the light. Mr. Walsh couldn't see if she closed her eyes. She wondered if he could see her at all. If he was even looking. It didn't matter. Let him look. A strange woman in a skirt. This wasn't her. Not the real Sara. The real Sara had moved off somewhere beneath her hat.

". . . it's a shame really . . . a boy with his potential. . . ."

Yes, she nodded. Of course he was right.

". . . his grades are suffering . . . he's slipping behind. . . ."

Sara was slipping into the wide spaces of the man's great bald face, the pouches beneath his eyes, his jowls, his round, shining skin . . . if she didn't move her eyes, she would fall away . . . fall into the spaces of his face and disappear.

"Of course it's not too late . . ."

But Sara was afraid that it was. Yes, if he wanted to know the truth, she really was afraid it was.

"That's why I called this meeting when I did . . ."

Too late. She was slipping. She knew it. Why didn't Harry come?

"Mom. Mom."

Sara's hand fell off the armrest. She didn't bother to replace it. Her son was calling her. It was like a dream. A moment ago she had thought of something to say, now she couldn't remember what it was. *Please, Harry, please.*

"There's always time to mend our ways . . ."

Is there, Mr. Walsh? Is that what you think? Is that what the good, kind man smiling at her now, standing up, extending his hand, thinks?

Sara stood up too. One foot was asleep. Her whole leg up to her knee tingled painfully as she shifted her weight. She wanted to sit back down, to let the paralysis creep up, take over her body. She aimed her hand toward the man's and turned her dead ankle. Mr. Walsh lurched across his desk, Justin grabbed for her from behind. They were both too late. Sometimes it is too late, Mr. Walsh, you see. But it was all right. She hadn't fallen to the ground, hadn't really disgraced herself. She had merely stumbled and caught the edge of the desk for support. She was all right now. Everything was all right now. She was shaking the man's hand, stroking the side of the boy's face.

Out in the hall she bumped up against a girl with green eyes. A face she had seen before, a look she had seen on that face. Her children lurked in the darkness. Islands of safety, she had intended them, not witnesses to her undoing.

IX

Friday, June 1. The morning of the fourth day off the pills. Sara had done it. She'd broken her record and was on her way to becoming a normal person. That the fourth day should fall on the first of the month she took for a sign. A bleak sign. The month, as she lay in bed staring up at the ceiling, unfolded before her blank, eventless. A dry month, a straight month. Was this how other women did it, she wondered. Did they wake up knowing however they felt when they first opened their eyes was the best they were going to feel all day? No peaks to look forward to, no transformations?

It was an accomplishment to have reached the fourth day. She looked into the off-white ceiling, followed the line of peeling paint. Why did it feel so like a loss?

At breakfast, Julia looked at her admiringly and gave her an extra hug as she was leaving for school. "Hang in there, mom. You're doing great."

At her touch, tears sprang to Sara's eyes. There were other systems of support in the world, it seemed. But should it be one so young, she wondered, so untried? Julia seemed more a mother to her now than a daughter. It was she who, these last three days, had looked after Sam and William while Sara slept, had made their meals and picked up their rooms when Sara couldn't drag herself off the bed.

Yes, Sara said, she'd try. She'd hang in there all right. Seeing them out the door, she made silent promises to each of them to be a better mother, a better person— more reliable, sane, and stable. She would not rush at them with knives or shout at the top of her lungs making their eyes open wide in fear.

The fourth day was definitely the hardest. Sara had evidence of that now. Depression— thick, black, all-encompassing—it weighed on her movements, pressed on her mind.

She had thought once to get her ideas into order about having a proper life. When she got away from home, finished school, she'd decide on a career. But she never did. As soon as one possibility came forward—sculpting, teaching—she pushed it back. After all, she wasn't actually bright enough to be a teacher, good enough to be a sculptor. She had been working at the clay again, though, these last few days, her fingers gradually reaccustoming themselves to the task. And several little animals—some of them actually quite good, if she did say so herself—sat around the living room now, the better ones up on the mantel, others lower down on the shelves where Sam could reach. He liked to play with them on the floor, devising a series of barnyard games which he tried in vain to teach to William. Even Justin had picked up the goat— one of Sara's favorites—and said how good he thought it was.

But nothing had come of these vague hopes of hers for a different kind of life. So Sara believed she had just slid inevitably into marriage, gently pushed by her parents' subscription to the prevailing wisdom of the day. What else was there for a woman? Even a college educated woman? And she wasn't much good on her own. Even among friends, and she didn't have any close ones besides Jennifer, she felt stiff and revealed and looked about for cover. It wasn't surprising, then, Sara thought, for marriage, the perfect camouflage, to be waiting. But how dreadful to feel her life all these years later spreading out around her unclaimed, uninhabited. If this was being straight, she didn't want it. It was too bleak, too unadorned. She thought she might just go back to bed again, lie still and not move, sink way down into the mattress until she sank right through the cover and into the stuffing itself. Harry would sleep on her. The children would crawl on her, bouncing themselves silly. Where's mother? they would ask. Mother's gone, mother's at peace at last, made of mattress ticking.

If she wasn't going to die, she'd have to have a pill to keep her alive. The house was waiting to swallow her. She dug her hands into her pockets, pulled loose threads out under her nails. One capsule was all she wanted. What use was a broken record if it broke her spirit as well? She'd give her life right now for fifteen milligrams—a dose that any other day would hardly get her off the ground.

Tomorrow would be easier, Harry had said. *You're on your way*, he told her. *If you can just hold out for a week*. A week? Another hour of this would kill her. *If you absolutely can't make it*, Harry had said, *I could hospitalize you. Readdict you to something else. Barbituates, most likely, then take you off slowly*. He wouldn't want to do it, he said, and he'd hate to risk the publicity, but. . . . No, Sara had answered. No hospitals. She'd stay here quietly at home.

Holding William on her lap, waiting for his food to heat, she thought being the last, he was in some ways the most precious to her. "Everything I am comes to an end in you," she said to him, tracing the shape of his nose, his cheeks. William's little fists closed over her fingers. He drew himself up onto his feet in her lap, pulling against her with all of his weight. What if her strength gave out and she dropped him? What if he fell to the floor? It was an awesome responsibility being alone with a child. *Hire a nursemaid*, Harry had said, and Sara had had them on and off with all of the children. Strangers in her house. Letting outsiders in. And in the end, she'd let them go.

Harry didn't understand. It was more than the fatigue and depression of withdrawal that got her down. More than the inability to function in her house. It was the humiliation of having another person take over her job. The degradation of being replaced. The house won then. Strangers won. It was a double defeat. Sara was stripped of her center, and worthless as well.

Things would be different now. "Mommy's going to be a new woman," she said, placing William in his highchair. A sense of endings came over her then, an end to drugs and child-bearing, an end to old dependencies. And to unmeasured highs as well?

Feeding William was a kind of dance. The spoon goes into the jar, alights on the rim. William's toes wiggle and twitch, his fingers clutch and grasp. A normal child. All parts perfectly formed. Sara remembered that other child—Theresa Bower down the block. A normal child too—from the waist up. She had no legs. The spoon goes into William's mouth, rides inside in the dark. Sara had gone to see Theresa when she was born. A pink blanket covering her, she looked like any other baby. Any normal baby. The spoon comes out. If they never lifted the blanket, never looked underneath, no one would know. If her parents kept her dressed in skirts, they would never have to look. It was fortunate she was a girl. Then maybe she would die. But she didn't die. Not enough of the Thalidomide babies died. The spoon rises, William's mouth opens. Theresa grew. Every part of her grew, except her legs. After a few years, they moved away.

The spoon goes in, the mouth closes, the spoon pulls out. All her babies were normal. Normal babies from a normal mother. Thus had she fed three others before him. But four was enough. William was the last. No more babies now.

The spoon moves again, catches a trickle of food running down his chin, reintroduces it to his mouth. Could she still be feeding him? Could it still be only lunchtime?

The spoon dips into the jar, into William's mouth. All her children were normal, thank God for that. No Thalidomide for her, only Dexedrine for strength, for life. What she wouldn't give for one now.

How she'd love to crawl back into bed, take a nap, feel her head on the pillow, the covers up to her chin. The clock ticks on the shelf but its hands never move. 12:22. The spoon rises and lowers. William's mouth opens and closes. Shadows creep on the wall. Sara does what William does, opens and closes her mouth, licks her lips. William laughs out loud. Another mouthful accomplished. 12:23.

A solitary bird sings outside. William's birthday is coming. One year old next week. He would go out into the world, leave her behind. Back and forth the spoon goes, into the jar and out. She'll give him a party out in the yard. Into his mouth and out.

Sleep would release her. Tears would release her. She could run out of herself on tears.

Now all the jars are empty. Her baby's belly is full. Sara drops the spoon in the sink, carries William and his bottle and toys out into the living room, puts him down on the bright, red rug.

Sinking into her favorite chair, Sara looked around the

room. Clutter everywhere: Julia's shoes, Justin's record
Harry's journals strewn on the floor. Broken pencils, toy car
bats, balls, and Sam's blocks lying where they had lande
when he kicked them over on his way to school. There's n
a single empty, open space for the eye to rest. Why can't
be neat? Why can't it be pretty. Sara imagined flowers in
vase, starched curtains at the windows, the tables cleared, th
floors polished. She longed for a touch of beauty in her hous
A Parian figurine, perhaps, some bit of colored glass to catc
the sun. But anything she loved, anything delicate, the childre
broke at once.

She hung her legs over the arm of the chair. There wa
so much that needed to be done and she didn't have th
strength. Straight, she was worthless. And even high, th
house won. It arose before her day after day, a challenge sh
could never meet. Even the other Sara, the real Sara, couldn
conquer this house. Down she dove into the midst of unmad
beds, dirty diapers, dirty clothes, spotted floors, dishes t
wash, children to mind, up she struggled through the debris
surfacing a moment, gasping for air, plunging down throug
it all again. The house closed over her. There was no way o
winning, no final victory. Sara started to cry.

Oh, Christ! She sat bolt upright in her chair. I can't cry
There isn't time. Jennifer's coming to lunch!

She had to make some food, do something about th
house. This hopeless, mocking house. Harry could give he
something to calm her down. What she needed was somethin
to raise her up. She couldn't make it this way. She knew sh
couldn't. It was no good. Just one. A hit of something . . .
Preludin, anything. She lunged at the table, tore open a drawer
shook it hard. Something rolled in the back . . . brown, round
She slapped her hand down on it as she would a bug, and ha
it halfway to her mouth before she saw what it was—a button
a damn button. She hurled it across the room, searched th
other drawers. She clawed through loose papers, broken pens
old photographs, pulled apart bundles of sewing, grabbed a
pages Sam had torn out of books and she had stuffed in ther
to glue. "Shit!" she yelled and slammed the drawer and re
proached herself for disturbing him as she saw William star
violently on the rug. "Hush," she said as he began to whimper
"Hush up now."

She searched the room, trying to divine hiding places, even running her hands over her body as if her own person might conceal a stash. Oh God, let there be one. Just one. I'll give them up tomorrow, I swear I will. She ran up the stairs to the linen closet, pulled the towels out onto the floor, shook the sheets loose—queen sizes, doubles, singles, even the ones fitting the crib. They fell like dead birds at her feet. Nothing. She grabbed the pillow cases and napkins, shook them out as well. Nothing. Tablecloths, washcloths. Not a single hit of speed. Gulping sounds started in the back of her throat. Nothing for it anywhere. She had picked the closet clean, given the last chance she had to Harry.

Sara went back downstairs and sank into her chair. Without the pills, she'd just as soon die. Harry didn't want her anyway. He wanted someone younger, prettier. Well, let him have her then. She wouldn't stand in his way. Death didn't seem to her so very terrible. An end to this climbing and sinking. An escape from this house whose walls one day inevitably would crush her. She would like to take things into her own hands now. But how? How does one repossess one's life? Does one go from room to room, scraping it off the walls, the floors? Reclaiming like dust all traces of oneself from beneath the beds, the tables, from under the rugs, behind the drapes. *Here, life, here*, does one call? *I want you back now*. And if life proves obstinate and refuses to come, what then? Gas? Pills? She didn't have any. The window? It wasn't high enough. A gun? She was afraid of guns. Slitting one's wrists in a hot tub? That was painless and quick. She had read so in a medical journal of Harry's.

That would be it then. The bath upstairs, a fresh, clean blade. She sees her blood escape, running as freely from her body as on a single capsule she would run from all such preoccupations. Everywhere around her there is only red—red blood, red water rising, spreading over her feet, her legs, her chest, closing now over her head. Head submerged but eyes still open, she looks up at the underside of red water. Eyes bleeding red, she looks into the vacant place where once her body had been. Her head sinks and now that head begins to bob . . . slowly it turns one way, then another . . . that small, fragile, precious head . . . and William who has nodded off to sleep lies still as death in the middle of the bright red rug.

Sara leaps from her chair. It's one forty-five and Jennifer'
coming at two!

She scoops her baby up from the floor. He doesn't wake
For the sake of her children, a mother must live forever. Sh
takes him up the stairs to bed.

The house was empty, no one in it making noise. A dea
house housing a dying remnant. Sara drew her knees up to he
chest and rocked herself. Dr. Harold Richardson. Was he God
then, to give and take away? Dr. and Mrs. Richardson. Sh
followed his title, attached to it by a conjunction and a uni
versally understood form of possession. She sat in her chai
rocking herself and all that she rocked was his.

Suddenly, there's an insistent kind of banging . . . like th
sound of Sam's wooden mallet . . . up and down . . . bangin,
a peg into place . . . up and down . . . but Sam was at schoo
and all the children were accounted for . . . banging softly
incessantly . . . Oh, Christ! It's Jennifer at the door.

Sara runs to answer it. "Jenny!" she calls, flinging ope
the door. She does feel better. The nap has helped. "I'm sorry
Forgive me. I must have dozed off."

"It's okay, I just got here. The bell was broken, so I ha
to knock."

Jennifer holds out her arms. How does she stay so thin
Sara hugs her, leads her through the house. She's consciou
of their arms about one another, of the smell of Jennifer'
freshly-washed hair. "It's so good to see you," she says. "It'
been much too long."

"I know," Jennifer says. "You'd think we lived in dif
ferent towns. Well, let's see . . . How've you been?"

"Oh fine, fine," Sara says. "Hectic of course, but fine
Oh God, look at this mess." She throws a sneaker off th
couch, moves a load of clean, unfolded wash to make a plac
for Jennifer to sit. "I meant to straighten up, to have thing
looking nice for a change. But . . ."

"It doesn't matter, you know. You don't have to clea
up for me."

"I wanted to do it right for once. Have lunch all made
the table set and I haven't done a thing . . . except quit," sh

added after a moment, remembering. "I'm off the stuff for good."

"You are? Really? You quit? Hey, Sara, that's great. You really did it? Just like that? Just quit cold?"

"Yup. Fourth day. That's why I asked you over. A celebration of sorts."

"That's just great. Four whole days?"

"Well, the beginning of the fourth."

"How do you feel?"

"Terrible."

"I'm so proud of you, Sara. It's tremendous, really. That stuff's lethal, you know."

"Now don't go sounding like Harry. 'They'll rot your teeth, they'll destroy your brain.' I've heard enough of that."

"Okay, but all the same . . ."

"'They'll wreck your heart, make you bald . . .' Some nerve from the guy who got me started on them in the first place, wouldn't you say?"

"That's right. It was Harry who . . ."

"Sure. He was always pressing them on me. 'For pep, for energy,' he said. 'To help you lose weight.' Really to help me stay awake at his lousy doctor parties."

"Okay. But that's all in the past now."

"You can't imagine how I dreaded those parties. The wives seemed there only to be inspected. We were dragged in by the hand and passed around from doctor to doctor like curious new diseases."

Jennifer laughed and Sara thought how good it was to hear a full, round, female laugh—a sound that hadn't been heard in her house for far too long.

"Now tell me," Jennifer said, tossing her hair. "What have you been up to these days besides renouncing drugs?"

"Oh, the usual. Children and house. One or the other always needs attention."

"That's not all, I see," Jennifer said, catching sight now of the ceramic figures around the room "You've been working again."

"Playing, I call it. It gives me something to do with my hands when I'm trying to quit."

"Hardly playing," Jennifer said, picking up an animal,

examining it, putting it down and picking up another. "They're wonderful, Sara. So lifelike. Really, they're wonderful."

"Glad you like them," Sara said and turned away. It embarrassed her to hear herself complimented, and yet how good it felt to have someone admire something she had done, something other than a child that had come from her.

"You're really very good, you know," Jennifer continued. "You always were. You could even take it up professionally."

"Oh, sure," Sara snapped. "And when would I get the time for that? Having four is not the same as having one, you know." The minute she said it, she regretted it. "Forgive me, Jenny. I'm sorry. I didn't mean to snap. It's just that coming down makes me so irritable. I say things I don't mean."

"It's okay. Forget it."

"I didn't mean it. Honest."

"It's okay. You're right, of course. I don't know where you get the time to turn around with four kids."

"Not that I haven't thought about it," Sara admitted. "The house filled with ceramics . . . little animals all over the place . . . pots, planters, mixing bowls . . . and huge sculptures too. I mean *huge* ones. Life size. A bust here, a full-sized figure there, a hand, a head. . . . You see, Jenny?" She laughed. "Even in fantasy I can't escape the litter."

Jennifer laughed too. "Well I think they're just fabulous," she said. "And I'd hate to see you give it up because you can't find the time." Jennifer put the little frog she was holding back on the shelf and turned around. "The kids must love them too," she said. "Speaking of that, how are the kids?"

"Ubiquitous," Sara answered and Jennifer laughed again. At least, Sara thought, she could still make someone laugh.

"I don't know how you do it," Jennifer said, opening her arms to the room. "A house this size . . . four great kids. I couldn't, that's for sure."

Again, a sense of things spreading endlessly before her came over Sara and a feeling of fear took hold.

"I can't either straight," she said, suddenly serious. "I know I can't hold out. I need the stuff, Jenny. I can fool myself that I don't, but I need it right this minute."

"No you don't, Sara," Jennifer protested. "You can kick it if you want to. . . . Four days already . . ."

Sara shook her head. "It's no good. I know myself. It

on't last. You know how long I've been on it. It's a part of
me now. The best part."

"Don't say that, Sara. That's not true."

"It is, Jenny. It's better to admit it. Anything I've ever
been able to accomplish—keeping up with the kids, the house,
making a few things out of clay—it's only because of speed.
Without it I'm nothing. Hardly alive. I can't function, can't
do anything except sleep. And you don't need to be alive for
that."

"None of that's true, Sara. You're just saying it because
you're so depressed. I know what coming down does to you."

"Sometimes I think I'd rather be dead. . . . Once I woke
up after a sleeping jag and found a strange woman in William's
room. I thought she was trying to kidnap him, so you know
what I did?"

"No," Jennifer said. "What?"

"Chased her out of the house with a breadknife. How's
that for rational behavior?"

"Well, if you thought she . . ."

"No, don't try to excuse it. The kids thought I was crazy.
You don't know what that's like—frightening your kids, acting
crazy in front of them. Sometimes I think it would be better
for them if I were dead."

"Oh, Sara! That's nonsense. You must be more depressed
than I thought. Who was the woman anyway?"

"Just someone Harry had hired to help out. Imagine—
chasing her out of the house with a knife in front of the kids."

"It'll be all right now. You'll quit. You'll stay off."

"I won't, Jennifer. I know myself. I feel worthless when
I'm off. That's not a feeling I can live with. Harry doesn't
understand, of course. He thinks it's just a matter of willpower.
You know how he is, so damn sure of everything. He doesn't
know what the word worthless means. . . . And unless you've
been on them, unless you've known that power, that control . . . that feeling of having it all there in your hands. . . .
You'd have to be really crazy to want to give that up." Sara
stopped and shrugged her shoulders, and for a moment neither
of them seemed to know what to say.

After a while Jennifer broke the silence. "God," she said
softly. "The house is quiet without the kids."

Instantly Sara shot her a glance. "What do you mean by

that?" she asked. A woman with only one child. Either she took her with her family or not at all.

"I only meant the noise," Jennifer replied. "You must admit it's easier to talk when the kids are out."

Yes, Sara said, of course she did. She didn't mean to be suspicious of her friend. But to her it wasn't noise. It was only the sound the house made when it was occupied.

"Sorry, Jenny. There I go again. Snapping. Irritable. I've been sort of adding up my life these past few days, the way one does occasionally, you know. And it doesn't seem to me to come to very much. . . . I have a sense of things ending. Slipping by. I think it has to do with William's birthday."

"His birthday?"

"Yes. I know this sounds absurd, but he's the last of the bunch. There won't be any more babies. And even he will be gone soon."

"Gone? William? Sara, he's only a year old."

"But that's the beginning. Oh I know I'm not making sense. It's just a feeling that everything's coming together wrong. I can't bear the thought of them leaving. I love the children. Really I do. I'd die without them. . . . Yet everywhere I look they're there."

A sense of suffocation overwhelmed Sara then as she thought of her life composed of human bodies she herself had created. Everywhere she looked she saw a child. With every step she took she bumped into one. Somebody somewhere was always needing something. She heard them calling, she saw the appeal in their eyes. Like those of anxious seamstresses, their fingers grabbed at her, plucked at her flesh, taking her in here, letting her out there, making darts, making tucks. They twisted her out of shape. They stood in her way so she had to push them—push them aside, her own children!—to take a step.

"They're always in the way," she tried to explain. "Always underfoot."

Jennifer was smiling. "I know," she said. "I know."

But she couldn't know. She only had one. And suddenly Sara wished she wouldn't smile. "Stop it!" she said. "This isn't funny." This was what was killing her, being surrounded by bodies and Harry never at home to help.

"I hate them, I do!" she yelled and heard herself say the

words and couldn't find the strength to be appalled. "I can't stand it," she cried, hearing the fighting begin, the screaming, the endless demands. And just when she saw a space for herself between it all, there was a cough in the night, a pillow soaked with sweat, and one of them was sick. "Do I have to wait for the last of them to grow up and leave?" She was nearly crying now. "Is that it, Jenny?" She didn't want to cry. She didn't want them to leave. "Do I have to postpone my life until they're gone?" She hadn't had them for that. "It's not that I don't want them. I do. You know I do. But it just isn't fair." She loved them. She hated them. "It's just not fair." The children were killing her. Without them she'd die.

Then Jennifer's arms were around her. Jennifer was holding her tight. She didn't have to hide her tears. Jennifer was her friend.

"My God, Sara. You're utterly exhausted."

Jennifer understood. Those lovely arms were around her, holding her close. They'd been at school together, they'd walked across campus, sat in coffee shops. Sara liked to look at her—at her narrow waist, her long legs. She'd often found herself comparing, seeing Jenny's hips, her slender thighs, comparing them with her own. Now here she sat with Jennifer's arms about her, thinking she had never felt so close to any man. What did it mean, then? That those school years and this one moment were more to her than seventeen years of marriage? That this was who she was? What her life should have been? No. The notion repelled her. She wasn't like that. The very idea revolted her. Yet here she sat sobbing in a woman's arms and making no attempt to stop.

"Sara, this can't go on," Jennifer said gently after a while. "You've got to get yourself some help."

Immediately Sara was on her guard. "A psychiatrist, you mean? A shrink? Is that what you think I need?" She felt empty now and sick with herself. She ought never to have trusted her. She knew better than to let herself go like that.

"No," Jennifer said quickly. "I meant some help with the house. A cleaning woman is what I meant."

But it was no good now. Sara withdrew her body from Jennifer's touch. If only she could as easily withdraw her confidences. It was a mistake, she knew, had always known, to give herself away like that. People didn't understand. However much they protested, they had only their own best interests at heart.

A moment ago, she had felt closer to Jennifer than to anyone else on earth. But that was a mistake, Sara knew. It was not to be. Speed kept her apart. Closeness was not for her. What felt like joy one moment, a transitory and insubstantial lifting of the spirit, fell away again the next, and a moment later was gone entirely, submerged beneath the skin.

She needed her pills, needed to feel the embrace of the drug. It never betrayed her, never led her on with promises of euphoria unfulfilled.

"Sorry, Jenny," Sara said, straightening up, pulling back. "I'm just no good like this. I'd take anything I could get my hands on right now. And I don't even have an aspirin in the house. I cleaned it out. Gave everything to Harry to take away. Dumbest thing I ever did."

"Maybe not," Jennifer said. "Maybe it was the only way. But you do look exhausted. Why don't you go up and take a nap?"

"No, Jenny." Sara shook her head. "A nap won't help. What I need are my pills. Can't you see I'm no good without them?"

"Don't talk like that, Sara. You'll do it. I know you will. It's been four days already. That's a start. A great start. How long does it take? What does Harry say?"

"Harry?" Sara could hardly remember what he looked like. "Harry's too busy to say much of anything. Saving lives takes up most of his time." He was tall, she knew that. Tall and extremely busy. "The rest of his time he spends screwing his nurses."

"What? Harry? Oh I don't believe that. Not Harry. Not for a minute. You've got to be kidding."

"Do I? Well, whatever you say." Tall and busy and involved with a younger woman. But Sara had never meant for Jennifer to know. "Forget it, Jenny," she said. "Of course I'm kidding. Sometimes I don't know what I'm saying. The words just come out. . . . Harry's probably right . . . it destroys your brain. . . . Let's forget it, okay? Let's talk about you. How are you, Jennifer? What have you been doing? And Peter? How is Peter?" Peter was fine, Jennifer said. "And the photography? How's the photography going?" The photography was going well, Jennifer answered. Her new series was nearly done. Peter was fine and the new series was nearly done. Good. Everything was going well. They were on safe ground again. "And Edward?" Sara asked. "How is Edward?" She'd almost forgotten him—young Edward, nearly nine years Jennifer's junior. Edward was fine, Jennifer said. Everyone was fine, it seemed. Sara didn't understand it. Younger men wanting older women. Older men wanting younger ones. All she wanted was the ecstasy of speed.

"Listen, Sara. . . ." Jennifer began. "Isn't there something I can do?"

"Do? No. Nothing." Everything was fine. What could anyone do? Sara didn't understand it at all. Her brain was paralyzed, her mind was going to sleep. She was only half human like this, half alive. "Yes, there is," she said, suddenly knowing what she had to do. "There is something you can do. Lend me your car." Amphetamines to awaken her. Dexedrine to bring her to life. "I've got to go out. Please, Jenny. Mine's in the shop."

"Out, now? . . ."

"Please, Jenny. Lend it to me."

"But now, Sara?"

"Yes, now. This minute. I have to. It's the only way." She grabbed her bag, ran for the door. "The keys, Jenny. Please." She held out her hand.

"But where? . . ."

"Just give them to me, please." Jennifer hesitated a moment, then dropped the keys in her hand. Sara pulled open the door, turned back. "Thanks," she said. "I love you for this. Oh, Christ! I almost forgot. William's asleep upstairs. Could you stay with him, please? Just until the others get home? An hour or so?" She looked at the clock in the hall. It was a quarter to three. "Oh, God, look at that. I'm sorry, Jenny," she said. "I'm so sorry. I wanted to do it right." Tears were blinding her eyes. "I wanted it to be nice. To have everything clean, everything ready. And look at what I've done." Tears were running down her face. "I invited you for lunch . . . you see, not even that . . . not even the least thing straight . . . I asked you here and never made us any lunch at all."

X

Jennifer's car was neat, clean. Like Jennifer's house. Like Jennifer's hair. Clean. Bathed every day. Washed her hair every day. Nothing out of place in Jennifer's house or Jennifer's car either. Sara's car, on the other hand—her own, not Harry's Mercedes, but the big Buick that was in the garage—was always a mess. Chauffering four kids around, trips to the park, trips to the supermarket, how could it be otherwise? But the car of a woman with only one child was neat. No gum wrappers in the ashtray, soda cans rolling under the front seat. No odd socks and dirty sneakers in the back. Harry's car, too, was spotless. So clean it might have been sterilized. Sara could picture him going out to it at night, sponging it down with alcohol. The steering wheel squeaked in one's hands. The fenders and hub caps shined in the dark. Spotless, sterile. Just like Harry to have a car clean enough to operate in. And always finely tuned, ready for any emergency. Good for Harry. Always prepared, possessed of a steady, rational mind. Good. Let him be prepared for this.

Tearing down the highway, Sara felt herself being reeled in. Steadily, surely, hand over fist, New York City and Harry's office pulling her toward her destination. Mile after mile the distance steadily diminishing, the outcome a foregone conclusion. This time she could not fail.

Everything was happening as if it had already happened. The roads bumping up and down beneath her, the highway signs, the sun racing along beside her, then suddenly glaring straight into her eyes as she made a turn. She had seen it before. It was meant to be. Preordained. Infallible. Sara knew every inch of the road, every hill in the landscape. She was safe in that knowledge. There would be no hitches, no problems this time.

There wasn't a highway cop in sight. She could go as fast as she liked. And if one suddenly materialized, an appropriate story would occur to her. She was on an errand of mercy, a medical emergency. She was the emergency and long overdue for mercy. Houses and trees flew by. The top of the bridge leading into the city came into view. Seeing it, Sara's pulse raced. She was so close now, she couldn't fail. Blood pounding in her ears, she made her plans, went over her lines. Harry must see her position. It was her life, she had a right to make her own decisions. He must be made to see that.

Coming upon the city suddenly, experiencing that abrupt switch from greens and quiet to the heart of steel and glass, honking horns and changing lights, a certainty like rock took hold of Sara. She was an adult in charge of her life. She had a right to ask for what she needed. Harry must be made to see her need. He must give her what she asked. It was that simple, she thought, catching the light on Park Avenue, feeling it settle like a rock within her, that simple and violent obligation to herself.

Double-parking in front of Harry's office, she twisted the rear-view mirror, ran a comb through her hair, applied some color to her lips. A Park Avenue address, after all. One had to look presentable.

Everything was neat inside, compartmentalized. Reception area off to the right. The woman in white behind the desk, on the phone, looked up in surprise. Waiting room to the left. Filled with Harry's fancy patients. Matching shoes and bags, signature scarves, signature coiffures. Suddenly Sara was no longer so certain. She should have changed, put on a dress, done her hair.

"Why, Mrs. Richardson, how nice. . . ."

Margot—combination secretary and R.N.— Sara took one look and knew she wasn't the one.

"Be with you in a minute," she said, putting her hand over the mouthpiece.

Sara shook her head, kept on walking. She couldn't wait, wasn't that clear? Wasn't it obvious she couldn't go in there and wait among the pure silks and genuine leathers?

115

"Just a minute. I'm afraid you can't. . . ."

Margot got up from her desk, smoothing her white skirt down over her hips. If they'd just leave her alone, Sara thought. If everyone would just stop telling her what to do.

"He's with someone right now."

Margot stretched out her arm . . . straight, white, directive. "Won't you wait. . . ." Sara shied away. ". . . in here? . . ."

"No. I'm afraid I don't have the time to wait. I'm double-parked."

Margot hesitated a moment, then went back to her desk. "I'll tell him you're here."

Sara started for the door.

"Wait! Let me buzz."

Sara continued down the hall. Pulling open the door to Harry's consulting room, she nearly collided with the woman coming out. The other one in white. She was the one. One glance and Sara knew. *With someone,* was he? So that's how they did it—covered for one another. How nice. How sisterly. A regular sorority they had going here.

"Hello, Mrs. Richardson." Helen's eyes flashed in her small face. "How are you?"

"Perfectly well," Sara answered, shoving past into Harry's office.

Harry looked up from his desk in surprise. "And to what do I owe this honor?" he said, glancing at his wife, glancing at the door.

"Relax. No one recognized me if that's what you're worrying about," Sara said and slammed the door. "She's the one, isn't she?" she asked, gesturing behind her. "Very pretty, Harry. Very young."

"What can I do for you, Sara?" Harry said, standing up, motioning her to a chair.

"How old would you say she was? Twenty-three? Twenty-four? Somewhere in there? Odd, isn't it? I was exactly her age when Justin was born."

"Did you come for something specific?" Harry was leaning forward, speaking calmly. "As you must have noticed, I have a bunch of people waiting."

"Yes. I noticed. Your brutal schedule. Well times certainly have changed, that's all I can say. Once women were mothers at twenty-three. Now they're husband stealers."

"Sara, I don't have time for this."

"No. I shouldn't think you do. But you seem to make the time, don't you? You seem to be very good at making time."

Harry sat down and reached for the phone.

"What are you going to do? Call the police? Have me thrown out?"

"I was going to find out who's waiting, that's all." He buzzed Margot, asked her who the next two patients were. "Tell Helen to give Mr. Marks his shot," he said. "Then put him in room *A* and Mrs. Bailey in *B*. Get blood and urine samples from her and tell them both I'll be along shortly." He hung up and turned back to Sara. "Now tell me what I can do for you."

"I didn't come here to make trouble. I know you're busy, Harry." Sara sat back in her chair, crossed her legs and looked at him. "My, you look so nice in your office, so forceful. The place really suits you. I should come here more often. It's quite impressive, really. You must make a strong impression on your patients, sitting there so confidently, so sure of yourself." Sara looked around the room. "You look exactly right sitting in this room in that chair, behind that desk. Everything suits you exactly. The leather chairs, the books, the lights. Everything arranged just the way you want it. It must be reassuring to anyone coming through that door. Anyone in pain. All those books around you, those scholarly journals, those diplomas hanging on the wall. Very reassuring. I can see how people would readily come to you, offer you their pain, their illnesses . . . even their hearts, to cure. I can see that, Harry. Really I can. I don't blame her. I did it once myself, didn't I? When I was young. Younger than she is now." Sara began to cry.

Harry inched a box of Kleenex toward her across the desk. "Would you like a tissue?" he asked. She took one and blew her nose while Harry tapped his finger against his upper lip, expelling a quiet stream of air. "You don't look at all well," he said after a moment. "I'm going to call Leon right now and make an appointment for you." He put his hand on the phone. "What you need is a complete physical. The works. Head to toe. I've been meaning to set it up for months, but there's never any letup around here and it keeps slipping my mind."

Sara shook her head. No, not that way. He was a helpful man, a concerned physician. But that wasn't the kind of help she wanted from him today. "Not now, Harry," she said. "I'll call Leon, I will. I'll make my own appointment. But not today. That isn't why I came."

Harry put the phone down, but kept his hand resting on top of it. It was reassuring in a way, thought Sara, the fact that he had whatever he wanted at his fingertips.

"I know you're busy," she said. "I know people are waiting." Harry kept glancing over her head at the door behind her. "All you have to do is give them back and I'll leave."

"Give what back?"

"You know what." Sara met his eyes. Dark, direct. He was so tall. Even sitting down he looked tall.

"Oh, Sara," Harry shook his head and tilted back in his chair.

Even from that position he took command of the room. "They're mine, Harry." she said. "I want them back."

"You were doing so well."

"Write me a prescription."

"How many days has it been? You almost had it licked."

"Make it renewable. Don't make me beg every month."

"I thought you might really do it this time."

"No you didn't. You never thought that. Spare me the lies at least. You never thought I'd do it." Sara felt the tears burning again at the back of her eyes. "It's just a game you play, waiting for me to lose."

"That isn't true." Harry's finger went up and down against his lip.

"Well, take a good look then," Sara said, letting the tears spill over. "I've lost. I've failed. Is that what you wanted? Are you happy now?"

"Sara, keep your voice down."

"Damn my voice! And damn you too." She held out her hand. "Just give them back."

"This is my office. I won't have you shouting in here."

"Your office. Your practice. That's all you care about."

"Someone might hear you. I won't have my patients upset."

"Your patients! And what about me? I'm upset, Harry. What about me?"

"Calm down, Sara, try to get control of yourself."

"Control. Willpower. That's all you think there is. I don't have any, then. Is that what you want to hear? All right. I'll admit it. I don't have any willpower. I'm weak, I've failed. And right now I'm begging. Is that what you want, Harry?" Sara lifted herself out of her chair. "Do you want me down on the floor?"

"Stop it this minute. Sit back in that chair."

"I did that once, remember? I'll do it again if that's what it takes. If you want me to crawl, I'll crawl."

Harry pulled open his drawer, took out a vial of pills and shook two loose in his hand. "What I want you to do is take two of these right now."

Sara reached across the desk, slapped the pills out of his hand. "Nothing of yours!" she shouted. "Nothing. I want my own pills. I want them back!"

"Lower your voice, Sara. Let's talk about this calmly."

"Ah, yes. I almost forgot. The precious patients." Sara readjusted herself in the chair, folded her hands in her lap. "All right, I'll be calm." She glanced around the office again. "Everything is arranged for your convenience, isn't it, Harry? Everything at your fingertips. Books on the shelves, medication in the drawers. Ailing patients waiting in line and whenever you get the urge, a twenty-threeyear-old woman in white."

"Sara, that isn't so."

"Is this where you do it?" She asked it quietly, gazing down at the thick gray carpet. "Right here on the floor?" She looked back at Harry. "Or there across your shiny black desk? Or perhaps you take her in the back, put her feet up in the stirrups?"

"Stop it, Sara."

"What's the matter, Harry. Can't you stand it?"

"No. I can't. I can't stand to see you this way."

"What?" Sara had to look twice to see if he was serious. "You who see people in pain every day of your life?"

"But you're my wife."

"Nice of you to notice. Have you informed little Helen of that?"

"There's nothing going on between Helen and me."

"Oh, don't make me laugh. I can see it. I can smell it." Sara tossed her head. "Be a sport, Harry. You've got what you want. Give me what I want and then we'll be even. I'll go away and you'll have peace and order restored."

"And what will you have? A coronary before you're forty?"

"I'd better hurry then, hadn't I? Time's running out. Wouldn't want to miss the deadline, make your prediction wrong. You're not much good at being wrong, are you? You could take a few lessons from me in that." Sara stopped, struck by the look on Harry's face—he did care, she thought, he was serious. "Trust me, please," she continued. "I can handle it. I've been taking them long enough to know how to keep it under control." Harry's dark eyes were staring into hers. "One a day," she promised. "Honest. Like vitamins. No more than that, I swear. But I can't quit cold, go off entirely. I just can't. Harry, please." The tears were rising again. Her voice was beginning to quiver. But the look in Harry's eyes was kind and concerned. He did care, he did. "It gets worse every time I try. It hurts me, Harry. Can't you see that? Can't you see how it hurts?" She put her head on the arm of the chair and began to cry. "You take care of everybody else's pain, why not mine?" She covered her head with her arms to stifle the sound of her sobbing. Harry's patients were waiting. Harry's patients might hear. She put her hands to her mouth to stop the sounds, she wouldn't disgrace him for the world.

The sound of papers being shuffled on the desk before her. The sound of drawers opening and closing, a chair being rolled back, footsteps on the carpet.

"Would you try an antidepressant instead?"

Sara shook her head.

"A tranquilizer then?"

"No," she said.

"Thirty milligrams of Librium?"

"No, Harry."

"Not even Librium?"

Harry's voice was low. He sounded disappointed.

"It's a nice drug," he told her. "Good for headache, premenstrual blues."

"No, Harry."

"It combines well with Tofranil. Try it, Sara."

"No," she said. "No Librium. No Tofranil."

"For anxiety, tension, agitated depression. . . ."

Sara shook her head.

"Valium then?"

"No, Harry. No Valium either. My own pills. That's all want. Nothing else." Sara held out her hands and saw that hey were shaking.

"Please, Harry."

Harry's eyes were kind. He would give her what she sked. He would take her pain away.

"I'll stick to the dosage. I promise."

Harry was in front of his desk. The paper bag was in his hands. Meeting his eyes, Sara thought she saw something huge and unmanageable open within them. A moment later it was gone and Harry looked away.

"No more than one a day," he said.

"I swear, Harry. I swear."

"You know how dangerous they are."

"I know it, Harry. I know they are. I'm going to quit some day for good. Only not today. Don't ask it of me today."

"When, Sara?"

"Soon. You'll see, Harry. Some day soon. When I'm tronger. When the weather's nicer. Only don't bully me, please." She reached for the bag. She didn't want to fight any more.

Harry was silent a moment, then said softly, "I suppose hey can't be any worse for you than what you're going through right now."

It was alien to him, Sara knew, this dreadful dependency, this need. As much as he tried not to, he closed himself against it. She saw the almost imperceptible movement—something within him taking a step back. Harry had never been sick a day in his life. He watched his weight, got the proper amount of exercise, and depended on nothing at all but his own inner strength to get him through. Sara admired that. Harry played golf in the summer, squash in the winter and never let himself dwell on things. If she had his knack . . . if she only knew how. . . . She'd be like him if she could.

"Withdrawal like this is probably impossible anyway," Harry continued, speaking slowly, carefully weighing his words. "It might even do more harm than the addiction itself." He stopped then and looked up at her directly. "Fifteen milligrams, Sara. Tops."

"I swear it, Harry. I swear." He was giving in, Sara saw, but try as he might he couldn't sympathize. His training, his background held against it. A healthy body and a healthy mind was Harry's code. So much of his work involved interpreting symptoms, he felt it imperative that he himself manifest none whatever. And here she sat before him, trembling, twisting her fingers in her lap. How he must despise her, Sara thought, and how ironic that he should, when all she was trying to do was make herself more like him.

"I hate to see this happening to you," Harry said softly and handed her the bag. "Everything's in here just as you left it. You can use my bathroom, if you like. I'll write you a prescription while you're washing up."

"Make it refillable, Harry, please."

"I can't do that," he said. "It's a Schedule II drug. A new prescription is required each time. Go on, now. I've got patients waiting."

"Yes, Harry. Thank you." Sara nodded. She'd do it again then, if she had to. "I'll be fine now, Harry. Thank you." Next month. And the month after. "Just fine, Harry. You'll see." Month after month to the end of her life. "Thank you, Harry. Thank you."

XI

Very early on Sunday morning, Sara ran down the front steps and out onto the narrow pavement where the children played and rolled on the street and fought one another, where the new grass was already trampled down and bicycles were left to rust in the rain. She ran past Sam's tricycle, past some sturdy pull-toy that had lost only its paint through all kinds of weather and all kinds of treatment, around corners, across streets without looking to the left or right. She ran past long stretches of white houses like her own with green trim, and gray houses with white trim. She ran into the center of town past the camera shop, the meat market, past the library, the post office and all the people who turned to stare.

She didn't notice them now. Impervious to their looks, indifferent to their judgment, Sara ran. Those places where such things usually got at her were sealed up now. As other pills protect women from pregnancy, so Sara's protected her from the world's regard.

She ran into the path of an oncoming car, slowed to let it pass, changed her mind, speeded up and raced across the street. The car whizzed behind her, horn blaring at her heels.

A lapse like that could destroy her. Hesitation at the last minute. She wouldn't hesitate this time. She knew what she had to do. Repair whatever damage she had done. And protect herself from harm. Harm from friends. Danger from friends. A careless word, a misplaced confidence leaving one at another's mercy.

Sara knew she had been careless last night. Inexcusably, she'd dropped her guard. It must have been the wine, or the hour—two or three in the morning, she didn't quite remember now. The conversation itself was foggy too, as if they'd had a bad connection. Maybe she hadn't actually done it, had only thought of doing it, or dreamed it. It might actually have been a dream. But she remembered the phone in the kitchen too clearly, felt it in her hand. She was sitting out there by herself drinking wine. It wasn't a dream. She remembered Harry's voice, Harry's words. She remembered the need to pass it on. No, she knew she hadn't dreamed it. Neither had she rid herself of his words. All she had accomplished by that incoherent call was to relay to Jennifer some information Jennifer had no business knowing. Why couldn't she learn to stay off the phone when she had a bottle of wine in her hands?

Sara ran on down the street, hearing the awful words—hers, Harry's—repeating in her mind. Had she told Jennifer everything? No, she didn't think so. Not word for word. She couldn't have done that. Even drunk and speeding, her sense of self-preservation was too strong for that. But the essence . . . yes, she'd certainly relayed the essence of that Saturday night scene. *I don't feel anything at all with Harry*—she remembered herself admitting that, admitting her whole sexual life was a fraud. Not one moment of real physical pleasure gleaned from seventeen years of marriage—she had admitted that. Had told Jennifer that. Dropped that bit of information like a precious stone into the phone at three o'clock in the morning. And at the other end, Jennifer had picked it up. It was hers now. She could do what she liked with it. Leave it untouched or reach for it to admire, turn it over in her hand and upon any whim, display it. Sara couldn't let her do that, she had to have it back.

Even as she ran, she saw how Jennifer would look at her, rushing through the door, as if she were looking at someone who was not a real woman. Sara felt nothing for her husband—she had told Jennifer that. No more than a branch is moved by the rain that drops on it was she moved by him. That was what she was then—a branch, a stick of wood. Jennifer knew and might tell. Tell Edward. Tell Harry. Tell her children. Tell the whole neighborhood that her friend was no more than a stick of wood. Sara had to stop her. Everyone would laugh. They would all despise her. Her own children would despise her. Jennifer must be stopped from telling.

She must be convinced it was a lie or a joke, that it had never happened, had never actually been said. That shouldn't be difficult, Sara thought. She lied so often, so easily—everyone knew how she lied. Why shouldn't she have been lying then? No one tells the truth on the phone at three o'clock in the morning.

Sara tried to remember how it had actually happened. Running down the last few blocks to Jennifer's house, she tried to reconstruct the scene. Harry was leaning over her, yelling into her face. *Right, Sara? Right? Isn't that right? I know it is. I know that's right.* Harry was pinning her shoulders. Sara couldn't move. *It makes you sick, doesn't it?* He brought his face down close to hers. *It makes you gag. You only do it for the pills.* He pinned her shoulders to the bed. *That's right, Sara. Isn't it?* He tossed her away from him and turned his back. He hung his feet down over the bed. Sara pressed a handful of Kleenex to her mouth. *Go ahead,* he said. *Spit it out.* She hated it. *I won't ask you to do it again.* She buried her face in the pillow. She hoped he meant it, she hoped he would never touch her again. *Sex without children disgusts you, doesn't it?* he asked. *You have to go on and on procreating. That's it, isn't it, Sara? Isn't that it?* And finally the yelling had stopped. The weight on the other side of the bed lifted off. Harry was standing up. *You must really need them bad,* he said, walking out of the room.

Jennifer must be made to believe it was a lie. She must be stopped from telling. Sara saw her house just ahead. She ran to the door, caught her breath and rang the bell.

In an instant, Jennifer was there. Neat, clean, composed.

"Well, hello, Sara. What a surprise."

Suspicious too. Her eyes were suspicious, Sara saw it at once. Already Jennifer found her repulsive. Less than a woman. A freak. In a minute she would be barring the door.

"How are you this morning?" Jennifer asked. "Come on in."

She has to ask, of course. But she knows she's dealing with a freak.

"Beautiful day, isn't it? But what on earth is wrong, Sara? You look awful. Come in and sit down."

Jennifer's house is quiet. Neat and clean and quiet. Mind

your p's and q's, and don't forget to curtsy when you leave. Next she'll be serving tea.

"You're all out of breath and you look like you've been up all night. Didn't you get any sleep after we talked?"

There she goes, bringing it up the first chance she gets. Sara was right to hurry. God only knows how many people she might have told about that call by now.

"How about a cup of tea? I was just about to make some."

Tea! She knew it. No matter how extreme the situation, etiquette is not to be abandoned.

Jennifer is up in a flash. "I won't be a minute," she said and went into the kitchen.

As soon as she was alone, Sara dug through her bag for another pill. She needed more than one today, she needed the whole month's supply.

Jennifer's floors had just been vacuumed. There were no clothes thrown on the chairs, no toys strewn about the room. The vase of spring flowers was reflected in the polish on the coffee table. Sara's house, too, could look like this, she thought, if she lived alone and had only one child. A place for everything, everything in its place. The lover too. She mustn't forget the lover. Jennifer probably had a place for him as well. But where, Sara wondered, where was there a place for a man in all this neatness? Did the order conceal a flaw? Was Jennifer, too, a liar? Was the lie buried somewhere in the neatness of her house, concealed perhaps in the wash flapping on the line, or in the humming, swishing cycles of her kitchen?

Jennifer returned with the tea, bringing some cookies as well. Sara put one in her mouth and tasted nothing. A texture like cardboard, a certain thickness.

Seated there across from her, Jennifer still looked like a young girl, Sara thought—narrow face, pointed chin, intense blue eyes. Her black and white striped smock accentuated the lean lines of her body. She had been working in her darkroom, presumably, when interrupted, but now like the good, old faithful friend she was, she was giving Sara her undivided attention.

"Tell me what's wrong," she said.

A hunger for even more details? Hadn't last night been enough? "Wrong?" Sara asked. "Nothing's wrong." One mustn't be gluttonous, she would advise her friend. Or was she pretending to have forgotten? "Why should anything be wrong? I felt like taking a walk, that's all. People don't walk enough in the suburbs."

"But you looked so upset when you came in."

"Did I? Must've been the light. It's awfully bright outside. The sun was in my eyes."

Jennifer sipped her tea. She looked distracted, preoccupied. Maybe she'd been working.

"Were you working?" Sara asked. "Did I disturb you? I don't want to stay if I'm bothering you."

"No, no. Not at all. As a matter of fact, your timing's perfect. I finished printing a minute before you rang and I was just taking a break."

"You sure?" Sara asked, wishing now she hadn't come.

"Of course I'm sure. I'll show you the pictures when they're dry if you'd like to see them."

"Yes, I would. I'd love to see them." Did Jennifer doubt it? Did she imagine she was such a stick of wood that she didn't care about her work? "Is this the contest series you're working on?" Sara asked.

"Yes, it's finally finished." Jennifer leaned back and smiled. "And just in time, too. The deadline's tomorrow. . . . Wouldn't it be something if I won?"

"I hope you do," Sara said. "I hope you win first prize." She really meant it. She could at that moment imagine no reason for having come other than to wish her friend success. "Here's to luck," she said, raising her cup and tapping it against Jennifer's. Jennifer would never try to harm her. They were friends. They felt only affection for one another.

"Thanks, Sara," Jennifer said. "First prize would be great but I wouldn't turn down second or third either. The top three winners get a month's showing in a really good gallery."

"No problem then. You're bound to be one of those. And you really deserve it, Jenny. You've worked so hard." An idea was occurring to Sara. She thought it might be a way of handling things. "Harry and I were talking about that just the other evening . . . about work, how important it is for a woman to have some work of her own. . . ." If she could just convince Jennifer of this, show her that she and Harry were close, that they did talk. . . . "And Harry agreed with me completely. He understands that need entirely. Harry can be very understanding, you know."

"I'm sure he can," Jennifer said quickly. "Most doctors have a . . ."

"Oh, no," Sara said at once. "It's not because he's a doctor." It was important Sara convince her it wasn't his training that made Harry understanding, but his capacity to respond to her. "Just as a man, I mean. As a man he can be very understanding."

"I'm sure he can," Jennifer said, refilling Sara's cup, but Sara sensed she didn't quite believe her. Was it so hard for her to believe that she had a man—a man like Edward, no, better than Edward, Edward was practically still a boy— couldn't her friend believe that she, Sara, despite everything that was wrong with her life, had a man who understood her? Why should that be so hard to believe? "With the kids too," Sara said firmly, for that was true and she wanted Jennifer to know it. "Harry's being a lot more understanding with the kids lately. He really is. Especially with Justin. About the garage, you know." Sara stopped, searched for herself in Jennifer's eyes—blue, intense, waiting—searched for some sign, some way of continuing. She felt suddenly at a loss, couldn't remember the point she was trying to make. What was Harry being understanding about? Something was confusing her— the pills or the tea or both on an empty stomach. "Oh, yes," she said, remembering now the story she'd meant to invent. "The class. He said by all means for me to go ahead and take it."

"What class?" Jennifer asked, pulling out a cigarette.

"The pottery class," Sara answered sharply, annoyed by the cigarette. She hated seeing people smoke. It was such an unhealthy habit. "Didn't I tell you?"

"No, you didn't. What pottery class?"

Sara was sure she had told her this before. Unless she was making it up. Her heart was pounding in her chest. Was she making it up or not? Her thoughts were confused. Did this class exist? Had she told Jennifer about it? Her confusion made her angry and Jennifer sitting there, smoking, waiting patiently for an answer made her angrier still. Her patience was patronizing and the smell of smoke filled the air. "You really shouldn't smoke, you know," Sara said. "Why don't you give it up?"

"Oh, I don't really smoke," Jennifer said, shrugging and looking at the cigarette in her hand. "I have maybe three or four a month after dinner or when I've been working especially hard. It relaxes me, that's all. That's not really smoking. Now tell me about this class."

"You know," Sara said, certain now that she had told her before. "At the pottery barn. Mrs. Thompson's class on Tuesday nights. Harry thought it was a great idea. Really he did. He said . . ."

"Emma Thompson?" Jennifer interrupted. Her face looked serious, her voice sounded strange.

"Of course Emma Thompson," Sara snapped. "Who else? You know she's been giving that class for years." But Mrs. Thompson wasn't the point. Harry was the point. Jennifer was leading her away from her point. "Harry even said he'd babysit." That's what she wanted to tell her. "Can you imagine that? Harry babysitting?" That's what she wanted her to know. How helpful Harry was, how understanding. "Even if he does put most of the work off onto Julia as I'm sure he will, it was sweet of him to offer, don't you think?"

"Yes, certainly it was, but . . ."

Jennifer didn't believe her. She didn't believe Harry could be sweet. "He can," Sara insisted. "He can be very sweet when he wants to be." Why shouldn't Jennifer believe her? Why shouldn't she have a man who could be sweet? Was it because of what she'd said on the phone? Was that it? Sara couldn't go on. Her thoughts were confused. The story was a lie. Why had she ever made that damn call?

Silently, Jennifer helped them both to more tea. Sara had the impression they were in a Chinese restaurant. Fortune cookies would be next.

She tried to concentrate on the stripes in Jennifer's apron. Her heart was pounding, her pulse racing. She'd like to know her fortune, she thought, as the stripes began to vibrate. Know how it all would come out.

Black, white, black, white. Sara couldn't make them stop. Pulsating strings on a musical instrument. Music was buzzing in her ears. The black strings were breaking apart now, spilling over into the whites. Millions of tiny black specks splitting off from their stripes, dancing freely about. Dancing to the music. Sara could do that. She could dance. She could sing. She could refuse to be contained. For suddenly there was nothing to hold her down. Bodiless, weightless, she had snapped free. Other things in the room too—the chairs, the tables, the stereo, the flowers in the vase—were dancing, jumping about, coming loose. Multi-colored dots swam freely around the room. The new Sara was falling free from herself, leaving the old Sara behind.

"I think I'll start with planters," she said. Her voice was sharp, clear. Each word distinct, unattached. "They're the easiest and will give me a feel for it. A good way to get the touch back, you know. Then I'll go on to cups and saucers, bowls and pitchers. I'll make you a vase, if you like. Or how about another ashtray for your rotten habit?" She reached out, grabbed Jennifer's wrist, pulled the cigarette out of her hand, stubbed it out in the ashtray. Jennifer stiffened in surprise. Instantly, Sara felt remorse. "Oh, I'm sorry," she said. "I'm sorry, Jenny. Did I hurt you? I didn't mean to hurt you." She didn't mean to hurt her friend. She never meant to hurt anyone. Jennifer shook her head. No, she said, she wasn't hurt. Sara was glad of that. She didn't mean to cause anyone harm. She only wanted to reclaim herself, to have her confidences back. Some things ought never to be spoken. People didn't understand. They let you go on, listened while you exposed yourself, even encouraged you to do it. Then they lowered their eyes and pulled away in disgust. Sara had to get those words back, but first it was important to tell Jennifer about the clay. "I can feel it already," she said. "Oozing through my hands. I love the feel of it squeezing through my fingers." She glanced at the cup she was holding and saw it break into a thousand specks of energy. She felt her own energy welling up inside herself now, breaking apart, rising free, rising beyond the ordinary, bounded reality of her life. She could do anything now, anything she wanted. "You believe me, don't you? You believe I'll do it?"

Jennifer swirled her tea around inside her cup.

"And Harry will be proud of me then. He used to love the things I made." Anything at all was possible. "And the kids too. They'll be proud. I'll make a whole new set of plates." She could do anything she put her mind to now. "Soup bowls. Dessert dishes. And I'll do fabulous pieces too . . . huge figures in bronze . . . a bust of Harry . . . I'll show you I can. I'll show you all. You believe me, don't you, Jenny? Say you believe me."

"Sara, I . . ."

"Say it."

"Sara . . ."

Why couldn't she say it? "I want to hear you say it."

"Sara, listen . . ."

"I want to hear somebody say they believe me. Say it, Jennifer. Say: Sara, I believe you."

"Sara, Mrs. Tompson died last month."

So what? What was that to her? What did she care who died? Who was Mrs. Thompson anyway? "Mrs. Thompson? Emma Thompson?"

"Emma Thompson. Yes."

"She died?"

"Yes."

Sara laughed. She really had to laugh. Mrs. Thompson was dead. "Well, she can't very well teach a class that way, can she?" she asked and laughed. She had to keep on laughing. "Died, did she? Imagine that." Just when she'd started to believe in the class herself. Just when she was beginning to feel the wet clay in her hands, to feel it oozing through her fingers. "Just up and died? That's funny. It really is funny," she said and laughed and reached out to pick up her cup and saw her hand shake and the tea splatter on the tabletop.

"Here, let me," Jennifer said.

Jennifer knew what to do. Already she was sopping it up. Coaxing the spilled tea up into the yellow napkin, repairing things while Sara laughed.

At least she thought she was laughing, assumed the sounds coming from the back of her throat in short, quick gulps were the sounds of laughter, the tears squeezing from the corners of her eyes, the tears of laughter.

"Well, I'll have to think of something else to do with my life now, won't I?" she asked and looked up at Jennifer and laughed. Bubbles of water, rain splattered on a windshield. The bubbles burst, the rain is cleared away. Sara raised the flat of her hand to her wet face. Her sides ached beneath her ribs. Laughing till her sides hurt, laughing herself silly.

"Hey, Sara. . . . It's okay."

"Okay? Sure it's okay." She opens a yellow napkin to cover her eyes and nose. It covers her mouth too. She holds it flat against her face with the palms of her hands. Breathing in, breathing out, dry paper invades her mouth, blows away. Eyes and nose streaming, soak the paper. Tears of laughter, running tears. Oh, what a fool she was. Making up stories, telling lies. To have it backfire like this. Any fool could have seen it coming. It was enough to make her laugh.

"There must be other classes around," Jennifer began.

Or cry. But it wasn't a story, a lie. She meant it. "I meant it, Jenny," she said. "I really did."

"I know you did."

Wet napkin soggy in her hand, a wet yellow ball. How did this happen? This wasn't what she meant. She stared down at the soggy yellow paper. She'd intended it to be a piece of clay. Wet clay oozing through her fingers, being molded into life.

"Do you hate me?" she asked. "Do you think I'm crazy?"

"No, Sara. Of course I don't."

"Sometimes I have to do that," she tried to explain. "Make up a story, say it out loud to see how it sounds. Talking about it as if it's already happened makes it sound real. That isn't a lie. Does that sound crazy? Not exactly a lie. Do you understand? It fixes it in my mind so I can go ahead and do it. I really was going to do it, I was. Say you understand, Jenny. Say you don't hate me."

"Of course I don't hate you, Sara. We're friends."

"Yes. I want us to be friends." That sounded right to her. Really right. She and Jennifer were friends. It made her eyes overflow and she was laughing again. Or was she crying? Did Jennifer really mean it? Was this another story? Sara couldn't tell. Nothing now was what it seemed. "Be my friend," she said. "Tell me I'm okay."

Jennifer was next to her, leaning close. Her small, intense face, her strong arms. Sara didn't want it ever to stop. She was safe within those arms, protected by that face.

Yet the tension within was overpowering. Pressure was building up, an explosion was imminent. Sara had to do something fast to save them both.

"Get your prints," she said. "I'm dying to see them."

"All right," Jennifer said, getting up, heading for the door. "They should be dry by now. You just stay here and relax. Put your feet up. I won't be long."

Relax? Sara jumped up the minute Jennifer left the room. How could she relax? She was churning inside. She had to move. To lift things, walk around the room. A spacious and dangerous energy was building up inside her. She didn't belong in Jennifer's neat, clean house. She was too unwieldy to be contained within this room. Everywhere she looked she saw something she might break, some fragile object she might knock over. Wrapping her arms around herself, she tried to keep still. Only in her own house was she safe. Here, outside, alone, she was exposed to any number of insults, any number of possible dangers. It was better to run, to leave this neat, quiet house before Jennifer returned, before she could do her friend any harm.

But Jennifer was coming back now, carrying the prints in her arms, moving the flowers aside to make room on the table. She laid the pictures out side by side, carefully lining them up as she spoke. "See," she said, straightening out the corners on one. "This is the order I want. If they're chosen for the exhibit, I want them hung like this." She pointed from picture to picture. "See how the snow is mounting here and here . . . the banks getting higher, the people smaller . . ." She gestured over the photographs to explain what she meant. "Look at this little boy. You see him here . . . and again here . . ." She pointed to the boy to show Sara where he appeared. "Here once more, and in this one he's almost gone. You can see only the very tip of his cap." Sara watched her while she spoke. Clearly she loved her work, loved what she was doing with her life. Sara envied her that. "Everyone's being swallowed up by the snow," Jennifer was saying. "Does that come across? The enveloping whiteness. Have I captured that?"

"Yes," Sara said, bending over to look more closely. "Yes, you've got that." She didn't really respond to photography. "You've certainly captured that." She didn't want to look at any more snow. It was spring now. She had had enough snow. William's birthday was on Friday. That's why she'd come. To remind Jennifer of the party. That was the reason she was here. What was she doing looking at pictures of snow?

Photography was too one dimensional for her. Too neat. Like Jennifer. You were always being told not to touch. Like Jennifer's house. Sara liked a messy art, an art you could get you hands into. "Very nice," she said, staring at the photographs. "They're very nice."

"Do you really think so, Sara?" Jennifer said. She sounded delighted. "Oh, I'm so glad you like them. I hoped you would."

"They're awfully good," Sara said, touched that Jennifer should sound so pleased. That she should care at all for her opinion. Sara would try to take more of an interest, to be a better friend. "Can I see that one again?" she asked, reaching for the photo where the child had all but disappeared.

"Careful. Don't smudge it."

Sara picked it up, then quickly put it back down and sat away from the table. She didn't want to ruin anything. She'd die before causing offense. Did she offend? Did her breath smell, did she have body odor? All that running had made her sweat and on top of it, all that tea. Well, she couldn't do anything about it now. She'd just have to keep her distance, think of Jennifer as a photograph, not get too close.

"They're really good," she said again. "Awfully good, Jennifer. Thanks for letting me see them. Well, I guess I'd better be going now." She got up out of her chair. "Don't forget the party on Friday. Remind Peter too. And Edward."

"We haven't forgotten. We're all looking forward to it. A year already. It hardly seems possible."

Sara wanted to leave now. She walked toward the door. "I hope the weather holds. I'm planning to have it out in the yard."

"That sounds lovely. Edward said to tell you children's birthday parties are his favorite things."

Edward again. "How is? . . . ." The lad, Sara almost said. "How is Edward?" she asked.

"Oh fine. Just fine." Jennifer dropped her eyes as she spoke and seemed to blush.

Sara couldn't believe it. Was it possible the very mention of this practically still adolescent male caused her friend to blush? Sara moved back to take a closer look. "Jennifer?" she said. "What's going on?"

"Oh, nothing. Well, as a matter of fact something," Jennifer admitted and broke into a smile. "It's just that things are going so well I'm almost afraid to talk about it. Jinx it or something, you know. He really is a darling. . . ."

"It's true. I can't believe it. It's actually so. You're blushing."

"I never expected to be this happy with a man again," Jennifer confessed, rubbing her cheek as if to remove the blush. "And he's so good with Peter. They adore one another."

Something in Sara was going wrong. She should be happy for her friend. She was happy for her, of course she was. And yet this other feeling . . . something hard, perverse and set against it, wanting to ruin it. . . . She should get out of there at once.

"And he's so great about my work," Jennifer continued. "He really understands what it means to me. . . ."

Sara wanted to leave, run for the door, but Jennifer wouldn't stop.

"I've never known a man like that," she was saying now. "Peter's father . . . you remember . . . he always seemed to resent what I did. Was jealous of every minute I spent in the darkroom."

Jealous? Was that what it was? Was she jealous of Jennifer's happiness? "I've really got to go," Sara said, but Jennifer didn't seem to hear.

"And he's so gentle. You wouldn't believe it. There's a quality about him . . . an almost boyish tenderness. . . ."

Sara didn't want to hear this.

"We hadn't planned to tell anyone yet, but there's no reason I can't tell you. . . ."

She wanted to block her ears, leave the room before Jennifer could say what she was starting to say.

"It looks as if we're going to have to do the boring, conventional thing and get married."

No, she wanted to say. No, don't. "Marry Edward?" Sara felt a need to warn her. Marry that scrawny, gangly, practically prepubescent youth?

"Yes. I can't seem to do without him."

"Really marry?" Sara felt them both in danger now. She didn't know what to say. "Oh, Jenny, that's . . ." Jennifer was waiting. A smile on her lips, her eyes delighted. "Wonderful," she said. "That's wonderful." Marry Edward? He was all right to play around with, she supposed, but did one actually marry

135

a boy like Edward? "Really wonderful." Boyish tenderness, indeed. He would take Jennifer away. Sara put her arms around her friend as if to keep her still and as she felt the swell of her breasts against her own, something within her threatened to break free and Sara remembered why she had come—last night's conversation, the reckless confidences—and what she had to do. "What I said about Harry," she blurted out, "wasn't true."

"What about Harry?"

"You know. Last night. It didn't happen."

"What didn't happen?"

"You know, Jennifer. Don't pretend you don't. What I told you never happened. It was all a lie. Everything I said was a lie. There's no trouble between us. Everything's fine. Perfectly fine." She was talking too loud, too fast. The speed was taking over but there was nothing she could do. Jennifer had to be convinced. "He's not having an affair," Sara announced. "How could he be?" She threw back her head and tried to laugh. "You know me, Jennifer. My jealous nature. I'd kill him if he was. I'd kill them both, you know I would. I wouldn't let that go on for a minute. Not for a minute. Harry's mine. You don't think I'd let anyone else take him, do you? He's the only one who would ever put up with me. Do you think I don't know that? No other man could stand me the way I am. I know that, Jennifer. I'm not a fool. Harry's the only one. I know that. . . . Everything else I said was a lie too. We're perfectly compatible. Perfectly. Whatever I may have said about that last night was a lie too. I want you to forget it. Just forget it, okay? All of it. I was lying. I lie all the time. You know that. Everybody knows that."

Sara looked around for the door. She'd better leave at once. She didn't want to harm her friend. Her friend about to be married, to marry the lover, the young lover, her friend who knew all about love.

"Sara, relax," Jennifer said, reaching for her. "You're all uptight."

Sara jerked away at Jennifer's touch. "No I won't relax." She didn't mean to be doing this. "Everybody is always telling me to relax." She hadn't meant it to go this far. "You don't understand, do you?" She didn't want to hurt her friend. "You'd better watch out," she yelled. She hadn't meant to yell. "You'd better get out of my way." She started for the door. Jennifer held her back. Sara swirled and approached the table. "All right, Jenny," she said. There was Jenny. Pale, thin, young, sweet, frightened Jenny. Jenny was afraid. Sara threw out her arms to protect her friend. Jenny jumped away. "Fuck you then!" Sara shouted. "If that's the way you want it. Fuck you and your child-lover and your untouchable art!" Sara looked up. The teapot was in her hands. Tea was pouring out of it over the pictures on the table.

Instantly Jennifer was on her knees. Sara moved back out of her way. She would move right back through the walls if she could, right into the walls and out of the house. Jennifer was mopping at the pictures with the yellow napkins. Sara had done that, had actually done that. Napkins soaking up the tea. Tea-stained yellow napkins in her hands. "My God, Jenny. I'm sorry. I'm sorry. I didn't mean . . . I didn't . . . I warned you . . . I told you . . . you wouldn't let me go. . . ." Yellow napkins turning brown. Tea-tinted photographs. Bleached images. Fading memories in the snow. "I'm sorry," she said. "So sorry." White on white, disappearing boy in white. "So very sorry." Dead boy, dead words. Sorry, sorry, sorry. A dead body, dead life. Sorry. She had watched herself do it. Watched with dead eyes. Sorry. Dead words. Dead eyes. "Oh Jenny," she said. "I'm sorry. Your pictures. Your beautiful pictures."

"It's all right," Jennifer said after a while. She had stopped mopping at the pictures. She was sitting back on her heels away from the table, looking up now. "I have the negatives," she said quietly. "I can print them again."

There was nothing to be done. They didn't move. Nothing would ever move in that room again. Sara thought they might die where they were—she rooted to the spot, Jennifer sitting back on her heels. Then a key turned in the lock. Jennifer was turning her head, moving her body. She was getting up, going to the door, embracing Edward.

Sara watched them hanging there together as if attached by magical threads. Jennifer's head on his chest, Edward's arms around her. Magic puppets. Enchanted puppets. Their bodies holding together, holding each other against her.

Arm in arm, barricades of irrational love, they moved across the room toward her.

137

"Hello, Sara," Edward said, then spotted the soggy yellow napkins on the table. "What happened here?" he asked and took a closer look. "Oh, God, Jenny, your photos!"

"It's all right," she said. "It was an accident."

"But those were the ones for the show."

"I can print them again," she told him. "They might even turn out better the second time around."

Edward walked to Jennifer's side, took her arm, pulled her close as if the threads that had bound them at the door bound them still. Sara watched them come together. She saw them sit . . . Jennifer in the boy's lap . . . she saw Edward's legs stretch out, his arms swing around to hold Jennifer's body, and something in Sara's mind cleared and receded and something else came forward. Like that moment in a dance when the man steps forward, then back, and the woman steps out to curtsy, so Sara's mind divided and shifted, and what had been foremost in it was pushed to the rear and what was in the rear came to the front. She couldn't bear to look. She shielded her eyes and turned away.

After a while Edward asked, "How've you been, Sara?"

"Fine," she answered. Her throat was dry. Her hands were trembling. Jennifer's hands were holding Edward's. A hollow ache, something needing badly to be filled, opened within Sara. Jennifer's arms had surrounded her, she had felt herself contained within them. Now those arms were around that boy. Edward's arms were around her friend. He was touching her, caressing her. His hands on Jennifer's skin, his fingers on that delicate neck. He was unworthy. A boy. A mere boy. Sara tore her gaze away from Edward, as if her very eyes might do him harm. She must stop this. She must not cause any more harm here today.

"How're the kids?" Edward asked.

"Fine," Sara said. His hand on Jennifer's arm. She wanted that too. "Everybody's fine." She wanted to feel what Jennifer felt. "I've got to go now," she said, moving toward the door, averting her eyes. "Don't forget the party," she called, pulling the door open, looking away from them. It hurt her eyes to look.

XII

On the morning of William's birthday, Sara opened her eyes warily. There it was again: 4:33. It was going to be a long day. Being careful not to wake Harry, she pulled open the drawer in the bedside table and felt around in it for a Dexedrine.

Swallowing the pill, she lay back against the pillow and listened to the sounds of Harry's breathing.

She'd been cheating a lot that week, but each time she had a reason. The party was coming up, a specific task, a difficult chore, a long day. Only for that reason, that day. She'd be good again tomorrow. And the next day or the one after that, she'd keep her promise about the dosage.

Yet it wasn't normal, she knew. Frightening people, stabbing them, pouring tea over their photographs. Was Harry right? Was her luck beginning to run out? The thought frightened Sara. She threw herself into her household chores, taking more and more speed to propel her through the days and keep the thought away. People were afraid of her. Jennifer. Harry. Even her children were afraid of her. Sara didn't want to be like that. She didn't want to frighten her children and friends. Why couldn't she be like everyone else—just normal, she'd settle for that.

4:52. Good, she thought. The earlier the better, it would give her a good start on things. She got out of bed quietly— Harry didn't move—went downstairs to the kitchen and put a load of wash in the machine. She could clean up in here, start breakfast and make lunches for the children before anyone upstairs was even awake.

Crashing

The day must be properly marked for William, Sara had set her mind on that. It was important to keep the significance of the occasion. Age one, after all, was a milestone: an end to infancy, a beginning of personality, of clear likes and dislikes, of eccentricities even. And, yes, she thought, unloading the dishwasher, it was an occasion for herself as well. People didn't very often make the connection at her children's birthday parties that whatever age they were—four, fourteen, eleven, one—just so many years before had she lain in the delivery room at Dunsdale Medical, struggling to produce a form from her body which would make her a mother once again. This was her day too, as well as William's. Her baby, she thought and smiled at the thought of him, her gentle, wide-eyed William. Life was a source of joy for him, not something to be battled against as it was for Justin. Not something to be skirted—as if it were possible to manage by just slipping around the edges—as it seemed for Julia. But life for William—exactly like his sandbox—was to be reveled in. He jumped to the center of it, squatted down and dug in.

Sara felt her body coming to life now—energy coursing through her veins. She mopped the kitchen floor, thought ahead to the packages still to be wrapped, the yard to be cleared and decorated, the cooking and cleaning to be done. She wanted everything to be nice for William—her last, her special baby, the one that was hers alone. With Justin's birth, Harry had his son and it seemed to Sara that something had been settled for him after that. He grew increasingly casual over her succeeding deliveries. *The hospital's only minutes away*, he said. *Call an ambulance if I'm not home.* And he managed not to be with each of the other three, leaving his office with less and less time to spare, arriving at the hospital later and later. With Julia, he arrived after Sara had been taken in to labor; with Sam, after she'd gone on to delivery; and with William, Harry didn't arrive at all until the infant was already several hours old. William belonged to her alone—the last, the end of a cycle.

Sara looked out into the predawn stillness of the yard and thought she hadn't been downstairs this early since William began sleeping through the night. She used to feed all her children down here in the kitchen when they woke for their bottles at just about this hour. And the feeling of warmth,

darkness, peace, she had felt then, as she sat inside with a
baby in her arms looking out at the dew sparkling in the yard,
returned to her now and she remembered how she used to love
this time of day.

She thought of her life as a painting: fixed and set apart
from the mainstream of things. Within the frame Sara applied
herself to house and children. Outside, the world went on. She
longed to break through, to let her life run over the edges,
break the frame. Harry's practice increased his information
about the world. At the end of any given day, he knew far
more about his patients than their medical histories. He knew
their politics, the mechanics of their jobs, their performances
in bed. He had discussed sports, history, economics, finances,
and philosophy with them. He was privy to their minds as well
as their bodies, and merely by opening his ears had poured
into them words, facts, ideas, theories, criticisms, beliefs—
evidence of an ongoing world which Sara, surrounded by children, bombarded by their needs, hardly knew existed. She had
to wait until the children were in school or in bed, were eating
or had finished eating, to read a book or magazine. She had
to wait until each was asleep or accounted for to listen to the
news and even then she never got it all, for at any moment
a child might wake or walk in out of nowhere and demand she
attend to him at once. She had to pay for every scrap of worldly
information she accumulated. It cost her the children's pro-
tests, it cost her the price of a sitter and her own internal pangs
of guilt to spend an hour downtown. She ran the risk of ne-
glecting her children, of damaging their psyches, to learn more
about the world. These were criminal offenses. Harry had only
to open his door for artists, vice presidents, professors, and
chairmen of the board to walk in. The world paid office calls
on Harry. Sara had to incriminate herself for it.

Dishes done, clothes in the dryer, coffee made, one cup
consumed, Sara went upstairs and dressed. She brushed her
teeth and downed another pill and pulled on her jeans and went
to see if it was time to get Harry up.

6:01. He'd said he wanted to get an early start. "Harry,"
she whispered. He lay on his stomach, face to the right, arm
flung up over his head. She hated it when he asked her to
wake him this early. What if he'd changed his mind in the
middle of the night? Would he be angry? Would he yell at

her? "Harry," she called softly. He slept so soundly. Sara
envied him the depth of his sleep. Her own was so shallow,
so fitful. She'd kill, she thought, to protect a sleep like this.
"Harry." She touched his arm. "It's after six."

"Okay. I'm up," he said and turned on his side. He was
awake now. Instantly alert. Sara marveled at the way Harry
could awaken on the spot in the dead of night, his mind active
on a moment's notice. A phone call, a voice in the night and
he was there engaged in the problem. Listening carefully,
noting symptoms, weighing remedies . . . *fever?* . . . *bleeding?*
Ticking off possible diagnoses in his head, suggesting im-
mediate action. Was it something he'd been taught in medical
school, this ability to switch from the world of sleep to waking,
to trade the unconscious for the conscious at will? Or was it
yet another example of Harry's will. Needing sleep, he willed
himself to sleep. Knowing himself needed, he willed himself
awake.

Harry sat up and looked at her and, in the focus of his
eyes, Sara could almost see his thoughts falling into place,
plans for the day being made, problems resolved, actions
taken. What a sense of power he must feel, she thought, to
awaken with his energies immediately and non-chemically
available like that. It took her forty-five milligrams at least to
reach the place Harry was the minute he opened his eyes.

"Been up long?" he asked.

"A while."

He nodded. He knew. Already he had it figured out.

"Trouble sleeping again?"

Not even her sleep was natural. Pills to make her drowsy,
pills to wake her up. She longed to have Harry's power, his
strength to make it on her own. But not everyone was equipped
as Harry was. People were not created equal.

"It's William's birthday," she said. "You won't forget
the party? You'll come home early?"

"The little man's birthday? Why so it is." Harry got out
of bed, and pulled up the shade. "Of course I'll be home for
that."

"It's going to be a nice day," Sara said, looking out the
window, seeing there was more to do out in the yard than
she'd thought. "I'm so glad. I want it to be really special.
Decorations, balloons, Everything."

"Don't overdo it," Harry said, going into the bathroom, turning on the faucet on the sink.

"Why not?" Sara shouted over the sound of running water. "A first birthday should be something special."

"I just meant . . . well, you know," he shouted back. "Take it easy."

Sara liked to watch him shave. Careful, overlapping paths through the lather with his razor. The same safety razor he'd used for years. Electric ones had no appeal for Harry. In some things he stayed deliberately behind the times, careful and safe.

He shaved first, then showered, never reversed the process. He dressed too in an unchanging order: underwear, socks, shirt, pants, shoes. It was a comfort to Sara to watch him. It was possible to impose order upon life, to believe in causality, to establish routines.

Going to the dresser, Harry returned to his pockets everything he'd removed from them the night before. Shaved, showered, dressed, pockets filled—Harry was complete. No additives required. He was ready as he stood to go out and enter his day.

"You look nice," Sara said, admiring him a moment from a distance, then going closer, straightening his tie.

"Thanks," he said and stood still to let her fix his tie, adjust the hang of his jacket.

For a split second Sara thought she would give all that she had for Harry to take her in his arms just then, to press her against his strong, reliable body; and when he did, swiftly and without a word, so much was it in the nature of an answered prayer, it nearly took her breath away.

"You want me to bring anything home?" he asked.

"Maybe some more balloons," she said. The moment was gone. "You can never have too many balloons."

Now it was beginning, she was getting off. She felt that solid rush of energy tingling in her palms, traveling up her legs, telling her the drug was taking hold. She went downstairs and had a second cup of coffee and stared at the cereal box she had put on the table for the children's breakfast. The print jumped out at her, the letters wiggling uncertainly as if each were impaled on the point of a pin. A clear, moving halo of light surrounded the print, lifting it off the box. *Brawny buck-*

wheat with a snap of maple, Sara read with difficulty. What on earth could that mean? The letters grew blacker, the space around them whiter. She looked around the kitchen. Everything—stove, sink, refrigerator, even the table at which she sat—everything was taking on a new reality, pulsing with life.

The words on the cereal box were not merely words now. They were actions, textures, emotions. Sara could feel movement pounding within her. A new order of life was being established. Sharper, brighter, more intense. The chairs and the faucet, the squares of linoleum, the empty soda bottles on the floor, everything around her was coming to life. Her skin tingled, her eyes widened. Sara loved this moment. It was like those first few seconds in an airplane when the engines raced, the jets ignited, and the whole cabin churned with the anticipation of takeoff.

Now she flew into action. She could wash the window over the sink and the glass portion of the door that looked out onto the yard before Harry came down for breakfast. Halfway through, with water dripping down her arm, she heard the first chirping sounds, like beeps tapping out a Morse-coded message, coming from William's room above. The birthday boy was awake. William's morning sounds were happy ones—quick, sharp stabs in the air, then silence, then more sharp, quick calls—not calls expecting an answer, but brief, happy statements announcing his presence to the house. Sara knew he would go on like that for some time yet without requiring her attention and today, especially, she loved him for it. He was the only one of her children to wake so cheerfully to the world. The others as babies had demanded instant feeding, instant changing, instant mothering. They shrieked, they yelled, they woke their father. *For God's sake, Sara, do something!* But William found his own amusement until she came.

Sara finished the window and the door and looked through to the cluttered yard beyond. She'd get to that after the children left for school. The sun was still pale in the sky, but Sara could tell from the way the leaves were buoyed on the air and from the sounds of the birds in the trees that it was going to be a lovely day. She felt her own powers rising with the sun. Like its emissary, she would go through the house cleaning, brightening, bringing light, bringing cheer. And it would be entirely due to her own personal store of energy that the party that afternoon would be a success. And it would be a success, Sara was sure of that. A party to end all parties. When the children came home, when Jennifer and Peter and Edward arrived, when Harry came back from the office early as he had promised, she'd make them a party they'd never forget.

"Happy birthday, darling," Sara called, running into William's room, taking him up under his arms, swinging him around. "Happy, happy birthday!" William squealed at each revolution and held his breath for the next. His warm little body felt light in her hands. She loved the sound of his voice, the smell of his skin. "It's all yours today, my love," she told him. "The sun, the sky, the world—take it, my sweet. It's yours." She put him down on the floor and grasped the little hands he wiggled up at her. Together they danced around the room, William squealing, Sara chanting to her birthday boy. "William is one. William is one today."

As insubstantial as a paper pinwheel, Sara spun through William's room. Effortlessly, things got done. They got dusted and straightened. William got bathed and dressed and put down on the orange pile rug now catching the first rays of sun creeping up over his windowsill. "There you are, my love," Sara said. How William loved the sun. He shrieked and darted in and out of it, laughing and reaching for its rays. He lay down and rolled back and forth across the rug letting shafts of sunlight pass first one way, then the other, over his rolling body. Sara stripped the crib and sponged its slats with Lysol; she fitted a clean sheet over the mattress, folded the blankets and stacked them at one end, changed the pillow and plumped it at the other. She wiped the chest of drawers, the radiator cover, the woodwork around the windows and doors. Pulling William's crib further into the sun, she put him back into it and immediately he ran for a sunny spot, bounced up and down in it on the mattress, hammering his little legs into the springs. As Sara kicked back the rug and began to damp-mop the floor, she heard Harry's voice behind her.

"You're a real dynamo today."

Instantly she whirled and motioned him back. "Don't walk. It's wet."

"You mean I can't even come in and say happy birthday to William?"

"Oh come ahead," Sara said, relenting. "But watch where you step."

Harry lifted William from his crib. "Happy birthday, little man," he said, planting a kiss on his cheek and giving him a toss in the air. "There's one from your old man." Catching him, he held him close against his body for a moment.

Watching them together, Sara thought Harry's face looked different somehow—older, not in years but in remembrance. It was a face he used to have—softer, more vulnerable, filled with wider perspectives. A rush of still photographs swept through Sara's mind: portraits of Harry taken years ago—profiles, closeups, action shots of Harry playing with the children, holding them as babies, or posed around the Christmas tree. His face, she recalled, his eyes, then as now were softer, freer. A face he'd worn before he met success.

Harry returned William to his crib and watched him prance across the mattress in the sun, raising his knees high, laughing up at his father. "What a little show off," Harry said. "I think he knows it's his birthday."

"He's showing off for you," Sara replied. "He loves you, you know."

"Isn't he too close to the window? I wouldn't want him catching a chill." Harry pulled the crib further out into the room and, delighting in the brief ride, William clung to the rail and grabbed for his father's tie. "Now, now, little man," Harry said, smoothing the tie back down inside his jacket. "Don't mess me up. Daddy's got to be neat and clean for the office. . . . Don't worry about breakfast," he said, turning to Sara. "I'll get my own. I know you've got a lot to do today."

"Thanks, Harry. The coffee's made and I put the juice out."

He kissed her cheek. "Watch yourself, will you?"

"Sure," she said. "Be home early."

"Early as I can." He waved and walked out the door. "Happy birthday, son," he called over his shoulder on his way down the stairs.

"Don't forget the balloons!" Sara shouted, picking William up and carrying him into her bedroom. By the time she had made the bed and was vacuuming the floor, she heard Harry's car pulling out of the drive.

Watch yourself, will you? Sure she would. Every step of the way. The other children needed to be awakened, their breakfasts made, rooms attended to. Sara went into the bathroom and took another pill. With all the work she had before her, this, as Harry was so fond of saying, was bound to be a brutal day.

"Morning, mom."

"Morning, Justin. Morning, Julia."

"Morning, mommy."

"Morning, sweetheart."

William sat in his highchair, pushing pieces of banana through his fingers. Justin helped himself and Sam to cereal, passed the box to Julia. Julia put a muffin in the toaster, got the milk from the refrigerator, passed it down the table.

Sara watched her children eating. Such good children she had, so helpful, so loving. There were parts of her life that couldn't have turned out any better. And everything would go well today. "Listen, you three," she said. "How about saying happy birthday to your little brother?"

"Oh, that's right. Hey, I almost forgot."

"Happy birthday, old man."

"Happy birthday, squirt."

Justin and Julia threw William kisses from the table, while Sam sat and loudly slurped his cereal. "When's my birthday, mommy?" he asked.

"September, Sam. And we'll have a party for you too then." Sara poured herself some more coffee, filled Sam's glass with juice. "Justin," she said. "You come *straight* home this afternoon, understand? No stopovers. No garage. You too, Julia. Straight home. And Sam . . . Jennifer's picking you up. You wait for her by the school gate." Everything would go off like clockwork. Nothing could stop her today. "We're going to have a lovely party," she told them. "The sun will shine and the yard will look like magic. You won't believe your eyes when you get home."

"Can I stay, mommy? Please. Can I help?" Sam was picking up her rhythm now. "Make magic in the yard?"

147

"No, you go on to school, Sam. I want it to be a surprise."
And what a surprise it would be. Sara saw it before her: colored
balloons, crepe paper flowing, mountains of presents, cascad-
ing satin ribbons. "It's going to be the best party anybody
anywhere ever had."

Julia and Justin exchanged quick glances.

"Oh, oh. Look out," Julia said. "Speed queen rides
again."

"Go, speed racer, go."

They laughed.

"Cut it out, you two." They shouldn't laugh at her. They
shouldn't make jokes.

"Flying high . . . speeding along . . ."

"Julia, that's enough!"

Sara picked up her cup, knocked it against the table edge
as she put it back down.

"Easy, mom," Julia said.

"It's just the coffee," Sara explained, wiping it up. "You
know it makes me nervous."

"How many have you had?"

"Three or four cups, I guess. I've been up since dawn.
Nothing's wrapped yet and you kids left the yard in an awful
mess."

"I didn't mean the coffee."

"Don't hassle me, Julia," Sara snapped. "You don't know
anything about it." She wished that were true. She wished they
didn't know anything about it. She wished they had never
heard the word, the street names, the stories, the lies, the
boasts. She wished they hadn't seen enough to frighten them
into making jokes. But she hadn't meant to yell at her. "I'm
sorry," she said to Julia and went over and arranged her hair
about her face. "Don't worry," she said, giving her a kiss on
the top of her head. "You worry too much, you know that?
Just be my sweet little girl and eat up your breakfast. . . . All
of you now. . . ." She went from one of them to the other.
"Eat up and stop worrying and get on to school and let me get
to work." She stood over Justin, looking down. "And you,
young man, never mind those looks."

Justin swept his eyes from her face back down to his
plate. "Okay, mom," he said, finishing the last mouthful and
taking his dishes to the sink. "Whatever you say."

She'd give anything for them not to know. "I'd do it differently if I could," Sara said, feeling a sudden need to explain herself and they were looking at her then, uncomprehendingly. "Don't play judge," she said into their bewildered faces. "And above all, don't you ever . . . well you know the expression . . . do as I say, not as I do." Justin was staring at her. She was a disappointment to him, she knew. She'd embarrassed him at school. She was sorry about that, she'd never meant to do it. There were so many things, it seemed to Sara, she did that she never meant to do. "Don't worry, honey," she said to Justin, pulling him against her, holding him there a moment. "It'll be all right. Trust me."

That was all she'd ever really wanted, Sara thought, feeling herself taking off now—someone to trust her, to say he believed in her. She couldn't do it alone, no one could. Amphetamines were called upon to stand in for human trust.

But she was almost through now, through the time-bind, the body-bind. "Don't be late for the party!" she shouted to the children she had fed and kissed and now was sending out the door. "Don't be late!" she called, standing in the doorway with William in her arms, hearing her voice blend with those of generations of mothers, both before and after her, seeing their children off to school. "Be careful crossing the street. Wait for the light. Don't be late. Pay attention in class. Eat your lunch. Be good. Be strong. Be smart."

She had to shade her eyes because the faces of her children were coming at her between great sheets of blinding light rising white out of the east . . . light crossed here and there by shadows . . . birds, she thought, or branches, or overhanging leaves still wet with morning mist . . . beautiful faces, young faces . . . now swinging free like masks close before her, now at a distance, reduced in size. "Hold Julia's hand, Sam," she called. "Pay attention now. Stand up, Justin. And Julia, brush your hair out of your eyes. Goodbye now. Have fun. Be good."

Her children were leaving her. "Sam . . ." She called them back. "Don't forget. Jennifer's picking you up. You come home with her today."

They were walking away. "And Justin . . ." They turned again. "Come *straight* home, understand?"

They walked ahead. "All of you, now . . ." They stopped. "Straight home." They nodded and waved and walked on.

"Will daddy be home?" Julia called from the corner.

"He said he would," Sara answered. "He promised."

They walked ahead. "Julia!" Sara shouted. They turned again. "I told you to take his hand!"

"I've got it, mom. I've got it."

"Bye," they called.

"Bye."

"Bye, mommy," called Sam, only a year ago, her baby.

"Bye, darling."

"Come along, birthday boy," Sara said to William, tossing him in the air. "We're going to make you a cake." His body left her hands, returned to it, no heavier than a doll's. "What sort would you like, my love?" she asked, catching him on a giggle. "Chocolate? Angel for an angel? And what about the filling? Lemon? Apricot? Banana? Your slightest wish is my command." She put him down, rushed ahead into the kitchen. William, babbling in that fantastic, preverbal language she loved, followed at her heels. Harry put such emphasis on words: *What's he trying to say, Sara? What's he mean?* Listen to the rhythm, she told him. The meaning is in the rhythm. "But daddy doesn't understand that, does he?" Sara lifted William into his highchair and pulled it close to the countertop so he could watch her work. "Daddy thinks you have to be explicit," she said. "Point to where it hurts with one finger. We know better, don't we?"

William pounded his hands impatiently on his metal tray. "All right, my love. All right." Sara got to work. "But you'll have to leave when I ice it. That's a surprise."

Truly Harry didn't understand. He talked to her about drug dependency and side effects, about psychotic agitation and paranoid psychosis. What did that have to do with her? She wasn't psychotic. *Not yet,* he said. *But you're working up to it. It can trigger a true psychosis.* Harry longed to be a psychiatrist, loved throwing those words around. Maybe he even did it to frighten her, she'd suggested once. *Why would I want to do that?* Why indeed? "Why do you suppose, William?" she asked her baby, pulling spoons and beaters out of drawers, sticking her head in low, dark places, coming out with pans and bowls, thermometers and measuring cups. "Why would daddy want to frighten me?"

William slapped his hands on his tray, responded with an enthusiastic rush of sounds. "He just doesn't understand," Sara continued. "All his talk about antisocial behavior and dangerous side effects. That's not what it's about at all." It's about having some backing, Sara thought, suddenly remembering how she used to paste paper dolls to cardboard for extra strength. It's about strength and confidence and euphoria. But Harry didn't understand that. There was so much Harry didn't understand. Or care to. Sometimes when she talked to him she saw him watching her with the cold, objective eye of his profession. She could almost feel his fingers on her words then, testing and judging, pruning out the ones not medically significant.

Sara found the bowl she wanted, took some eggs and milk from the refrigerator. William urged her on. More, more, his fists insisted on the tray. Sara measured and poured, mixed and stirred. William's squeals pierced the air while Sara boiled and cooled, beat and whipped.

"Irrational fears, he says, paranoia . . . violent rages. . . . That's all he understands. Not the sudden confidence, not the transformation." Sara dipped her finger in the batter and licked it. "He doesn't have to," she said to William, dipping it in again and letting him lick it. "Your daddy's happy with who he is. He wakes up with his self intact. I have to go chase mine."

The bowl was tilted, the batter ran into pans, the pans went into the oven, the oven was lit. William's fat little fists went up and down on his metal tray. Sara had made the cake, her baby son had approved the cake, the gods were happy and all was right with the world.

Carrying William into Harry's study, Sara walked over and put him down in the maroon reclining chair next to Harry's desk. "There you go, little one. Your daddy's reading seat." William rocked back and forth in the chair while Sara dusted the shelves and furniture. She straightened the papers and magazines on top of the desk and put the wastepaper basket near the door where she'd be sure to empty it.

It was feeling she wanted from Harry, not expert testimony. "Isn't that right, William?" she asked. "Isn't that what we want? Not daddy's articles in medical journals. Not his name among the foremost." She picked up a magazine, slapped it back down on the pile. William laughed at the sound. "You think it's funny, do you? Well, you're right. It is funny a man that smart can be so dumb. *Willpower,* he says. He doesn't know what he's talking about. Not a clue. A smart man like that. You're right, sweetheart. It's very funny. For we all know how smart daddy is, don't we? There's not a doubt in the world about that. Look at this. . . . Listen now. . . ." Sara leafed through tear sheets of Harry's most recent articles, reading out the titles and waving the pages in front of William. " 'The Advisability of Extensive Changes in the Nature of the Dietary Fat Intake,' by Dr. Harold Rice Richardson. How do you like that? Or how about: 'The Causal Relationship Between Blood Cholesterol Levels and Heart Disease.' Smart. Oh he's smart all right. And here we have Dr. Harold Richardson on blood vessel disease, on the chemotherapeutic treatment of depression . . . of insomnia . . . of weight control. . . . That's a good one for daddy, he's an expert on that. And here the famous Dr. Richardson discusses chlorpromazine for hyperactivity in children . . . Tofranil for bed-wetters. . . . Now nobody said he wasn't smart."

Sara returned the articles to their folder. Her heart was racing. Neatening and straightening when what she wanted to do was tear the den apart. "But where does he talk about feeling strong? Where's the article on feeling good about yourself? He thinks we're born with it. He thinks we're all like him. Come on, baby." She plucked William out of the chair. "This room is clean enough. I need some air."

Sycamores and chestnut trees ringed the yard, their leaves offering some shade from the sun. William's sandbox sat out directly in its path and the sand already looked hot. But William didn't seem to care. He toddled straight for it, climbed in and went to work with his tools while Sara walked around the yard picking up the papers and bottle caps strewn about, throwing them in the trash and gathering toys, returning the ones that belonged in the sandbox to it, arranging the others neatly at the side of the yard. "It's a perfect day for a party. Look at the sun," she called to William, pointing up. "It's shining just for you."

It takes so little to make him happy, she thought, watching

him in his sandbox, working away with his pail and shovel, exulting in the sun.

Sara was pleased now by the way the yard was shaping up. The day could not be more beautiful she thought, looking around at the branches swaying faintly overhead and at the peonies and azaleas blooming by her feet. After lunch and a nap, William would wake refreshed and bright for his party. The finest party anyone ever had. First and finest. Only one thing left to do out here—move that picnic table and benches. Sara wanted them in the center of the yard—center stage, she saw it clearly, everyone sitting around the table, laughing, talking, eating, the children jostling one another, the wind making gentle partings in their hair, all turning now to look at William at the end of the table . . . the honored end . . . the guest of honor opening his presents, cutting his cake. She heard his shrieks of laughter. She heard them wishing him well: *Happy birthday, William. Long life, little one. Happy birthday, son.* She saw the adults lingering on around the table, sipping coffee, talking quietly. She saw the children slipping down from their places, running off to play. She saw Harry looking handsome, looking proud. *Nice party, Sara. You did a fine job.*

It was a heavy redwood table and usually she needed Justin and Julia to help her move it. But today she had the strength of gods. She didn't need any help from children. The birds sang louder than she'd ever heard them sing and William's shouts, too, reached her amplified across the yard. Sara flung an arm over the table, put a hand beneath its edge. Encountering hardly any weight at all, she lifted it easily and carried it across the yard. Whatever had made her think she needed help for that? Centering the table near the swings, she went back for the benches.

"There" she said, standing back, admiring her work. "That's fine now." Lifting William from the sandbox, she held him close. "Just you wait, little boy. You'll see what a party you're going to have."

XIII

While William took his nap, Sara decorated the yard and made the icing for the cake. Beating egg yolks, pouring droplets of syrup into a bowl, whipping the mixture until it was hot, whipping it again until it was cool, she had gone through these motions, she calculated, thirty-five times over the years for her other children, but this was the very first time for William. She added the butter and vanilla, beat it until it was creamy and soft. The world had come round to June again and William had lived an entire year. Round and round her spatula went, pressing frosting onto the cake, refining memories from year to year; Justin's birth, and Julia's, and Sam's. William being born and brought home from the hospital, thrust into a household of big, noisy children. William with roseola, William in the sun. She had called a sitter for Sam, called herself a cab. Harry's at the office. Harry can't be disturbed. Yellow and blue butter cream pushing through the paper cone. Waiting for Harry to come. Being wheeled into delivery. Waiting for Harry to arrive. Blue and yellow flowers dotting the cake. Wondering through the whiffs of gas if Harry was at the door. Push, they said, and she pushed down hard and a single scream shot up from her mouth and flew to the ceiling and vanished in the electric light while she became one once more and William drew his first breath of life. Tiny rosettes taking shape on William's cake. Mother and baby doing fine. They sleep. They wake. The hours wearing on, her distinction wearing off, fading into pale green gowns, into the comings and goings of hospital life. Harry comes at last. It's all been done without him. Mother and baby doing fine. Tiny flowers ring the cake.

Sara had transformed the backyard into a pastel wonderland. Pink and blue balloons, streamers of white and green, lilac and the palest yellow were hung from the limbs of trees and from the bars of the swing set. Painted clowns juggled golden balls on paper napkins, rode carousels on cups and plates. The paper tablecloth was weighted down at points by bowls of fruit and sprays of baby's-breath. Candy baskets and small blue forks and spoons marked each place.

Amid the paper clowns, Sara sat wrapping presents for her William. Cutting ribbons, tying bows, folding colored tissue paper: red for the wooden horse, orange for the fire engine, purple for the lawn mower that rolls to the sound of bells within. Paper lanterns strung from branches bobbed approval. A fluttering pastel expanse laid out beneath a glittering sun, a fitting place for the adoration of the child prince, her fourth-begotten, bright-eyed, curly-haired year-old baby son.

The guests would be arriving soon. Sara didn't want to risk coming down. She dug into her pockets and tried to remember how many she'd taken. Two? Three? Something like that. Well, another wouldn't hurt. She could handle anything today. Anything at all, she told the trees and the hanging streamers. Anything, she said to the clowns and the chirping birds. It was her baby's first birthday. Nothing could go wrong today.

"Hi, mommy! I want some cake!" Sam grappled with the gate and took off across the yard. Edward and Jennifer, just behind, were loaded down with packages and Edward was fumbling with something that looked like a bottle under his arm.

Old grudges forgotten? Trespasses forgiven? Sara looked at Jennifer and hoped that for today, at least, it could be so. "Champagne!" Edward cried, pulling the bottle out by its neck. "Jenny made the exhibit!"

"Oh, Jenny, that's wonderful!" Sara called, running to her friend and throwing her arms around her. "You made it! I knew you would. I'm so happy for you. Now we'll have a double celebration."

Sam was pulling at William's presents. "Can I have these? Can I?" he demanded.

"No, Sam. Don't touch," Sara shouted, running over to him, whisking him away from the table. "Those are for William. It's William's birthday today, I told you. Yours is in the fall." Sam's face, large and wounded, swayed unsteadily before her. "Let him open his own presents, okay?" Sara wanted to make him smile, to take the hurt look away. "He'll let you play with them later, I'm sure he will." Edward's face and Jennifer's, too, were coming and going before her, now lazily at great distances, now without warning catching her up short. The trees were beginning to spin and blood was pounding in her ears. That must stop. She must make things settle down, get control of herself. "When it's your birthday, darling," she said to Sam, drawing him to her, glad to have his body to hold on to, "I won't let anybody else open your presents. You'll be the first to see them and then if you want. . . ." But now her arms were empty. Sam had broken free. He was running off across the yard, leaping into the sandbox.

"Come, sit down," she called to Edward and Jennifer, patting the bench beside her.

"The yard looks beautiful," Jennifer said, looking around her. "Really lovely . . . the lanterns . . . the balloons . . . and those streamers on the swings . . . it's like a fairyland. You must have been working all day. Why didn't you call, Sara? I would have loved to help."

"Oh, it wasn't hard," she said. "I enjoyed it." Her special gift to her special child.

"It really does look great," Edward agreed. "Nothing like balloons and streamers to make a party."

A wail went up from the sandbox.

"William broke my pail!" Sam was holding some misshapen toy aloft. "Mommy! He broke my pail!"

Sara didn't want any trouble today. No fights, no screaming. She thought she must go to Sam but the distance from him to where she sat seemed all at once impassible, and she was grateful to see Edward go in her place. He seemed to rise into the air before her and float effortlessly across the yard, propelled by her silent gratitude. Reaching Sam, he sat next to him on the edge of the sandbox and inspected the toy.

"It's only bent," Sara heard him say, his words now rushing back at her as if they were riding in on a pounding surf—now lost, pulled out to sea again—and she had to strain

o hear. ". . . handle's come off . . . little dent . . . easy to
fix . . . not broken . . . see? . . ."

Edward was good with children, just as Jennifer had said
he was. Sara watched, entranced as the handle was reattached
. . the dent smoothed out . . . the child appeased . . . it
seemed a scene from a play . . . she could watch all afternoon
. . everything being resolved, coming out right in the end.
A voice was interrupting . . . she didn't want to be distracted
. . . she wanted to watch the end of the play . . . a voice at
her elbow . . . soft, insistent, "Can I?" it asked. "Sara?" The
man was so good with the boy. "Can I?"

"What?" Sara said, watching the man with the boy. "Can
you what?"

"Do something." Jennifer was laughing. "Is there anything I can do?"

"What?"

"Can I help you? Can I do anything?"

"Oh . . . yes," Sara said, there was, now that she mentioned it. She could keep an eye on things out here for a
minute, on Sam, if she didn't mind. "I've got to go in and get
something."

"Okay. Sure," Jennifer said. "What do you have to get?"

Get? Jennifer's questions didn't make any sense. Get
what? Oh, William, of course. That must be what she meant.
"I've got to get William," she said. "He must be up from his
nap by now."

"There you are, my beauty." Sara walked into William's
room and, finding him awake, scooped him out of his crib and
hugged him tight. "Now let's get you dressed."

Perching him on the edge of the bathroom sink, balanced
against her body, she rinsed out a washcloth and caught a
glimpse of her face in the glass. It was a pale bluish white,
with the taut drained look it sometimes had on the first day
of her period. Little pieces of dry skin flaked on her cheeks.
Her dark eyes seemed lost, floating in the white skin. How
could she look so terrible, she wondered, when she felt so
great? Maybe she was coming down. It was early for that, but
possible. Tucking William under her arm, she reached for a
pill and found the feel of it so familiar in her hand she thought

she must just have taken one. Or perhaps she was always taking one, swallowing it down, reaching for another. Well, what did that matter? Today was a special day. As she clapped the pill to her mouth, William tried to grab it from her. "No," she cried out, swatting his hand away. "For mommy," she said, frightened by the thought of that pill in his hand. "Not you. Never for you I hope." She swallowed it quickly with a toss of her head. "We're off now, little one. Nothing can hurt us now."

White shirt and pants. White socks and shoes. Birthday boy in white. The very first time she had dressed him, it was all in white. Tiny white garments laid out on the bed. William is going home today. The father carries the baby out. The father isn't here, he's a doctor, you know. Yes, we know but the father carries the baby out, those are the rules. Follow the rules. Wait for the doctor.

White pants. White socks. Clean white shirt for the birthday boy. She could fly with him now, race down that hospital corridor. You can't do that. Run with her baby in her arms. Come back here, you're breaking the rules. Fly with him out of reach. Stop her, stop that woman. Oh, doctor, thank goodness you're here, the doctor's here, your wife wouldn't wait. Trapped then. She had to wait. Stop. Yield. She had to yield. The father carries the baby out. She relinquished her child. She obeyed the rules. Home-going infant all dressed in white.

"Here he is, everybody!" Sara shouted from the kitchen door, holding William up for them to see.

"Hooray, the birthday boy!" they shouted back.

Arms waving, voices raised, kisses planted, best wishes offered. Carrying him out past Sam's black looks as a thousand voices flew at her at once. "Hi, mom!" "Hello, mom!" "Hey mom. We're home." "We're here." "Hi, everybody. Here's Peter!" "Hiya, Sam." "Hey, William. Happy birthday to ya!" Sara turned her head this way and that, opened her mouth, stretched out her arms, tried to catch each word before it fell. "Hello, Just...hi, Jul...how was...how are?...." The children's voices spun around her. "Hi, Jennifer!" "Hello, Edward!" "Hi," they said. "Hi, William." "Hi, Sam." Clutching at words, names, juggling questions before they fell, at

taching responses, it was so important to get it right. "Fine
. . . yes . . . good . . . hello . . . come. . . ." But her direction
was off, her vision hazy. They were close now, now far. The
ground came alive with forms and sounds. Bodies walked,
ran, tumbled here and there across the yard. Voices called,
shouted. Colors moved on the ground, floated free in the air.
Only moments before . . . but it was inconceivable . . . could
it be no more than a matter of moments before that she had
been alone? Now she was scattered. Forms everywhere. Not
a single still place for the eye to rest. The ground was moving.
Stones spurted across it, lay still and spurted again. Knot holes
skipped places along the trunks of trees. Children's bodies
crouched close to the ground, then shot overhead on swings.
A young boy was running toward her. "Hello, mom." Sara
turned. The boy ran past. Peter running for Jennifer. Julia
unfastening her hair . . . such pretty hair . . . how it caught
the wind. Justin called to Edward, held something up for him
to look at. Something he had made in school? Sara strained
to see. Why was he showing Edward? Why not her? Sam was
tugging Justin by the hand. "Come, Justin. Come see." How
he adored his older brother. That was good, she was glad of
that. Or was it good? Cars. Garages. That wasn't good. Would
Sam, too, settle for that? Sara wanted so much more for both
of them than that.

"Justin," she called.

"What, mom?"

What? Sara stared at him. She didn't know what she'd
meant to say. Sorry, came to mind. Perhaps she wanted to say
she was sorry. To tell them all she was sorry for the way she
was. Or to say she loved them, she loved all her children. She
couldn't say that.

Edward was speaking loudly now. He was holding the
champagne up in the air.

"Listen, everybody," he shouted. "Listen!"

He was waving the bottle in the air.

"We have an announcement to make."

We, he was saying and reaching for Jennifer. *We have
an announcement to make*. Sara didn't want to hear it. Blood
rushed to her ears to block his words. He was putting his arm
around her friend. His lips were smiling, his mouth opening
and closing. His teeth flashing in the sun. Jennifer put her

hand over his mouth. Good. It was going to be all right. Jennifer was stopping him. She wouldn't let him say whatever it was he wanted to say.

"Wait," Jennifer said. "Not yet. Not without Harry. Harry's coming, isn't he, Sara? We have to wait for Harry."

It was all right now. Sara knew what to say. "He'll be here," she said. "He'll be here soon." The bottle came down out of the air. Arms were disentangled, voices dropped, the children went back to their games. "Harry will be here soon," she said and found it comforting and found herself disgustingly weak for taking comfort from it. She who could do anything today—transplant redwoods, lift whole trees with her bare hands—could not endure the sound of Edward's announcement without Harry by her side. It wasn't like her, it wasn't worthy. Yet here she was, taking comfort from the prospect of Harry's arrival. "He'll be here soon," she said.

"We'll wait then," Jennifer replied and Edward put down the champagne.

They had found a quiet corner of the yard. Jennifer was talking softly. "It's really fantastic the way you put this whole thing together by yourself."

Edward was playing a game with the children . . . Peter, Julia, Justin . . . even Sam was involved. William sat in his chair in the sun, happily ripping the wrapping off his presents. And there occurred one of those splits in her day which left Sara both bewildered and grateful. To look around and find no one requiring her attention, she was divided and thrown off balance. It was wrong, it couldn't last. She had to do something about it at once. A question was pressing urgently on her mind. A question about doing things right. "How do you know? . . ." she asked Jenny. "How can you tell? . . . I mean really sure?" Jenny must answer. "Sure you're doing the right thing?" That wasn't what she meant. "I don't mean right . . . I know it isn't right . . . not right or wrong . . . it just is. It's the way things are. The way I am. Maybe they shouldn't be, I shouldn't be . . . but they are, that's all. . . ." What was the question, the urgent question Jenny must answer? "How do you know if you're doing harm?" That's what she meant. "I don't want to do them harm. I don't want to be a bad mother. Do you think it does? Do you think it harms them?" She was talking too fast, but she had to say it all. Jenny had to understand. "By example, I mean. What they see. What they know." Jenny would tell her. "And kids see everything, know everything. They even make jokes about it. Speed queen, speed racer . . . they think it's funny but they shouldn't call me that, should they, Jenny?" Her children shouldn't laugh at her. "Do you think I'm a bad influence? Is that it? That's funny, isn't it?" She started to laugh. "Your own mother a bad influence. How can you avoid your own mother? I've heard of children actually allergic to their mothers. They break out in a rash. Can't stay in the same room with them. Chemistry of the skin or something. But I don't want to hurt them, damage them like that. . . . Do you think it does? Do you think it makes a difference?" Jennifer looked confused. "Influences them . . . entices them to try other things? Do you, Jenny?" Sara didn't want her confused. She wanted a sharp, clear answer. An answer before Harry arrived. "Do you think it'll turn them into addicts . . . lead them to acid or heroin or something like that?" Sara shook her head, waved her hand through the air to wipe her words away. "Oh, that's stupid. I know it's stupid. Of course it won't. I don't know why I brought this up. Come on, let's forget it; let's have some champagne."

Jennifer put her hand on her arm, held her back. "No, wait. What's the matter? What are you trying to say?"

Trying to say? Did she think she couldn't say what she meant? Did she think she had trouble thinking? "Nothing," she said. "Forget it." Jennifer's face looked dark, then suddenly phosphorescent. Sara pulled her arm away. She wanted all that to stop . . . things popping out at her, shapes changing in an instant, faces going darker, then brighter. "I'm sorry," she said. "Forgive me."

"There's nothing to forgive. I just don't understand."

"That's the problem, I guess. Unless you're hooked, you don't understand. And if you are, you can't help. Once you've known that feeling . . . nobody in their right mind would want to give it up."

"But it doesn't make you happy."

"Happy? It's better than happy. It's power. It's freedom. It's knowing you exist. Without it, I'm not even sure of that."

Sara turned away. She'd give anything to have those

words back. Nobody on earth could be expected to understand that. The distance between herself and Jennifer seemed at that moment immeasurable. It followed narrow dark meandering paths through the trees, then spread out in great expanses of new grass and warm sunshine. "It's always like this," she said in despair. "Either one thing or its opposite. I'm here now, alone with you. Whole. That's everything . . . feeling whole. But it never lasts. They'll start coming, you'll see, and break me into pieces. They'll come from all directions and divide me. The only way to stop them is to die. If they think I'm dead or asleep I can have a minute's peace. But only a minute's. And so I'm quiet. I hold my breath and tiptoe from room to room. But at the slightest noise . . . if I should cough or step by mistake on a squeaky floorboard or flush the toilet . . . even in the bathroom they follow me! . . . waiting for a sound, a noise . . . at the slightest noise they're on me. And I know what they want, Jenny. Don't think I don't. They want to get back up inside. Oh yes, they do. All of them . . . diving at me, clawing at me, thrusting their arms, their fingers into my mouth, my ears . . . their feet running after me, their eyes searching me out, their voices calling, their hands reaching for me, pulling at me . . . parts of human bodies always pulling at me. . . . Even Harry who's such a fucking famous doctor . . . they pull at me, they drag me down. And you know, the funny thing is, Harry's so against weakness, so abhors dependency, and yet in a way he depends on mine. He wants to keep me just the way I am. I know that, Jennifer, I do. Even though he's always telling me to quit, he doesn't want me to. Not really. No, I know he doesn't. No matter what he says, he likes things just the way they are . . . it does something to him . . . keeps him strong . . . in control . . ."

"Sara, maybe you should go in and lie down for a while . . ."

". . . keeps me coming to him, begging for prescriptions . . . he hates me then, but he has me where he wants me. Why does he do it, Jenny? Why does he hate me so?"

Jenny started to answer, but all at once her voice was submerged in a sea of angry shouts rolling toward them across the yard and Sara was afraid.

"You did too!" "I did not!" "You did." "I didn't." "Give it back." "I won't." "You will." "Don't have to." "Do too."

"Shut up!" "Can't make me!" "Can too." "Can not." "Bastard!" "Bitch!"

"You see, Jenny! You see!"

"Sara, get hold of yourself."

Jennifer's hands were on her shoulders. Jennifer's face was close to hers. Her friend was pressing her shoulders, peering into her face. What did she see there, a freak? A speed freak? *The lowest of the low,* Julia had told her. *Even heroin addicts think they're scum.* The voices were rolling across the yard, wave after wave of unremitting sound. Sara wanted to run, to vanish, to hide her face in Jennifer's body.

"It's all right, Sara," Jennifer was saying. "It's all right. I'll handle it."

"Mommy, mommy!" "Sam took William's toy." "Did not." "Did too." "Can't have it." "Can too." "Can not." "Julie pulled my hair." "Did not." "Did too." "Gimme that." "Let go." "Shut up!" "Mommy, mommy!" "Justin's hogging the swings." "I never get a turn." "You're just teasing him." "I am not." "You are too." "Gimme that." "It's mine." "Is not." "Is too." "Mommy, mommy!"

"It's all right, Sara," her friend was saying. "I'll take care of it. Why don't you go inside and take a nap?"

A smooth, calm, quiet voice. Sara wanted to hide in that voice. "But why do they hate me? Jenny, why? I love them so."

Jennifer planted herself in front of Sara. "Quiet now, Sara. It's all right." She held out her arms and knelt to receive Sam running full tilt into them. "Now what's this all about, Sam?" she asked, rising to her feet, keeping her body between his and Sara's. "What's going on here?" She took a step, holding Sam in front of her, keeping Sara to her rear. She took another step, and another, talking to each of the children in turn as she moved, her voice, low, calm, musical, leading the children away. "I see," she said. "Is that right, Sam?" She was walking away. "Is that what happened, Justin?" She was leading the children away. "Is that true, Julia?" She was gathering the children around her and slowly moving them away.

Sara's children were gone. She sat on the ground with her head between her knees and gradually her fear abated. For a moment she had thought she would faint, but that danger seemed to have passed now. Just when she had begun to think the noise would never stop, it stopped. The waves receded, the voices grew still. Slowly she raised her head and, incredulous, found herself alone. Not drowned in the pounding surf as she had imagined, not submerged beneath the waves of voices. She looked up at the sky . . . balloons floating freely in the air, crepe paper streaming from the swings . . . it was all right . . . she was all right . . . safe and free. . . . She looked at William, saw his highchair begin to tilt, leapt to her feet and cried out, "Grab him, Edward! Quick!"

Edward lunged for the chair, but it fell just past his fingers and the cry that came from William as he hit the ground stopped Sara's heart in fear.

"Here's daddy!" Julia shouted and ran to the gate.

"Hello, everybody!" Harry called.

On the ground rocking William in her arms, Sara saw in a split second the injury was not serious. Harry was coming toward her, his arm was wrapped around Julia's shoulders. The two of them there . . . father and daughter . . . the sun on their faces . . . their eyes on one another . . . something about it, something entirely appealing . . . Sara didn't know just what . . . but it seemed to her a new and different perspective, as if she'd looked up and caught them both at an angle she'd never seen before. She liked this view, she thought, Harry looking down adoringly, Julia looking up.

"What happened here?" Harry asked, coming closer, bending down to William on the ground. "Did the guest of honor take himself a spill?"

Edward righted the chair. Sam ran over and wrapped himself around his father's legs. He handed the toy that a moment before had created such dissension meekly back to William. William stopped crying and reached for it, and Sara got up off the ground.

"Here, let me help you," Harry said, taking William from her. "Happy birthday, little one."

A baby in his arms, Sam at his knees, Julia by his side, Harry was altogether transformed. Looking at him there before her, Sara thought for a minute anything at all was possible and let herself be drawn against him. She leaned on the arm he presented her, rested her head on his shoulder—a good place to rest a moment, she thought, in front of her friends, in front of her children.

"Hello there, you two," Harry said, turning now to Jennifer and Edward. "Hi, Justin. How ya doing, Peter?" he shouted across the yard. "How's the party going?" He looked around. "The place looks very nice . . . very nice indeed." He looked at the lanterns, the streamers, the balloons. "Oh, Christ, I'm sorry, Sara." He turned back to her and slapped his head. "I forgot the balloons. But you seem to have enough as it is. You've really done a terrific job. The place looks just great."

"Thanks, Harry," Sara said, feeling absurdly proud. "It turned out I didn't need them anyway, I had more than I thought. But come here now. . . ." She dashed to the center of the yard, motioning everyone around her. "Everyone over here," she called. "Edward has something to say." She turned back toward Harry. "We were waiting for you, but now that you're here. . . ." It was all right now. Harry was here. "Edward has an announcement. Let's hear what it is." She could hear it now that Harry was here.

"What's up, Edward? We're all ears." Harry looked at him eagerly.

Edward approached the group. Suddenly he seemed like a shy little boy at a loss for words. "Well . . ." he started and stopped and looked around. "Come here, Jenny. Stand next to me."

He flung an arm around her and with the other raised the champagne. "Something else we're going to celebrate with this." Edward's voice was low but steady. Jennifer's eyes brightened, her cheeks reddened . . . it was like a picture postcard, Sara thought, a scene from a film. She had the impression she had seen it before. The actors were posed. The words, too, had a familiar ring. But it was all right, Harry was by her side. Edward smiled and blinked and opened his mouth again. They were going to be married, he said, just as Sara had known he would. But it was all right, Harry was holding her hand.

It felt absolutely right, Sara thought, inevitable even. They should be married. Their happiness was clear. It circled out in waves of heat and light, carrying her off in the general commotion. Cheers went up from Harry and the children, congratulations all around. Peter seemed physically to expand, rising nearly off the ground, floating across it to embrace the pair.

"Wonderful news," Harry said. "I'm thrilled for you, really thrilled."

Harry as father, as friend. Sara was entranced. "So am I," she said, kissing her friend and her friend's intended. "It's wonderful, really wonderful." It was, she thought. Whatever they intended was right.

William, rising to the occasion, delivered a flood of his own high-pitched private language which everyone was pleased to accept as testimony of his personal good wishes.

"Really," Sara said. "I'm very happy for you." It was possible. It must be possible. Harry was by her side. She was happy for her friends. She wanted everyone to be happy, that's what everyone wanted. Words of happiness flew around her. *Happy. Happy. You'll be so happy.* What precisely did they mean? Hadn't she just been discussing that? It wasn't a question of happiness only . . . hadn't she just said that? But of being free. Happy and free. Powerful and free. Strong and free and certain of one's own existence. Strong as Harry, certain as Harry. Yes, that was it. To be like Harry.

"Champagne, everybody!" Edward was preparing to open the bottle.

"Hold on a minute," Harry called and ran into the kitchen and came out carrying four champagne glasses with a towel draped over his arm. "We have to do this right."

Harry could do things right. He was tall and confident and proper and right. He held out a glass while Edward struggled with the cork. It was a comfort to have such people in the world as Harry. They balanced things, Sara thought, they made up for people like her.

"Careful now," Harry was saying, moving the glass under the neck of the bottle. "Here it comes, look out.. . . . Oh! Great! I got it. I got it." The bubbling liquid filled the glass. "Good work, Edward."

The cork popped, the children cheered, they all took their places around the table. Everything fell into place. Sara knew exactly what to do. She was busy, she was cheerful, she attended to their every need. Nothing could get to her now. She was off on her own, distant and safe. She went to the kitchen, brought out the cake, went back for the ice cream, scooped it out onto the plates. She lit the candles for William, smiled as he blew them out. She held his tiny hand around the knife, helped him to cut the first piece, then cut all the rest herself and passed them around. She made certain Sam got a yellow rose and a whispered promise of something special for him later if he'd be nice and let William play with his new toys first.

Sara foresaw a host of accidents and neatly avoided them all: righting cups before they spilled; snatching plates back from the edge, napkins away from smoldering wicks; keeping Sam's fingers off the champagne, William's from being pinched in his tray. She intervened in fights, proposed alternatives. She was in a hundred places at once—passing food, settling arguments, keeping everyone happy, everything under control. Looking up once she nearly cried, "Look out!" For just for a second she thought she saw the car rolling backwards in the drive. But that couldn't be, she told herself. Nothing could go wrong today.

Harry was standing on the bench ready to propose a toast and the kids quieted down as, without a word, he commanded their attention. "To Edward and Jennifer," he said, raising his glass, "love and joy forever." All concurring, they sipped and drank, then Harry turned to William and proposed another. "To a very young man entering his second year of life. Happy birthday, son."

Shouts and cheers went up all around, and Sara looked at William—her smiling baby smearing his face with icing. She looked at Harry on the bench. Perhaps she'd been wrong about him . . . the thought flashed across her mind and then was gone . . . as she thought how impossibly tall he seemed, like a bridge into the sky . . . and he became unreal to her, closed and remote, a composite of ambitions from another world.

Suddenly Jennifer was behind her, bending over her shoulder. "Hey," she said. "You okay?"

Sara snapped back into place. "Yes. Sure. Why shouldn't I be?"

Harry was talking to Edward about the bookstore. Sara picked up words here and there . . . how well it was going . . . Harry had stopped in the other day . . . funny, he never told her. "You had such a crowd, I didn't have time to stay." But then there were so many things he never told her. The store was doing especially well right now, Edward was saying. "People get edgy in the spring. They want a whole new selection of books." Sara was edgy in the spring, summer and winter too. She followed the conversation, slipping in and out, losing track and taking time out for more champagne, then picking up another word or two . . . some talk about getting a partner . . . for Edward or Harry, she wasn't exactly sure . . . Jennifer thought it would be a help . . . "take some of the load off your shoulders." Edward, Sara guessed, for he was the one with the narrow shoulders. ". . . give you more free time." No, Harry it must be, for he was the one with the brutal schedule . . . but free time? . . . Wasn't all time free?

"Harry wouldn't know what to do with it," Sara heard herself saying. "He's not happy unless he's overworked."

"Not true." Harry shook his head.

She'd misjudged him again.

"But you're right, I do like running the whole show. Knowing exactly what's going on with each patient."

"Sounds like an awful responsibility to me," Edward said.

"I've got nothing against responsibility," Harry replied. "I like to keep on top of things . . . know who's getting what treatment, how they're reacting. Couldn't do that with a partner. . . . Oh, by the way . . ." He turned to Sara. "I just found out. Drumson's license is being revoked."

He'd turned too suddenly. She wasn't ready. "Whose license?"

"You know . . . Ben Drumson. I told you about him."

She couldn't quite remember.

"The investigation."

She nodded. "Oh, yes. That."

It sounded familiar. Ben Drumson being investigated for something or other . . . vaguely familiar. . . . But Harry liked to run the whole show, now that she had no trouble remembering. She had always known that about Harry. How he took control, hooked things together. She had been drawn to it from the start. It was a comfort, a reassurance. But somehow it had gone wrong. He'd hooked the wrong things, made a bad connection. And who was he talking about now?

"Drumson, don't you remember?" he asked. "Well, it

doesn't matter." Harry stood up. "Great to see you all but duty calls. I've got to be getting back."

"Of course I remember," Sara said. Had she shouted? Was that why they were all turning their heads? "I remember perfectly well."

"Don't go, Harry," Jennifer said. "You just got here. Have some more champagne."

Edward refilled their glasses. Sara felt the champagne rushing all at once to her head. A thousand bubbles rose free from the table, inside each a painted clown rode a dotted pony. Things were getting away from her. The children pushed back their plates, got down from their places. They were running away to play. The party was breaking up. Jennifer was right, Harry mustn't get away.

"Stay a little longer," she said to him. She held his arm, offered him cake, offered him ice cream. "Stay for William. For his birthday. Stay for Edward and Jennifer. It's not every day our friends get married. . . . Look at William, isn't he adorable, he's having such a good time. And Peter. . . ." She spotted him across the yard. "He looks so happy, doesn't he? His mother getting married. Children really are conventional at heart, don't you think? They don't understand anything but marriage. Not that they understand that, I don't mean that. Who does?" She turned to Harry. She must make him stay. "Do you? Does anybody? I certainly don't. I only meant they don't understand anything else . . . any relationship . . . certainly not between a parent and someone else . . . outside of marriage. I mean when that other person isn't also a parent. But then of course if both parties were parents . . . the child's own parents . . . they'd be married already, wouldn't they? That's not what I mean of course, but I think that's what children want, isn't it? At heart. To have both parents married to each other?" She reached out for Harry's hand. "Please stay, Harry." She had something to say to him she thought. She filled her glass again and raised it to her friends. Why were they looking so serious? Why were they staring so? Their faces widened and narrowed through the glass. Staring eyes, tight mouths, fish faces in the champagne, now bobbing up to the surface, now diving into the bubbling sea. Sara was dizzy and confused. She wanted them all to stay still. Stay and be happy. "Stay, Harry," she said. "To happiness." She drank to happiness, seeing it now within reach, now lost at the bottom of the glass.

Sara looked at good, solid, responsible Harry and thought he didn't really belong there at all. In this garden of streamers and clowns and children's balloons. How had he come to be there—a man of his ambition, his drive? He was out of his element. This wasn't what he needed. He didn't need her—speed queen, speed freak. She was no use to him at all. What he needed was a refined wife, a better wife. Well, she could be that too. She could be better. She was getting better and better by the minute. As long as he wrote the prescriptions, she could be anything he liked. She wouldn't disappoint him. Even now, drunk and speeding with shapes coming and going in and out of focus before her, she would go on playing the role he expected her to play.

"I'm delighted you all could come today," she announced abruptly and laughed at the artificial note, the elevated tone.

So the good doctor was out of his element, was he? Well, let him go then. She didn't want to waste his time. She was in her element now, time was her own and she had no intention of giving it up. Perhaps she could secure this time for herself even after Harry's death. Have it written into his will. The notion amused her. Dexedrine in perpetuity. Her own particular stab at an afterlife. She laughed again. Harry's face was close to hers. A serious, controlled, professional face. What was it doing here? What did he know of adapting his ways to others? Her life was nothing if not rooted in that, but people adapted themselves to Harry. They followed his orders, his diets, they took his pills, did his exercises, stayed in bed when he told them to, recovered when he expected it and died if they must; but only after first accepting his complete assurance that everything was going to be all right.

"More champagne, Harry?"

"No, I'm fine."

Yes, he was fine. They all were fine. Fine friends. Fine husband. How Sara detested them. Family, friends, she hated them all. Who did they think they were, coming here, messing up her yard, making her wait on them all day? And the children . . . Justin had grease beneath his nails, Julia never cleaned her room, Sam had to be told when to change his underwear. . . . But, no, it wasn't that. Why did it always come back to that? It wasn't that she didn't love them. She looked around. They were on the swings. They were running in the grass. They were playing frisbee. William was sitting in the sun. She ached with love for them. Certainly, it wasn't that.

"Is everybody happy?" she asked, raising her glass. She was master of ceremonies, mistress of life. "To happiness," she said. And to speed. She took a sip. To Dexamyl. To Elavil. She took another. To Preludin and Valium, to all mind-altering, pain-relieving, consciousness-expanding stimulants on the market. She finished her glass.

Edward and Jennifer were moving away. Watery figures slipping off the bench, sliding away into the grass. Come back, she wanted to call. I didn't mean it, I don't hate you.

Harry's hand was warm in hers. Big and strong and warm. "It was a nice party," she said. "Wasn't it?"

"Yes it was, Sara. Very nice."

She wouldn't do anything to disappoint him. "I can do it, can't I?"

"Of course you can."

"I can give a party. Make people happy."

"You did a fine job. I'm proud of you."

"Are you, Harry? Are you really?"

"Of course I am."

He was patting her hand. He was smiling at her. Things could be so simple if only she'd let them.

"I've got to make a stop at the hospital. See if you can take a nap while I'm gone. Sleep off that champagne. Let the kids clean up."

"I can do things right, can't I? Make things look pretty. The yard did look pretty, didn't it, Harry? It was nice for William, wasn't it?"

"It was very nice, Sara. Very pretty. You've worked so hard, you must be exhausted. Try to get some sleep while I'm gone."

"Don't go, Harry."

"I have to. I have to check on a patient in the hospital. It won't take me long."

His hand warm in hers. Her fingers clutching at his. "Please don't go."

His fingers wiping at her eyes.

"Sometimes people cry from sheer exhaustion," he said.

171

"Did you know that? I think maybe you overdid it a little today . . . and those other things don't mix with alcohol."

She pulled her hand away. "Oh Harry, don't start again."

"All right, not now. We'll talk about it when I get back. But we've got to do something. I know the party was a big job, but. . . . Believe me, Sara, if I didn't have this patient I wouldn't go. Maybe I have been letting my work take over . . . obscuring things a little here at home. But I've been so swamped at the office. Those people's lives are in my hands. I'm responsible for them, you know. I've got to be available when they need me."

"I know, Harry. I know. It's all right. Go on. Go to the hospital."

"When I get back we'll figure something out. There must be something we can do. A way to handle this dependency of yours."

"Oh, fuck my dependency! Just go on and get out of here."

"I only meant . . . well, we'll talk later. There must be something. Maybe some kind of therapy."

"Therapy? Shit!"

"All right, Sara. Quiet now. Sam's coming this way."

"I don't care who's coming."

"Well, hi there, Sam. How're things?"

Sam was tugging at her knees. It was this constant pulling and tugging she couldn't stand. As she raised him up, he reached for the edge of the table, missed it and grabbed a flap of paper cloth instead. The cloth tore, pulling ice cream and cake down over Sara's legs. Sam tried to catch the plate, caught only globs of chocolate ice cream in his hands and, pushing down on Sara's thighs, ground the mess into her lap. "Shit!" she cried. "Goddamn fucking shit!" Sam began to cry and Sara jumped up, spilling him to the ground.

"Come now, Sara," Harry said, reaching for his handkerchief. "You can't expect to have a kid's party without a few mishaps." He bent down and wiped off Sam's hands before picking him up. "It'll all come out in the wash."

"Then why don't *you* do the fucking wash!" Sara yelled and there was silence in the yard.

"Now, now," Harry said, bouncing Sam on his knee.

We don't want to hear that kind of talk on William's birthday, do we? And I think you owe Sam here an apology."

Husband and son appealed to her. Harry's clear, dark eyes. Sam's brimming with tears. She could lose herself in those eyes. Fly into their centers and away on their entreaty. All right, she would apologize. "I'm sorry," she said. She hadn't meant to hurt anyone. It was just that they didn't understand. She was the one who hurt. She had other needs to fill, other pains to stop. If she could be like them, she would. But it hurt so to do it straight.

Edward and the children were playing frisbee with the paper plates. Discs of white, splotches of color, now sailing on a curve, now high, now low, flew over her head. Harry was gone. Sara had downed another pill and produced another bottle of wine. Shouts assailed her ears. Happy voices in the yard. "Here! Here!" "Throw it here!" "Good catch!" "Look out." "Get it." "Got it." "That one's yours." Sara caught Peter's look of admiration as he watched Edward running for the catch, and understood why he had reason to be proud. So good with children. So good with Jennifer. Peter and Edward and Justin and Julia and Sam played around her. Peace was restored. William played in the sun. Happiness reigned. A space opened up. Through it Sara slid inward toward herself, confident and powerful and free.

"But only for a moment," she explained to Jenny. "There's no middle ground. All or nothing. Like this bottle here. . . ." She lifted it to her mouth. "Full or empty. Here today, gone tomorrow."

Jennifer was reaching toward her, saying something, but her voice was soft and far away and Sara knew that was where she'd like them all to be—far away. The trees at the end of the yard were painted on green glass. The paper frisbees stopped in their tracks. Frozen dots against the sky. Harry didn't want her. Harry didn't have time. Nothing moved. Nothing sounded. Then all at once, as on a single impulse, herds of people thundered toward her from the distance. "See, Jenny. You see!" They galloped across the yard. Their heads shot up, their legs crashed down, their feet pounded into the earth. Up they shot and down—high-stepping chargers against the sun.

"Can I, mom? Can I?" "Please, mommy. Please." "Do I have to take him? Do I?" "Wanna go to Justin's garage. Wanna go!" Sara knew there was some reason to say no, some reason she didn't want Sam at that garage. But already Justin was reconsidering. "Well, if you promise to be good. I've got work to do." "Promise, promise!" She didn't want that for Sam. "Sam. . . ." She started to say, but already he had turned from her. He was up on Justin's shoulders. "Well, okay, just this once." "Bye, mom. See ya later." So quickly it was decided. So quickly they were moving off away from her. Crooked patches of light and dark moving away across the yard. "Be careful," she called and now Julia was before her, her back to the sun, pleading for something in town at five o'clock. "Please, mom. Please." How lovely she is, Sara looked up, shaded her eyes against the sun. "I'm meeting the kids. Can I, please?" A child of hers, so fresh, so lovely. "I'll make my own supper when I get back. Thanks, mom. Thanks. Bye, now. Bye." And she, too, was gone.

"You see. . . ." Sara said, spreading her fingers wide for Jennifer to see. "Like water slipping through."

"Let me help you clean up," Jennifer said and started to stack the plates.

But Sara wanted her gone. "No," she said, taking the things out of her hands. She wanted them all gone. Now. Instantly. "I'll do it. I'll do it myself." What right had they to intrude like this, to insinuate themselves upon her when she most wanted to be free? Jennifer's arms were around her. She threw them off.

"Please, Sara. Let me help."

"No." She didn't want her here. "Leave me alone." She wanted her gone. "Go home and leave me alone." But still that woman persisted.

"Just let me clear the table."

"No." Sara pushed her hands away. What would it take to make her see? "I don't need any help," she shouted, but fortunately now the child-bridegroom was showing better sense. Edward was coming forward, saying something to Jennifer, whispering in her ear, pulling her away. At least he understood a person's right to be alone. They were going now. "Goodbye. Goodbye." Sara waved and felt relieved. "Thank you." "Goodbye." They had had a good time. She loved them for coming, loved them for going. She watched them gather their things . . . her friends gathering their things . . . nodding and waving and thanking her. She was capable of having friends, of showing them a good time. She watched them take some young boy whose name she had almost forgotten between them. "Goodbye," she called. "Thank you," they called. "Goodbye." She loved her friends, she loved her freedom. She waved them away. The yard was quiet. She loved them for leaving her alone in the quiet of the yard.

Sara looked around. Things came and went, black and slithering—snakes, no doubt, she didn't like snakes—at the base of the garden wall. Tiny particles of light flickered before her eyes and sank into the spongy depth of sky. Between those slithering snakes and flickering lights, Sara was divided.

How contemptuous she felt now of that condition of things—of life, of herself—that made people desirable only in their absence. Alone, she yearned to have them back. Surrounded by them, she thought she would drown. Whatever she experienced, some part of her longed for its opposite. Could she never be whole, then, but only a half crying out for its other half? No, she wouldn't believe it. She was as good as any of them, as complete. She didn't want them back. She didn't need them. They had deserted her. Let them go, then. Good riddance.

She grabbed the bottle of wine—there was only a little left—and swung it in time to her heavy, full-footed strides across the yard. Every so often she stopped and threw back her head, raising the bottle to her lips and taking another sip. Everywhere around her she saw a shabby, littered wasteland—crumpled napkins, squashed cups, torn birthday wrappings, crushed plates, broken balloons—the remains of the most hateful, ordinary, deadening domesticity. Wadded up splashes of color, clowns' faces, horses' hoofs, shredded streamers were strewn about her in the yard like clothes cast off by a drunk. William's new toys lay on the table soaking in pools of melted ice cream. Others were scattered on the ground, dropped one by one as his first fleeting delight gave way to the more substantial pleasures of his older toys. What did Sara care? She was beyond that now.

"Not for me," she asserted, raising the bottle to her lips. "Not this mess, this shambles. I want more than this." She wheeled and dropped the bottle. *"We* want more, don't we, my baby?" For there was William in the sun. "We want the sky. We want the world." She was off now, free and powerful. She could have whatever she wanted. She scooped William up, swung him around by the arms. "We want the sun, don't we, my love?" She held him to her, swung him away. "We want a little passion in our lives." Nothing could touch her now. Freedom, sun, light, and passion—it was all within her grasp. Dancing through the litter with William in her arms, spinning across the yard, careening through the mess, she was whole now, purely herself and free.

"Take it, my beauty," she said to him. "Stretch out your arms for life." Faster and faster she twirled—William shrieking, Sara circling—body spiraling, knees dipping. Nothing could touch her now. Nothing could bring her down.

Twirling at the front of the swing set, chrome and metal blazed like mirrors in the sun. "Take it, my baby," she cried and tossed him in the air. "Take that sun you love so well." She caught him and threw him up again. "Take it, my love. Take it all." His body was as nothing in her hands. She caught him again, threw him again, sending him higher and higher up through the streamers toward the sun. "Take it for both of us." She threw him again, his head parting paper streamers like a rocket the sky at lift-off and William's screams were no longer the screams of joy. "Take it, my Icarus," she called, sending him higher into the sky. "Take that sun you love."

Up through crepe paper trailing from the swings, up past the poles from which they hung. "Fly to the sun," Sara called after him as William reached his hands out wide. "Take it, my son," she called as at the top of his flight she thought she saw him smile, then wondered if it was a smile and saw, as he began to descend, either the wind or some unpredictable movement of his own shift him from the path he had traveled up— that path she had so carefully chosen to bring him safely down. "No!" she screamed, seeing what would happen, what she could not prevent from happening. "No!" she wailed, looking up, thrusting up her arms. There was no way to catch him now, the horizontal pole was in her way. William was off course. He was falling between two suns. "No!" she screamed.

The sun at his back, the sun's icy reflection glaring up at him from the metal pole directly in his path.

Sara leaped on a swing to cushion his fall but William's throat hit the pole with hardly a sound, and with an acrobat's eerie grace he bounced away out of reach and fell amid streamers dropping like dead leaves to the ground.

Sara fell to her knees by his side. She dug her nails into the earth and covered his body with her own.

Low in the west, the sun began its slow descent.

XIV

Flat white walls, steady lights, blinds pulled to even lengths. Arms stretched out on wooden table, two parallel lines. The clay in her hands, formless still, is worked through her fingers, shaped into a ball, softened with water and worked through. Shaped and softened and worked through.

My name is Frieda, Sara.

"Your fingers take to that clay as though they know what they're doing."

Shaped and softened and worked through.

Dead white walls, blind windows crossed with screens, shadows sliding through, becoming visions on the walls.

"Easy, Sara. Try to sleep."

Screams of sleep. Stabs of sleep. Violent images killing sleep.

"She'll come out of it? She'll be all right?"

"Yes she will. Sure she will."

Sleep slashed by voices. Words splattered like black drippings on a white wall.

"The coroner's inquest?"

"Out of the question. Look for yourself."

"Hysteria."

"No. Shock."

"Sara . . . Sara. She'll pull through?"

"Sure she will. Sure."

Light filtering through her eyes. Air currents shifting on her face. A fullness in the room. Bodies. Breath.

"Psychotic."

"No, Dr. Richardson."

"Prepsychotic."

"No, I think not."

A woman's voice. A woman saying no to Harry?

My name is Frieda, Sara.

"You've been excused from the coroner's inquest. You will stay here for a while. Work with me."

Clay running like water through her fingers. Running like life away from her. Tears running down her face, an endless, soundless stream.

"Just the two of us. No amphetamines. No crutches."

Empty dead white walls. Crocuses on the windowsill, potted tulips by the bed.

"You and I will work together."

Flashes of flowers, sycamores and chestnut trees, a fury of roses. Painted clowns, floating streamers, gleaming metal, a blinding glare. An immense and violent glare.

Voices by her head.

"Temporary drug-induced psychotic state. All psychotic symptoms disappeared completely within the first week."

"But reintroduce the amphetamines . . ."

"We have no intention of doing that. Have we, Sara?"

Have we, Sara? My name is Frieda, Sara.

"The amphetamines produced a transitory toxic psychosis."

"The possibility of recurrence . . ."

"Not so long as the drug is withheld. I am not treating the psychosis, Dr. Richardson. At this moment there is none. I am treating the dependency which led to abuse of the drug in the first place."

A woman who could say no to Harry.

The door opening and closing on a sound like rubber. Tears running down her face. Soundlessly, endlessly running.

"I want to die. I deserve to die."

"I'm not going to let you die."

"If you won't help me, Harry will. Get me Harry. Harry has what I need."

"I'm going to help you now, Sara."

My name is Frieda, Sara.

"Dr. Frieda Goffmann has a fine international reputation. She began the detoxification program in this hospital twenty-five years ago. You're in good hands, Sara. I want only the best for you. But you must cooperate."

Harry sitting by the bed. Nothing to do. No medical journals in his hands, no articles to read or write. Empty-handed. Fine, long fingers, skilled fingers, unemployed. Fingers twitching on the chair. *Cooperate. Only the best.* Fingers fluttering in his lap.

"The children are well. They send their love. I have a woman looking after them."

A woman in her house, looking after her children. One, two, three, four children. All hers. All of them. All four. A woman with four children. The mother of four. Four little lives running after her. Four hearts, four psyches. Running. Running after, pursuing her. Someone else looking after them now. Tucking them in. Running after. Finding Elsie. Where was Elsie? Elsie's gone. Elsie's lost. Would she ever be found again? Would her children ever want to see her again? Her children. Green eyes, defiant stance. Waves of hatred. Waves of fear. Running her down. Covering her over. Had she done that? Had she made them afraid? Had she made them hate?

"Give them to me, Harry. Give them back."

Harry's slender fingers twitched in his lap.

"Help me. Please."

"It's out of my hands now."

"Please, Harry."

"Dr. Goffmann's in charge of your case now."

Harry was gone. *Your case.* Frieda was by the bed.

"Just one. Just one to get up on." Sara was remembering how to be crafty, how to lie, to cheat. "Just one." It was coming back to her now. "Just one and I'll talk to you." It was all coming back. "I'll tell you anything you want to know. I'll cooperate."

"That isn't what you need."

"Get me Harry. Harry will help me."

"I'm going to help you now, Sara."

"Leave me alone, why don't you? Just let me die."

This woman before her. This doctor. A doctor in a clean white coat. What could she know about it?

"Go away and leave me alone."

This short, dark woman with stubby fingers. This woman who keeps repeating the word sure. *Sure*. *Sure*. Drawing out the vowel sound as if there were several.

"Go away. I'm not like you."

"Sure you are, Sara."

She closes her eyes. The woman is gone. She opens them, the woman reappears. Another day, another evening. Day or night the room is white. The white coat by her bed. The deep, reassuring voice. *Sure*. *Sure*.

The woman's hands are clean. Clean and useful. Productive hands. Hands engaged in life. Not like Sara's. Not dangerous. Not evil hands.

"Leave me alone and let me die. I don't want to live. I'm not like you. I'm not like anyone anymore."

"Sure you are, Sara. A woman like me. Look. We have the same form. We breathe the same air. Sure you are."

No. She wasn't human. She bore only a superficial resemblance to this woman who came every day in her white coat. Only outwardly were they related. Within, she was cast off. Isolated. There was no world, no corner of the earth to receive her.

White room. White dresser. White bed. White walls. Clean. White. Normal. A normal world. Not hers. No part of it hers.

The sun invades the room. Attacks her eyes, daring her to open them. She will not open her eyes, not look at the sun again.

Sunlight like lazer beams zoned on closed eyes. Like fire inside her eyes. She looks into her scorched, red eyelids. Burning like fire, red as blood. A dangerous and bleeding sun.

"How long have I been here?"

"Eight days. You slept through most of them. Now we begin to work."

181

The whiteness of the room is stark, hostile. Its cleanliness accuses her. Daring confrontation. This isn't her room. Not her house. She doesn't belong here. She sits in a corner of the bed, pulls the white flannel sheet around her. The room accuses her. Its whiteness, its normality accuse her.

Each day Sara opens her eyes onto the clean, white room. Meals are brought in, trays removed. Frieda comes and goes. Harry comes at night, his fingers flutter in his lap. The clay is squeezed through her fingers, shaped into a ball.

Life within these white walls proceeds in an orderly fashion. She is an alien in this room. An outcast. Nothing in her life will ever be normal again.

"Tell me about it, Sara."

"I can't."

"Sure you can. Try."

She is not human. She is an affront to this room. An insult to its purposes. Its white lines repulse her. She stands outside everything normal, everything human. All rooms are closed to her now. The rooms of her own house will never receive her again.

"What are you thinking?"

"Nothing."

No thoughts. No words. No memories. Crucial to keep the sun's image black. To keep memory stifled.

Reaching out, nothing in this room responds to her gesture. Crying out, her voice is neither absorbed by the room's furniture nor bounced back off its walls.

"I'm here, Sara. I'm listening."

The room repudiates her. Any room in which she might now seek refuge is closed to her forever.

Tears running down her face. Tears running in her heart.

"All right, Sara. That's enough for today. We'll talk again tomorrow."

All rooms forever closed to her.

Even the rooms of her own house where her children—her four, no three, no four, it must be four!—where four children sleep . . . the rooms where they hang their clothes and wash their faces, the rooms where they sleep and eat and play, the rooms through which they walk touching the walls with their hands . . . closed to her now forever.

Clay running like tears through her fingers. Clay caught in her hands, molded into shape.

"It's coming along, Sara. It's gaining a form."

In the mornings, the sun glittering on glass invades the room. Invades her heart. She will not look at it. The light casts its blade through her heart and she turns her face to the wall.

In the evenings, Harry comes and sits empty-handed by the bed. He talks of the children, says their names. There is one name missing. One name he doesn't say. Sara hears that name in every word he utters. That name and no other fills her ears as Harry speaks. Only that word. Only that name. In everything he says. In every word he speaks.

Now Harry has something to do. Suddenly his hands are no longer empty. They are carrying drawings, drawings from Sam. They are carrying letters, letters from strangers. One or two letters at first, more the next evening, more after that. Letters from people Sara has never heard of. Letters speaking to her, addressing her as if she and these strangers shared a common world.

Each night Harry hands her the drawings from Sam. They are signed 'love.' 'Love, Sam.' 'To mommy, love Sam.'

Each night Harry's fingers fly to the letters. His lips read words of support. His eyes glisten as he reads.

These letters addressed to her, addressed to Harry. *In your hour of great need.... Whatever comfort I might offer. ...* Strangers offering comfort. Telling her she is not alone.

Having suffered a similar tragedy, I am writing to say ... Voices from around the country. From people who had survived.

Night after night, the words grow clearer. Sara allows herself to hear. *With God's help.... Trust in Him.... Strength from within. ...*

"How do they know?"

"The papers. Things get out."

"Papers. Publicity. That's what you always feared."

Harry was sitting here in the room with her. Harry was reading these letters to her.

"How have you managed?"

"I lost a few patients, gained a few."

That's not what she meant. She wasn't talking about his practice. She let it go. She listened to the letters Harry brought.

Night after night, Harry read the letters. Sara listened quietly while he read. When Harry was finished, he leaned back in his chair, let the letters fall onto his knees.

"I never expected this," he said. "It's simply astonishing."

Letters of condolence, of understanding. They came from ordinary citizens and from inside prisons. They came from drug addicts and alcoholics, from murderers and child molesters, from women who had aborted their children, from men who had abandoned or massacred their families. Letters offering support where support could not be expected. Letters speaking of courage and of life continuing.

But how could she have courage or go on in life when he was not, when her baby was not? How was that possible? How was that to be expected?

There must be other letters, Sara knew. Hate mail, letters from people who found her, as she found herself, beyond redemption. But Harry didn't read her those. He read personal testimony to hope wrested from hopelessness, to life ending and beginning again, to meaning found in volunteer work and in nature and in acceptance of one's fate. One man serving three consecutive life sentences for stabbing to death his wife and two small children enclosed with his letter samples of inspirational verse. Others wrote of changing their lives through diet, by renouncing beef and alcohol, or by taking cures, recovering from breakdowns, repeating mantras, considering the needy or devoting themselves to the church. They reminded Sara of her duty to herself and to her other children.

Sara listened to Harry read. She watched his hands tremble and his eyes fill as he finished reading and let the letters fall onto his knees.

"He finds them comforting," she told Frieda. "I listen for his sake. I don't know what else to do. He pours over them. He seems so moved by them. Letters from strangers. From people he doesn't even know."

"Sure." Frieda nodded. "Voices from a distance are often easier to hear."

"I listen because he wants me to. What else can I do? There's so little anyone can do for Harry."

* * *

"Help me, Harry."

"I don't know how. I never did with you. All those people coming to me for help. Some of them right off the street. They saw my name on the door, walked in. Right off the street. And I knew what to do. But not for you. Never for you."

Clay on her hands, caked like mud beneath her finger-nails. Molding, squeezing, gauging out. Shaping a contour, firming a line, smoothing it over. Her fingers ache with fatigue. It isn't right. She smashes it down on the wooden table, picks it up, smashes it down again.

"It's hard. Sure. You're out of practice. Give it time."

June 21. The first day of summer, the longest day of the year.

"Let's fix you up. Your hair needs washing."

People shouldn't be made to look at her. She wasn't human. She didn't deserve to live. If they'd leave her alone, put a tray on the floor outside her door, she'd stay in her room where she needn't be seen.

"You're going to have a shower and wash your hair."

Rushing, pounding water, its driving force on her skin reminiscent of torrential rains and waterfalls and inner longings and all the energetic forces of nature outside herself—pow-erful, living forces, dead to her now forever. She stood in the shower and wept.

Frieda brought a towel and began to dry her hair.

"I can do it," Sara said.

"Sure. But I like to help."

Frieda's fingers worked vigorously on her head, drying her hair, massaging her scalp, causing it to tingle like a frozen limb precariously coming back to life.

"How can you bear to touch me? Don't you feel horror?"

The next evening, for the first time Sara asked Harry directly about the children. Had they grown? Were they eating? Were they getting enough sleep?

185

"Mrs. Landon's taking good care of them," he answered.

"But how are they really?" Sara persisted. "How do they feel? How are they acting? Does Sam cry at night? Is Julia eating properly?"

Would they ever want to see her again, she meant. And could she bring herself to face them, to reenter that house, go back into its rooms, his room, again as if nothing had happened. *It will never be as if nothing had happened.*

"They ask about you every day," Harry said. "They send their love. Sam sends his drawings. They need you, Sara. You've got to get strong enough to go home to them."

"Will I ever go home?"

I want to die.

It will be much harder to live.

"Of course you will. The lawyers say . . . but never mind that now. There's plenty of time before we have to face that. As soon as Frieda gives the word, you'll be released in my care."

Harry reached in his pockets, pulled out some letters.

"No, Harry. Please," Sara said. "No letters tonight. Tell me about the children."

"They're doing fine. Really they are. Don't worry about them, Sara."

"Of course I worry. How can I not worry? Tell me how they are."

"They're all right."

"Just all right?"

"Well, they're bound to be disturbed, of course, but they're handling it."

"Disturbed?" Sara jumped on the word. "What do you mean disturbed? What are they doing?"

"Not disturbed, exactly. But upset."

"Upset?"

"That's natural, Sara. They'll be all right. They're strong kids. They'll pull through."

"But how upset? How are they acting? What are they doing?"

"Nothing very different. Nothing to worry about. Please, Sara. I don't want you to worry. They're a little quieter, that's all. Subdued, you might say. But that's to be expected."

Sara nodded and turned away. Her children subdued. She

didn't want to think of it. Her children damaged, their young hearts scarred. She pushed the image from her mind.

"You don't have to worry about them. I know those kids. They'll be all right."

Upset, subdued. Her children disturbed. She couldn't bear to hear it.

"What's important is for you to get back on your feet now."

White discs sliding through the sky. Painted clowns, colored streamers, a pastel fairyland.

"Justin has really begun to pull himself together these last couple of weeks. He's still at the garage, of course, but not so much. And when he's home he sticks pretty close to Sam. He's showing a real sense of responsibility there."

Blue sky, bright sun. Cake and champagne out in the yard.

"I never minded his job, you know. It was the time it took away from his studies. I think he understands that now. I think he's going to do better in school next year."

White shirt, white pants. Birthday boy all dressed in white.

"And Julia's taken a sudden interest in my practice. Runs out to the car when I get home, wants to hear everything I've done all day."

Everything the way it was. Everything all right.

"All the clinical details. And I mean everything. A blow by blow account from the minute I leave her to the minute I get back."

Just as they were. Just as he was. William laughing in his chair. William waiting for her at home. Everything the way it was.

"She's particularly interested in Mrs. Kaplan's sciatica. Her current theory is that it's not sciatica at all but a slipped disc. Wants me to refer her to a surgeon. Exactly what I'm going to do, too, if she doesn't start showing some improvement soon."

White discs in the sky, colored streamers in the air, Julia's hair catching the wind.

"Sara, believe me. They'll be all right."

No blinding glare. No violent light.

"My daughter the doctor. Wouldn't that be something?

It's never what you expect. I always hoped Justin . . . Sara, are you all right?"

Harry and Julia in the sun, walking side by side across the yard. Just as it was. Everything back the way it was.

"Sara? Can I get you something?"

Children's voices, children's laughter. Playing frisbee with the paper plates.

"Do you want some water? Do you want me to stop? Maybe I shouldn't talk about them."

Her children. Her four children. Healthy, happy children. All of them. All four. Just as they were. No glaring sun. No immense and violent glare.

"Sara, tell me what you want. Tell me what to do."

"Julia's truly his favorite child," Sara told Frieda a few days later. "He never fights with her the way he does with Justin, never seems the least disappointed in her. She can simply be. And he adores her. The way he looks at her, talks to her . . . and she doesn't have to do a thing." Abruptly Sara stopped. "That must sound awful. I feel so ashamed. Jealous of my own daughter."

"Not of her," Frieda answered. "But of her relationship with Harry, perhaps. From what you've told me, you always longed to feel close to your own father but never did. I call that sad, not shameful. Your father's company preoccupied him just as medicine preoccupies Harry. Yet when Harry gets home the one person he finds time for is Julia."

Julia running to the gate. *Daddy's home!* Harry and Julia arm in arm. The sun on their faces, their eyes on one another. *That autograph you wanted.* Adoring eyes. *Oh daddy, you remembered!* Julia at the door. Shining green eyes. Eyes like jade in the dark. Like daggers in the night. Julia's scream. Crystal pure. Her eyes, her scream. *Daddy! Stop her, stop her!* That look of horror on her face. That fear disfiguring her daughter's perfect face.

"I never wanted to be like that," Sara said. "I never wanted to frighten them."

"We have a lot of work still to do."

Speeding cars, flashing knives, metal brilliant in the sun.

"I didn't mean it. I never meant it."

"Tell me about it, Sara."

She shook her head. "There's nothing to tell. Nothing happened."

Her baby's laugh, the sun in her eyes, his weight as nothing in her hands.

"Try, Sara. It might help."

"There's nothing to tell. Nothing happened. Nothing at all."

The sun at his back, the sun glaring up at him from the metal pole.

"I'll help you, Sara. Trust me."

"Get out of here! Get out! Nothing happened, I say. It didn't happen. It didn't."

Horizontal metal bar shining viciously in the sun.

"No, it's not true. It's not. Nothing happened. Nothing. Just go away. Go on and get out. Get out of here and leave me alone!"

Moment of impact, hardly a sound.

Sounds in the room. Frieda's breath, Frieda's voice.

"You were in a drug-induced psychotic state."

Calm, steady sound of her voice. *Drug-induced. Psychotic state.* Steady, flat rhythm beating a dreadful calmness into her. A calmness like peace. A calmness like death.

"It was a dreadful tragedy, Sara. Not deliberate. Not intentional. A terrible, tragic accident."

Frieda's words, Frieda's strength. Not Sara's, not hers. Nothing within her now but emptiness. A hollow space. No more babies. A living space petrified within. An absence at her center where once a life had been. An absence endlessly present, endlessly gestating. Forever denied deliverance.

"I'll help you, Sara. We'll do it together."

"I want to die."

"It will be much harder for you to live."

"You introduced Sara to amphetamines, is that correct?"

"For weight control. For energy. Only for that. I believe in people achieving all they're capable of achieving. If a substance produces the subjective experience of greater energy, greater strength and well-being—without harmful side effects, of course—I'm all for it. There isn't a drug you can name that doesn't potentially have harmful side effects. I have a good many creative people in my practice, Dr. Goffmann. Well-known artists, politicians . . . busy people doing important things. They must work at top efficiency on very little sleep. Amphetamines increase their efficiency. I don't deny I prescribe them in certain cases. But always with a medical exam and full history first. Nobody ever got a shot in my office without knowing exactly what was in it, what its side effects might be. But Sara . . . and I never injected Sara with anything. . . ."

"No one said you did, Dr. Richardson."

"Sara couldn't handle it. She thought it was more than it is. It's just a drug, a tool. A means possibly, in some cases, to better performance . . . but Sara thought it was the performance itself. She thought it was the answer. She thought. . . . She took more and more. I couldn't stop her. And when she tried to quit, when she crashed. . . . It was horrible. I couldn't stand seeing her suffer like that . . . but I'm not going to be blamed for this!"

"No one's laying blame, Dr. Richardson."

By the end of June, definite features had begun to emerge, a form was being extracted. The clay was taking on a life of its own. Standing back, studying the head, Sara felt the beginnings of satisfaction with her work. An order being imposed on the chaos within. Her will, her power to do that. To make order out of herself. To create herself through her work.

"But is it even possible?" she asked Frieda.

"It takes time."

"How long?"

"As long as it takes."

On the Fourth of July, Jennifer came to visit.

Seeing her friend standing there in a sunflowered dress at the door, her first daytime visitor, such a rush of longing overtook Sara—to be free, to be outside, to be a child again, to have a second chance, to feel the air, to take long walks in the open and breathe in again the smell of trees and grass, to feel the sun on her arms again and to feel in those arms her William once more warm with life. She wanted it all back again the way it was, and had to turn away a moment before she could look directly at the woman at the door and say, "Hello, Jennifer. You look terrific."

"You too, Sara."

Jennifer stepped lightly across the threshold, seemed carried into the room as if on sunbeams and small breezes, and by her presence it was transformed—warmed, humanized, touched here and there with the smell of kitchens, the routine of children, the feel of home, the past and grief. Neither woman spoke while they embraced. And love also entered with her friend, thought Sara, leading Jennifer to a chair.

As she sat, her skirt billowed out, exposing the side of one thigh. Sara's eyes were drawn down the length of her bare leg to her sandaled foot and the dirt between her toes. Dirt brought in from the outside world, acquired by walking down the path from her front door, along the pavement to her car, transported to these sterile surroundings, brought in through locked doors to this white room. Had she been stripped? Had she been searched?

"Doesn't seem right, does it? Me in a room this neat."

"No. It doesn't seem right. Not too bad is it?"

"For a loony bin, you mean?"

"Don't call it that. It's not that. It's just a floor in a hospital."

"The psychiatric floor."

"So what? You'll be out soon anyway, I hear."

"I guess so. If Harry and Frieda have their way. But I'm not sure I'm ready."

"You still haven't seen the kids?"

"No." Sara shook her head. "I can't."

"Well, I know it's hardly the same thing," Jennifer said, quickly reaching for her canvas bag, "but I brought you a substitute." She put both feet up on the table and braced the bag against the back of her knees. "I took it a couple of weeks ago," she said, reaching in and pulling out a large framed picture, holding it up with its back to Sara, "I just got around to enlarging it the other day."

She turned it then and as she did in a movement that seemed at once so real, so live—Sara had to gasp and look away, then quickly back, and seeing there were only three, away once more—Julia and Justin and her little Sam leaped out at her from the photograph. There they stood, a bit too stiffly but real enough to take her breath away, in too-clean clothes, just-ironed shirts, an unfamiliar scarf, her children. Her living children.

"They asked me to take it," Jennifer said. "It's their way of saying hello."

Looking closer, Sara saw they were not at all as she had remembered them. They appeared altered to her. All different, all wrong. Justin seemed miles too tall. Julia looked older. Sam's jeans revealed his socks. He'd never wear them that way. *They call them highwaters, mom.* She'd never thought of Justin's chin as quite so square and what was that around Julia's neck? "I've never seen that scarf before."

"Oh, that's mine," Jennifer said. "Julia admired it and it went so well with that shirt she's wearing I gave it to her."

"Did you?" Sara said. "Thanks." She nodded. She was grateful. But she couldn't quite take it in. "Justin's so . . . and Sam's so . . . and they're all. . . ."

The children stared back at her. They didn't blink or shift their weight from foot to foot. They didn't lick their lips or fidget with their hair. Resolutely they withstood her gaze as Sara's eyes filled with tears.

"They're doing fine," Jennifer said softly. "Really they are, Sara. They're healthy . . . eating well, sleeping. . . . I look in on them every day."

"You do?"

"They're all right. Believe me, they are. They miss you, of course. But they're all right."

They missed her. They were all right. "How could they be? How is that possible?" How could anything ever be all right again?

"Julia says she wants to be the first to visit, and Sam says to ask you to tell Mrs. Landon that he doesn't have to eat brussels sprouts."

Sara smiled at the messages relayed. "Thanks, Jenny," she said.

"Don't be silly. I have a great time with them. You've raised marvelous kids, Sara. We're going to surprise them all tonight and take them to the fireworks."

"Fireworks? You and Harry?"

"And Edward and Peter too. The whole group. It's the Fourth of July, you know."

"Is it? The Fourth of July? Holidays don't mean much around here. One day's pretty much like another. But that means . . . oh, of course," Sara said, just this moment realizing, "school's out." Time was falling into place again. "It's summer vacation. They're home all the time. What do they do with themselves all day?"

Jennifer laughed. "What all kids do in the summer. Loaf, hang around, see their friends. Swim. Ride bikes. Justin's working evenings at the garage. During the day he and Julia sort of take Sam under their combined wings. They're wonderful with him, Sara, really. You'd be proud of them. And Harry's spending a lot more time at home these days. He's got several doctors covering him . . ."

"Thanks, Jenny," Sara said again.

"For what?"

"Everything. For keeping tabs . . . for the photograph."

"Don't mention it: It's the least I could do. Hey, you're looking pretty good."

"Pretty fat you mean?" Sara put her hands to her stomach. "You know how they love to fill you up on bread and potatoes in places like this."

"A couple of pounds, maybe," Jennifer said. "But definitely not fat. And you'll lose it fast as soon as you get home and start running after the kids again, tackling that house and working out in the yard . . ."

Abruptly she stopped. The word seemed to reverberate in the room.

"I'm sorry, Sara."

One word. An image. It was all before her again. Unintentional, cataclysmic. Her world forever changed.

"If only I'd stayed . . ." Jennifer was saying. "I should have stayed."

Death at her hands. Her baby's blood on her hands. Herself set apart forever.

"I saw the state you were in. I should have made you let me stay."

Her friend was beginning to cry. Her friend who had come to see her out of a world changed to Sara forever was beginning to cry. "No, Jenny. You mustn't think that. You

193

couldn't have done anything." Was she still human? Still a person who could comfort a friend? "I wouldn't have let you. You know how crazy I could get. Honestly, Jenny . . ." Sara looked away. "There was nothing anyone could have done." She looked for a place to rest her eyes and found the portrait. "Thanks so much for that . . ." Her Julia and Justin and Sam. "I really love it." The world still left to her. "It brings them close. . . . But they look so young, so little. Are they really all right? Is that woman, that Mrs. what's-her-name, taking good care of them?"

"Mrs. Landon?" Jennifer was drying her eyes. "Yes, she's terrific. Does everything. Floors too. Even windows." Jennifer tried to laugh. "And you know how unusual that is these days."

"But Julia looks so thin. Is she on one of those fad diets again? And where'd she get that . . . oh, yes, you said. . . ." Sara looked up at her friend. "You gave it to her. Thank you, Jenny. Thank you." Jennifer's arms were sunburned. Her cheeks and nose were red.

"They're all pulling for you, Sara. They want you home."

"Do they?"

"Yes they do. We all do."

"But how can they?"

"They love you. They need you."

How could anyone need her again? And wouldn't they be afraid of her now? Wouldn't they shrink from her touch?

"Do they talk about it?" she asked quietly.

"Not to me. Maybe to Harry. They're dealing with it somehow. However children do, they're doing it."

Sara nodded. She would have to accept that. "Frieda wants me to see them. I'm afraid, I guess. . . . That's funny. I'm as afraid of them as I imagine they must be of me."

"You'll know when you're ready," Jennifer said. "Give it time."

Time was all she had.

"Come on," Sara said. "I want to show you something."

She led Jennifer down the corridor to the art room which was open to the patients at any time during the day, but was not formally in use on Sundays and holidays. The room had the aspect of an abandoned gallery. Drawings and watercolors hung from the walls, half-finished paintings were left propped on the backs of easels, and clay forms in various stages of evolution sat on the tables draped with wet towels as if to keep their identities secret. It was to one of these that Sara went upon entering the room and quickly snatched away the towel. As she did, she heard behind her Jennifer's small, sharp intake of breath.

"Oh, Sara . . . that's so good. It's really good. I had no idea . . . I mean, I always knew you were good, of course . . . but those were little animals and pots . . . and this . . . not that they weren't good . . . but this . . . nothing like this. I can hardly believe it, it's so like you. . . ."

"It's not nearly finished yet."

"No, I see that. But even so. . . ." Jennifer was walking around the head, examining it from every angle. ". . . even at this stage . . . it's so lifelike . . . and the resemblance . . . especially around the eyes. . . ."

"I've been working on it a little every day."

"Has Harry seen it?"

"Not yet. Not till it's finished."

"Well, it's wonderful, Sara. Really wonderful. You've got to keep it up when you get home. You will, won't you? You'll go on with it?"

"Yes, I really think I will now. If I can. I want to anyway. It feels so good doing it . . . just physically, you know . . . molding something in my hands. I always liked the feel of that."

They went back to Sara's room and talked of other things then. Peter would be going to camp for the month of August. Jennifer's pictures were beginning to sell. She and Edward had just about set the date—Labor Day, they thought. That would give Edward's parents enough time to arrange their trip east, they wanted to stop in Chicago on the way to visit the Art Institute.

"And isn't Labor Day as good as any to begin a new life?" Jennifer said.

When Jennifer was ready to go, they stood and silently moved into each other's arms. Holding her friend, feeling herself held in return—this was not a doctor, Sara thought, not a therapist whom she might never see again once their work was finished, but a friend, a woman and also a mother, a neighbor and fellow human being like all those others with whom she would have to live if she lived at all.

"Come home soon," Jennifer said and Sara nodded, feeling her friend's thin, lovely, sunburned arms around her shoring her up for life. Willingly, Sara leaned into them, for truly she had no other choice. Her three remaining children called to her. Some response awakened by her friend, something yet to be reached with Harry joined the call and Sara was bound to answer. If only . . . If only . . . she wanted to say and could not and began instead to sob, for what she wanted to say was if only things had been different, if only she had been different, if only it had never happened, if only now that it had she could reverse it and bring him back to life again, if only her grief were strong enough for that. If only the strength she was just beginning to find for herself could be used instead for him.

Jennifer held her while she cried and when at last Sara looked up, she saw she had not been crying alone. They both smiled then and wiped at their eyes and laughed a little, nodding their heads in a series of quick universal assents, and walking to the door in tears and laughter and with a sense almost of triumph for having resolved something between them, they said goodbye.

"But why, Sara?" Frieda asked.

William sat just out of reach. He sprang to a branch of a tree. She raised her arms to him. He jumped away.

"Why did you smash it?"

She stretched out her arms, he sprang to a higher branch.

"Why, Sara? For what reason?"

She reached for him, he moved further up the tree.

"William," she said. "My William. My baby. Oh, William, my William, my baby, my William."

"Will smashing the head bring him back? And just when you were making such progress. Not only with it but in our work here. Gaining insight, clarity. You've been off the drug six weeks now. For the first time in years you're completely drug-free. You were learning to use your talent, not paralyze it with drugs."

"How can I live with it? How? You tell me how. You've got all the answers."

"You're a strong, creative woman. That's what has always kept you going. Even when you were so heavily dependent on drugs, you got things done, you functioned. You never gave up. Don't give up now, Sara."

"How can I live with what I've done?"

"Raising those children, keeping that house, that took tremendous strength the way you were feeling. It's that strength you and I have been drawing on here. Sure it's hard. But you have the courage. You've always been a fighter, don't stop now."

No, she couldn't do it. She couldn't live with what she'd done. And yet she was. She was enduring it. She was surviving. She was living here in this world. Inside this hospital she was going on. She could look outside and see the clouds moving across the sky, the trees swaying with the full greenness of summer in their branches, the sun reflected on the duck pond just below her window in the afternoon. She could watch night falling, stars appearing, and know the world was going on. She was going on with it. She was enduring it.

Sara's sobs came from a place so deep inside her, it was out of reach. Frieda sat silently facing her while she wept.

"I will have to go home again, won't I? I will have to be a mother again."

The clay in her hands, beginning again. Hard, resistant. Working against her, resisting her. She plunges her fingers into the formless lump of clay, closes them over the solid, gray mass. She forces the mass through her fingers. Softens and squeezes and forces it through. Again and again. Resolutely imposing order. Willing it into shape. Again. And again. Again and again. And again.

"Speed made me better. Smarter. Quicker. Nothing could hurt me then."

"Go on."

"Nothing could get to me."

"You mean you couldn't feel it."

"Isn't that the same thing?"

"Poor sexual adjustment is common among amphetamine addicts."

"I never felt much of anything with Harry."

"Do you think that could change?"

"I don't think he's interested any more."

"He's here every evening."

"He has to be. It's expected."

"You sure that's all it is?"

"What else?"

"Everything you've told me about Harry . . . how much his practice means to him, his concern for his patients . . . you seem to see it only as power . . . his need to exert control."

"What else could it be?"

Clay in her hands, splattered on her wrists, caked like mud beneath her fingernails. The strength in her fingers making itself felt. Her hands taking hold, working themselves into the clay. Her fingers shaping, molding. Her vision slowly coming through, her form emerging.

Waiting for Harry in the evening, the thought came back to Sara as it had been coming and going all day, that it was exactly two months since William's death. Two hours, two days, a week, three weeks, a month. He would have been a month older, six weeks older, two months. The thought had never entirely left her since she'd entered the hospital. The world going on outside, herself going on, without him. People in motion, walking up and down corridors, opening and closing doors, wheeling carts in and out of rooms greeting one another in the morning, eating lunch, waving goodbye, going out the door. William never moving again, never laughing or crying, never growing older. A year and two months he would have been today. Would never be.

Like something trapped and fluttering in her mind—now at the forefront, now at the back, crossing it with shadows as it passed—that thought presented itself to Sara as she waited in her room for Harry. Not for himself alone, but for the world he brought in with him—news of the children especially, what they were doing, what they talked about, what messages they sent for her, how they looked, how they were getting along, any hope she could hear in his voice of reuniting herself with them.

Two months ago her world was different. She had a world then to which she belonged.

"Did you have much trouble getting here?" she asked the minute Harry arrived. "It's Friday night. Was the traffic bad?"

Reports on the traffic, the weather, the car, how his was running, what was being done with hers, were items of absorbing interest to Sara. News of Mrs. Kaplan's sciatica, the condition of his other patients, even the letters Harry continued to bring, conveyed to her ways in which the world continued, grew and changed even as she stood aside, progressed beyond her. In letters, books and magazines, in flowers and newspapers and word of the children, Harry carried the world in to her. He put it down on the tables, arranged it on the windowsills of her room. He put it into words and aimed them gently in her direction. He read her the words of others and gradually, as the very air in the room filled with the anguished and often inarticulate cries of strangers, anonymous voices of the world, Sara slowly began to hear her own voice among them. And Harry's voice, too, as he read became one with theirs, joined in human compassion—yet it also stood apart, particularized, the voice of this particular man sitting here appealing to her. Harry had changed. Nothing whatever was different about him, yet he had changed. There he sat before her, the same and yet different.

The walls of Sara's room were covered now with drawings Sam sent every night. Jennifer's photograph hung in the center. *I want you to see them*, Frieda had said. She wasn't ready, Sara had answered. *You're readier than you think.* "To mommy, with love," was scrawled on each of Sam's drawings. They loved her, they made Harry tell her, they wanted her home. But how could they? How was that possible? Wasn't it hate they really felt? *For the addiction. The consequences. Not for you. The addiction is finished. You're not the same person you were.* Was she sure? *Sure.* Would it last? How long would it take? They would work together every day, Frieda said. Even after Sara went home. Every day. *For as long as it takes*.

Harry's voice, the scent of his cologne, the way he walked around the room or sat in the chair, his shirt rumpled from driving in the heat, the smell of sweat and night air on his clothes, the humidity curling his hair brought the world into Sara and with memories of that voice, that smell, that walk, those clothes in other rooms, herself with them in other settings, came again the longing to believe Frieda was right, to see herself once more transposed.

"You really love medicine, don't you?" she said suddenly, unaccountably struck by the fact of Harry's dedication as she looked at him seated in the chair.

"What do you mean?"

"I mean all your research, your writing, the hours you spend at the office, even at home reading, finding out about new drugs, new treatments . . . my father was the same way about his company, immersing himself in financial reports, comparative studies of policy and structure . . . I always hated all that. . . . Sara paused, feeling a wave of insupportable loneliness sweep through her, both her father's absence and Harry's taking hold in a new way then, and she remembered how excluded she had always felt by both of them, how jealous of what they loved.

"You really love it, don't you?" she continued. "All those facts, the research, the new drugs . . . you love knowing about them. Love them for existing, for being there in the world where they can help people . . . and if they're not known yet, you love them for the possibility of being discovered . . . if not today, tomorrow, or next year or by the end of the decade . . . that's why you can never stop, isn't it? Always the possibility of new treatments, new discoveries. . . . Oh, I'm sorry, Harry. I know all this is obvious to you, but to me it seems like a revelation."

"What does?"

"The love involved in what you do."

Loneliness welled up again inside her, bringing tears to Sara's eyes. Loneliness not only for the world, its endless commotion and possibilities for change, but for Harry, too, and not only for the man serving these evenings as an agent for the world, but for the man himself, she felt, for that part of Harry she had never allowed herself to know.

"You never quite believed in your own success, did you?" she asked, all at once knowing it to be true. "At any moment you felt it could be snatched away. That's why you had to keep constantly alert, constantly one step ahead of everyone else."

"I'm not much good at failure," Harry said. "When a patient dies, I want to leave the room."

"And you saw me as your one live-in failure, didn't you?" Sara asked. "That's why you were so afraid of letting anything leak out about me."

"I suppose," Harry said, raising his shoulders, dropping them heavily. "I don't know."

"You don't know," Sara repeated and leaned forward and touched his hand. "I was always afraid of hearing you say that. It doesn't sound so frightening any more."

On the day of Julia's visit, which had been arranged for the second Monday in August, Frieda was helping Sara with her hair.

"See how it goes with Julia first," Frieda said. "Then she can bring Justin and Sam back with her another day. There. . . ." Frieda stopped and lifted the comb. "How's that?"

Sara looked at herself in the glass. She was older, the flesh on her face seemed to sag. All around the eyes, the color of her skin had changed. Thin and brownish, it seemed to ring her eyes with sorrow. The eyes themselves looked out at her with a kind of faded yellow light as if their former color—the rich, dark brown she remembered she had loved—had bled slowly outward into grief for what was gone and never would come again.

"I don't know," Sara said, looking at her hair. "Maybe I should have colored it. It's so gray in front. I don't want to frighten her."

"That's always been your fear with Julia, hasn't it?"

"Tell me something, Frieda," Sara said, turning around, taking her arm. "Not as a doctor. But as a woman, as a mother . . . Can you ever forgive me?"

"You don't need my forgiveness."

"Can you accept what I've done?"

"What's important is for you to accept it."

"No, I don't mean that. You have children of your own. Grandchildren. Babies. Would you trust me with them?"

"Sure."

"Would you let me hold them? Would you trust my hands on them?"

"Sure."

"Sure. Sure. You always say that. How do I know you mean it?"

"I don't say things I don't mean."

"Don't talk to me like that, like Harry would," Sara shouted, making fists with her hands. "Be straight with me, Frieda. I've worked very hard to be straight with you."

"What is it you want to know?"

So many questions rushed at Sara then. Could she be trusted . . . would she go back to the way she was, back to speed? Frieda had given her the recidivism rate on that, it was not encouraging. Could she live again among human beings? Could she live at all? Would her children ever feel anything but horror toward her again? Sara raised her arms helplessly, let them fall to her sides. As if responding to the anguish she felt but could not articulate, Frieda began to reply.

"William was the child still closest to you," she said gently. "In a physical sense, and perhaps in others as well. He had been out of your body for only a year. He was the most vulnerable part of yourself. The separation was hardly complete," she explained slowly, softly. "You weren't sure where you ended and William began. You said you could read his thoughts and that he knew what you were thinking too. When you threw him toward the sun, in your mind you were tossing him toward a fuller, more passionate life. Not death. In the irrational, drugged state you were in, you believed you were saving him. From yourself. Now you must save yourself. I will do everything I can to help you." Frieda was staring straight into her eyes. "I care for you, Sara. And not only as a doctor."

Sara's arms reached out for Frieda then and Frieda's opened to receive her as they heard a knock on the door and Sara, still reaching for Frieda, turned toward the door and saw on its threshold an unimaginably beautiful fair-haired young woman whom she recognized not at all and in the same instant, utterly. Passing before her in a matter of seconds as in accelerated films plant cycles complete themselves, she saw the child's purple face at birth, saw the first tooth come in, the first lost, she saw her in her crib, then walking, running, laughing, she remembered in a flash all the injuries that befell her, the scraped knees, cut lips, bloody elbows, she remembered the feel of chubby arms and legs wrapped around her, the sensation of lightness and loss as the limbs lengthened out and grew slender, she recalled the little girl breaking into a smile and running to meet her father, losing something of her hesitancy and that tentative look of infancy along the way, she remembered how gradually she had acquired a strength and assertion of her own, that new, clear gaze she now possessed, not her mother's or father's—although taking something from each—but altogether her own, distinctive now and almost all the way out of childhood, as Julia looked back at her from where she stood and seemed to say, it's all right, mom, I have come through. Sara took the arms that were raised to Frieda and swung them around toward this amazing girl to whom she had given life. Her arms stretched out and quivered there on the air and faltered finally and fell to her sides.

"Hi, mom."

"Hello, Julia."

"You look good."

"You too. You look marvelous. You've grown. You're taller."

"Hey, your hair's longer. It looks great and you're . . ."

"Fatter? I know. I'll lose it."

They laughed.

"No, I didn't mean that."

Somewhere in the midst of their greeting, Frieda slipped out the door.

"It's a nice room," Julia said, coming in and looking around. "Sunny. Bright. And oh, great . . . you've put them up." She went over to examine Sam's drawings on the wall. "You know what this one's supposed to be?" she asked, pointing to one in the middle. "You'll never guess."

"A field of flowers?"

"Nope, that's what I thought too. Sam was furious. Look again."

Sara studied the drawing. "Looks like flowers to me."

"Those things you think are flowers are actually invading spaceships," Julia explained. "And you know why the sky is green?" She tossed her head and laughed. "Outer space invasion turns it green."

Her daughter's golden laugh.

"Sam told you that?" More precious than any jewel on earth to hear it again.

Julia nodded. "Yup," she said. "He's got quite an imagination."

Her fine shining hair brushing her shoulders.

"How is he, darling? How are all of you?"

Were they eating enough, were they getting enough sleep? Sara asked all the questions she had to ask. Were they getting on with Mrs. Landon, was she taking care of them?

"Justin and I pretty much take care of ourselves."

"Oh, I know you do. Of course you do . . . I only meant . . ."

"We miss you, mom. When are you coming home?"

Home. Her daughter wanted her home.

"Well, Frieda says . . ."

"Frieda? She's your doctor, right? Daddy told me all about her."

Her daughter's clear, green eyes. Her sweet voice.

"I might be a doctor too. Been thinking about it a lot lately. Or a photographer. Jennifer's been showing me stuff. Don't you just love that picture?" She pointed to Jennifer's photograph on the wall. "She's been teaching me about lighting and composition . . ."

"Jennifer has?"

"Yes and about using the dark room, too. She's been great, mom, really. She comes over all the time, takes us for drives and out to the lake."

Jennifer. Rational and reliable. The ideal mother.

"She's been a great help to daddy too and Sam adores her."

"Adores her. Sam does?"

"Yes. He's even letting her teach him to swim."

Little Sam swimming. He'd cried so when she tried. He'd been so afraid.

"He's doing great, mom. You should see him dogpaddle."

Her baby paddling in the water. Her baby lying on the ground. Her only baby now.

Sara turned away. Was it as she had feared? Had she made them afraid? Of water, of life? Quickly she turned back. Her only girl. Had she made her afraid of becoming a woman? "I've changed, Julia," she said.

"I know you have."

"No. I mean it. I really have."

"I know. Daddy told me. You've stopped using." Nervously, Julia tried to laugh, like old times relying on jokes for support. "You've kicked the habit again."

"Not again, Julia. For good."

"Really?"

"Yes. Really. I mean it."

"That's great then. Congratulations. But you know if the FDA has its way, you won't have any choice. An outright ban on prescriptions of amphetamines for weight control is in the works. Daddy better watch it if that happens. He could be in a lot of trouble."

"I don't mean just the speed, Julia. I've changed in other ways too. I'm working awfully hard. I'm going to be different."

Sara saw it happen then. Like a veil from her daughter's face, the jokes were dropped, the screen of news events abandoned.

"How do I know that?" Julia asked sharply, adolescent anger and fear rising like a blush up from her throat. "How do I know you won't go back to the way you were before?"

Mother and daughter facing one another. Nothing between them now but blood.

"How do I know?"

Sara reached out to touch her, pulled back. Had she lost that right forever?

"Tell me, mom. How do I know?"

Where could she begin? How could she start to make her understand?

"You have every reason not to trust me," Sara said finally, her hands hanging by her sides. "Oh, but Julia, if you could give me a chance . . . it's going to take a long time and I'll need a lot of help, but, darling, if you thought you possibly could. . . ." Sara reached up then and put her hands on the

205

sides of Julia's head and looked into her daughter's splendid face. "I'll show you it's true, I promise. When something this terrible happens, you have to make a choice. Either you're going to die or you're going to live. And if you choose to live, you have to do things differently. Whatever happens, Julia, at the trial, or afterwards, I'm going to live. I'm going to be a good mother to you if you'll let me. To all of you. I love you all. I've always loved you all. I never meant anything but that. Never anything but that. . . . Help me now, Julia. Trust me. Be kind, if you can. You were always so kind and gentle with William."

Julia's whole body winced then as the sound of his name acted like a whip's lash on bare skin.

"And if there's any way that you possibly can," Sara continued softly, pressing her lips into her daughter's hair, drawing in the sweet fragrance like strength, "forgive me. I know how you loved him."

Julia began to weep then and Sara held her while she cried, experiencing again what she had thought she'd lost forever—the joy, the awesome responsibility of holding a child in her arms.

When finally Julia's sobs abated and, appearing to draw a new strength from her tears, she gradually composed herself and lifted her head, Sara, looking into those lovely wet green eyes, saw in a sudden flood of understanding that Julia, the child most like herself, had been the first to forgive and was now the first to offer support.

"Daddy's very optimistic," Julia said after a moment, wiping her eyes and going on in a rapid burst of talk.

"He's got the best lawyers in the city. They're preparing a really strong defense. . . ."

Sara could hear Harry's voice as Julia spoke . . . *preparing a strong defense . . . the best in the city* . . . Harry always had the best of everything.

". . . and the progress you've shown here . . . your rehabilitation, as it's called . . . it's all in your favor and daddy says with continued treatment they're almost sure of a suspended sentence . . . it wasn't intentional . . . no intent . . . you know, or even to cause bodily harm and that counts a lot in the law."

Sara took her in her arms again and held her. Her daughter

who knew all about drugs, now knew all about the law as well. So many things she wished she didn't know and Sara tried to explain to her that she'd never meant to frighten them or harm any one of them in any way. She'd never meant to show them anything but love. But her life had got away from her, she said. Somewhere along the line she'd lost control. She'd get it back, she promised. She'd do whatever she had to now to get it back.

Sara took Julia then and showed her the head she was working on and while Julia was examining it—bending down with her face close to the clay—Sara saw how it had gone beyond even what it was she thought she had intended. Not a self-portrait only, but capturing too something of her daughter's features—she saw it there in an expression in the mouth, the eyes, as Julia shifted her gaze—and Justin's, too, and Sam's, the clay incorporated them all. And one other as well. His face, too, small and still, embedded there with the rest.

Even after Julia had gone, a magical glow like the best high she'd ever been on hung in the air. Inside and outside, life was returning to her now. She could not shake it loose. It was filling her blood, her muscles. It was calling to her with her children's voices. For them, for herself, her obligation was to yield to life, to return to it as fully as she might.

Sara would be going home in a few days. This would be one of her last nights in a single room, a single bed. She was nearly forty years old. Her hair was partially gray. She was in many ways a different woman now and she was beginning to be able to envision, played out against the darkness of her room, a future for herself—one holding the possibility for change and even the hope of reaching something real with Harry. The night was her ally, and dreams were more than self-deception, she told herself, lying in bed in the dark.

The simplest route to life lay through her body and lightly, she moved her hands over her skin. Her arms were heavier and her breasts fuller than when she had first come here. The nipple, long unused, was slightly sore to the touch. She thought of babies nursing there, of Harry's lips, but there would be no more babies and whatever physical comfort she was to know she might have to learn to provide for herself.

To live, she thought, was to make her peace with this new and heavier body, to be responsive, to feel. She let herself move beneath her hands. Aroused, her skin began to tingle, the gooseflesh to rise wherever her fingers touched. Arms, chest, ribs, hips, thighs, to return to life was to reawaken feeling. Turning onto her stomach, slipping her hands beneath her, she let her fingers lap like tongues against her body's silken folds. The heat in her center rising up like a voice, one part of her body calling to another, her hands moving beneath her, her hips moving down into her hands. She guides her fingers along the parting of the lips to the hooded point of flesh waiting for them there. No one else's pleasure need concern her tonight. She is free to discover her own. Her body calls, a hollow aching call from deep within, her body answers, calling and meeting the call, one part of her body responding to another, just this, attending to her own needs, following the rhythms of her own pleasure and suddenly it's there, within reach. Straining for it now, her whole interior self seems to fall through its center toward one exquisite point where all that she is is perfect and, with a cry of delight at its perfection, her head snaps up and on a violent breath she sucks in the joy of her own sensations.

Then on the same breath and in almost the same instant, she let out a sound of solitary disappointment and, turning her head to the side, wept for all the lonely possibilities—for her husband whom she might never come to love, for herself, whom she might, and for the fragile hope she still stubbornly held out for them both.

Harry had brought her some clean clothes and was packing up the soiled ones to take away with him that night.

"I'm frightened, Harry," she told him.

"Don't worry. We've got the best lawyers in town. They're very optimistic. The case won't come to trial for months yet. Maybe even a year. That'll give you time to keep working with Frieda, keep getting stronger."

"I don't mean the trial. I'm afraid of going back into that house."

"Mrs. Landon will be there to help you."

"But actually going into it. . . ." Sara saw it spreading out around her as she spoke . . . the rooms . . . the stairs . . . the landing . . . " ". . . being in it again. . . ." the children's rooms . . . the one room she couldn't bear to enter. "I suppose it's just the same."

"William's room, you mean?"

She saw it before her: his little crib, his stuffed animals, his favorite teddy bear, his white wicker rocking chair. "You haven't changed it?"

"No. I haven't changed it."

Sara nodded and turned away. She cried easily these days. She saw his little face before her. She saw him lying on the ground. Every thought brought him back. "What will we do with his things?"

"The children's hospital would be very grateful for the toys, I'm sure, and . . ."

Sara leaned over and began to rock. William lay just under her heart. She pressed her body into his. His small, still body on the ground. The violent beating of her heart awakening no answer in his. William lay just under her heart. Peaceful and safe from harm.

"Don't Sara. Don't."

She stopped rocking and raised her head. Harry's was lowered now. The glare from the lamp picked up the ends of his hair and turned them white. Staring at those white ends, Sara saw something extraordinary in them. Something she had stopped seeing years ago. Harry had curly hair. Her own was straight. Julia's was straight. Justin and Sam, too, had straight hair. But Harry's hair was curly. Like William's. Thick and dark and curly.

"Harry," she whispered, staring at his head in pure amazement. "William had hair like yours."

She wept now at the sight of that hair curling there whitely in the lamp. Another head of curly hair lay beneath her on the ground.

"Sara. It will be all right. We'll manage, you'll see." Harry was speaking quickly now and softly. "I'll be more help to you. You won't have to do everything alone. I didn't tell you this before, but I've been seeing Tom Ornstein. He's one of the best in the city. . . ."

The phrase struck Sara as unspeakably sad. How Harry clung to the notion of having the best of things—best lawyers, best psychiatrist in the city. Something about it, innocent and pathetic and enormously vulnerable, flooded her with an unfamiliar tenderness for this man who could handle anything, who never asked for help from anyone, but now that death had touched him was forced to imagine himself safe in the hands of the best.

". . . I never thought I would . . . furthest thing from my mind," Harry was saying. ". . . but Frieda told me in the very beginning I'd have to change too if I was going to be of any help to you. And she was right, Sara. I'm trying. And with her testimony at the trial . . . it'll be a great help, you'll see . . . Frieda has always said at the time you didn't know what you were doing. The lawyers are sure the court will be lenient . . . and if you continue psychiatric treatment, and you've already agreed to that . . ."

Sara got up and went to the window. She had heard all this before. Reduced sentence, suspended sentence. She knew whatever the court decided her sentence was for life. The night looked close enough to touch and, even through the glass, she seemed to feel the warm summer breezes blowing up from the courtyard below, up through the trees and through the window and into her and swirling on up into the sky—warm currents of sheltering air, rising higher and higher overhead to form a perfect and protective unity. Forgive me, she said silently into the great dark encompassing universe. "Forgive me," she said softly to Harry at her back. Forgive me, she said to the stars shining above, and to William somewhere out there among those stars or below them in the new buds pushing up through the ground. William, within her now never to be taken away. Mother and child together in an indissoluble bond of continuity. An overriding sense of peace entered Sara, filling her soul with an absolute but momentary calm.

Oh, but never to see his sweet face again! Never to hear his laugh!

"Forgive me," she said again to Harry. "If there's any way that you can. He was your child too. I always thought of him as only mine."

She turned then and caught what she knew was the first totally unguarded expression she had ever seen on Harry's face. The bones and flesh seemed to give way, collapsing beneath his grief. She reached out for him, then faltered and stopped as Harry put his head down on his folded arms and seemed for a while to sleep. In just that position had she so often come upon Justin asleep at his desk. Something like love passed out of Sara then and moved toward Harry as she stood behind and watched him sleep, and later she could not recall exactly when it was she realized that he wasn't sleeping. Approaching him cautiously, she put her hands on his shoulders and found them—those shoulders, a doctor's shoulders—unaccountably shaking beneath her hands. Harry doesn't do this. Doctors don't behave this way. But here a man's shoulders were shaking beneath her hands. Here a man was crying. She had the power still within to comfort him. She stood with her hands on his shoulders while he cried. Harry's tears were new to her, unimaginable before this moment. Always her children's had been unendurable. Rather than face them she'd ordered them to stop. *Stop that crying,* she'd yelled at them. *Crybaby,* she'd hurled at them. At Justin and Julia and even little Sam. *Crybaby,* she'd said. *Stop it at once.* And flashes of her children then, their faces streaked with tears, passed before her. Their eyes running over with a grief she had not been home to share. She could cry now. They all might cry now. And as she listened to the low, unfamiliar sounds of Harry's sobs, she thought if in nothing else, in that she would be different. She would let them have their tears.

It seemed an immensely long time before Harry pulled his handkerchief from his pocket and blew his nose and raised his head. "Maybe I'm coming down with something," he said. "Lot of flu going around."

"In August, Harry?"

"Bad time for summer colds."

Sara smiled then and walked around in front of him. It might still be all right if he touched her. If he held her hand or stroked her hair. She sat down next to him. "You look tired," she said, holding out her hand, tilting his chin, as she so often tilted the children's chins to check for unbrushed teeth or sickly tongues.

"I'm all right," he said and took her hand and held it in his own.

"Want a B12 shot while you're here?"

He laughed then. "No thanks," he said. "No shots."

And Sara laughed, too, and wondered if even now she

weren't doing him an injustice. He was, after all, what he was, not what she would have him be. And tonight he looked to her old and lonely.

"You work so hard," she said. "You try to do everything alone." If there was any chance at all, she had to take it. "Funny . . . isn't that what you said about me? Seventeen years, Harry, we've been together. And each of us alone. Maybe we could do things differently now. . . . Maybe we could learn to help each other." Or was it too late? Was it beyond that now? "I don't know how people go on after something like this," Sara continued. "I don't know how anyone does it . . . or even if we can. . . . But maybe together . . . I'm getting stronger . . . I won't ask you to have all the strength anymore. I know how unfair of me that was . . ."

Harry was holding her hand. In the last few minutes she felt his shoulders shake. She had seen him cry. She looked at the hand that was holding hers—skilled, professional. And also, she remembered, a husband's hand, a father's. And remembering that, she thought perhaps it wasn't too late, perhaps she might yet find a way of looking into the sun again.

Frieda brought the children in after lunch and left them alone. Facing the door when they entered, Sara felt herself entirely turned to stone a moment, so beautiful did she find them. Her heart went out in gratitude to Mrs. Landon, whom she had never met, who had sent her children back to her safe and neatly dressed and somehow altered. Julia's green eyes had turned serious, Justin was no longer a boy, and Sam— yes, just as she'd guessed from the photograph—little Sam had grown. Her beautiful, clean, altered children. Their faces were bright, their hair washed. So short a time had they been away from her, yet long enough to return transformed. A space spread out before them now, an uncertain land alive with danger. Each of them, coming in the door, hung back a moment, then bravely crossed—Justin first, almost a man, he would be as tall as his father . . . Julia next, lovely and soft and closer, too, to her maturity . . . and finally Sam, her little Sam, happily still hardly more than a baby himself. Sam bounced in and looked around and drew back reaching for

Julia's hand, and raised his other arm and reached for Justin's hand as well.

Sara straightened herself and, with tears standing in her eyes waited for whatever would come. Hatred, resentment, she would not forestall it. But what she truly could not bear was the blurred, shimmering vision of these beautiful children standing before her forever withholding their forgiveness.

Then Julia's arms were around her, her daughter's body pressed against her own. Now Sam was in her arms. Little Sam. And Sara's hands were on him. On his face, his head, his arms, his back, and she was not afraid of her hands on him.

"Can I have William's teddy? Can I?" he asked and Sara withstood the swift pain of the question, coming as it did with such suddenness and force she knew Sam had been saving it up to ask her, could in fact have asked no one else.

"Yes, darling," she said. "Of course you may."

Then Justin came and stood before her. How amazing he was. The shape of his jaw, the fine flash in his eye. There was courage in the way he stood now, firm and tall before her. He would be all right, Sara knew. Like his father he would know success. And power, too, guided by love. Oh, but how appealing she found it to see this new, nearly ripe strength about to spring itself upon the world. Justin's feet, his hands, were as large as a man's. How was it possible? Her first-born infant grown into this. How amazing life was. How fantastic.

"How are you, mom?" Justin asked, and Sara held out her hands to him and as she had expected, Justin hesitated a moment before meeting them with his own.

Sara was choked with tears and didn't try to answer him, but only smiled and nodded her head a little up and down to show that really she was all right. He came closer then and embraced her and, drawing Sam into her lap and feeling Julia's and Justin's arms around her, she felt that really they were all right, too, that somehow it would be all right. Her children wanted her back and something in Sara leaped toward them as toward a state of grace and she was almost ready to go home.

* * *

"I'll leave this here," Sara said to Frieda, covering the clay head with a towel. "There's still a lot of work to be done on it."

"Sure," Frieda answered. "A lot of work."

"For as long as it takes," Sara replied and smiled and shook Frieda's hand. For as long as that and longer, she knew. For as long as she lived.

ABOUT THE AUTHOR

ENID HARLOW was for many years the fiction editor of *Harper's Bazaar*. She is now in her late thirties living in New York City and writing full time. CRASHING is her first novel.

RELAX!
SIT DOWN
and Catch Up On Your Reading!

THE LATEST BOOKS
IN THE BANTAM
BESTSELLING TRADITION

Bantam Book Catalog

Here's your up-to-the-minute listing of over 1,400 titles by your favorite authors.

This illustrated, large format catalog gives a description of each title. For your convenience, it is divided into categories in fiction and non-fiction—gothics, science fiction, westerns, mysteries, cookbooks, mysticism and occult, biographies, history, family living, health, psychology, art.

So don't delay—take advantage of this special opportunity to increase your reading pleasure.

Just send us your name and address and 50¢ (to help defray postage and handling costs).